T-Minus Two

KG MacGregor

Bella
BOOKS

2015

Bella Books, Inc.
P.O. Box 10543
Tallahassee, FL 32302

First Bella Books Edition 2015

Editor: Katherine V. Forrest
Cover Designer: Linda Callaghan

ISBN: 978-1-59493-452-0

Other Books By KG MacGregor

Acknowledgments

It shouldn't surprise you that I was frequently distracted by the research for this book. I'd go online to check a single detail and end up jumping from one link to another for the next two hours, before dragging myself back to my work. It's fair to say space travel is my new fascination.

Admittedly, I take considerable poetic license with the practicality of a manned mission to Mars, but the vision is hardly science fiction. There are some in the space community who believe the technology for colonizing the Red Planet already exists; in fact, experiments are currently underway on Hawaii's Big Island to determine optimal living conditions. While NASA has the first human touching down no sooner than 2035, private entrepreneurs at Mars One dream of getting there a full decade earlier. It will happen eventually. Why shouldn't it be a pair of women in love?

Thanks very much to my editor, Katherine V. Forrest, who always advocates for you, the reader. And to my reading team of Jenny and Karen, who find the important words I've left out, and the not-so-important words I've left in. A special shout out to the last line of defense—Bella's proofreaders, Ruth and Carla. They caught a few errors in this book that would have earned me a scolding from you.

I should probably add that this book is a work of fiction, and any resemblance to persons living or dead is coincidental. Except where it isn't.

About the Author

A former teacher and market research consultant, KG MacGregor holds a PhD in journalism from UNC–Chapel Hill. Infatuation with *Xena: Warrior Princess* fan fiction prompted her to try her own hand at storytelling in 2002. In 2005, she signed with Bella Books, which published the Golden Crown finalist *Just This Once*. Her sixth Bella novel, *Out of Love*, won the Lambda Literary Award for Women's Romance and the Golden Crown Award in Lesbian Romance. She picked up Goldies also for *Without Warning*, *Worth Every Step* and *Photographs of Claudia* (Contemporary Romance), along with *Secrets So Deep* and *Playing with Fuego* (Romantic Suspense).

Other honors include the Lifetime Achievement Award from the Royal Academy of Bards, the Alice B. Readers Appreciation Medal, and several Readers Choice Awards.

An avid supporter of queer literature, KG currently serves on the Board of Trustees for the Lambda Literary Foundation. She divides her time between Palm Springs and her native North Carolina mountains.

Visit her on the web at www.kgmacgregor.com.

CHAPTER ONE

"Ladies and gentlemen, seating in the lecture hall is arranged alphabetically. Please take your assigned seat as quickly as possible so we can begin."

Mila Todorov scowled at the announcement. So much for arriving early to get a seat near the front. How would she stand out among two-hundred-fifty-six candidates if she was all the way at the top of the room? *Not fair at all.*

At the doorway to the hall, she was greeted by a Pacific Islander wearing a yellow shirt with the words *Tenacity Project* stitched above a rocket emblem on his chest. He distributed bottles of water and gestured toward a tray of green capsules, each wrapped in clear plastic. "Energy tablet. Please swallow it when you reach your seat."

As Mila climbed the stairs to her assigned desk at the top, the din of conversations grew more subdued, replaced by the shuffling of papers in the information packets left at each seat. Clearly her fellow candidates were as eager as she to learn the details of what was in store for them over the next ten weeks.

Equally clear were the stakes. They had converged on the Big Island of Hawaii to vie for two seats aboard *Tenacity*, the interplanetary vessel that would establish the first colony on Mars—at least the first one known to scientists on Earth. The privately funded Tenacity Project had drawn over forty thousand applicants from all over the world. Engineers and physical scientists like Mila. Biologists, chemists, behaviorists, physicians. Pilots, soldiers, teachers, architects. Athletes, artists, journalists. Even a politician or two. If this were a reality show, they could call it *Dancing With the Planets*.

The finalists also included several alumni from space programs from around the world, mostly NASA and the European Space Agency, but also representing Japan, India, Australia and China. It was difficult to imagine beating out those who already had astronaut training, but Mila was determined to give it her all. She was only twenty-seven years old. If she missed out on this wave, there would be others.

"When you reach your seat, please review your profile and confirm the information is correct."

She found her packet at the third seat from the end, four rows from the top. Pity the poor W's and Y's, who were sitting above her in the dark. Already she planned a statistical analysis by last name of those who survived the next cut. *Not fair.*

Her profile photo—the same one that appeared on the badge hanging from a lanyard around her neck—was surprisingly good, considering it had been taken upon arrival in Hilo at the end of a twenty-eight-hour journey from Berlin. Long hair pulled back in a tie to hide its wilt, making it appear brown instead of dark blond. Mongolian eyes so dark the redness hardly showed. In place of a smile, she'd proffered a practiced look of sureness and satisfaction, as though she'd already been chosen to go.

The man in the next chair raised a mock toast as he swallowed his energy tablet. Even though he was seated, she could tell he was tall—perhaps even too tall to live comfortably in a space vessel. She celebrated that fact because it meant one less contender. On the other hand, the dark yarmulke that sat upon his crown afforded him a distinctive look the selection committee would notice and remember, since everyone was outfitted in the same khaki cargo pants, black shoes and blue microfiber T-shirt with the *Tenacity Project* rocket logo. *Not fair.*

"Good morning," he said, extending a hand. "Isaac Tobias. I saw you at the dormitory."

"I'm afraid everyone saw me at the dormitory," she replied sheepishly, recalling the stares when she'd clumsily dropped her well-worn Rubik's Cube at check-in, scattering colorful pieces of plastic across the hardwood floor. "Not exactly how I wanted to stand out."

"Don't worry about it. What they really noticed was how fast you put it back together."

Mila had gotten a perfect score on the analytical segment of their aptitude test, given almost a year ago during the second qualifying round. Science, technology and spatial relations were her strengths, along with anything else that sprang from the left side of her brain. Not so much with her artistic side, though she'd scored in the acceptable range thanks to her creativity with problem solving.

"I'm hearing an accent," he said. "Let me guess…Rumanian?"

Most people guessed Russian, but Isaac's ear was obviously better tuned to Eastern Europe.

"Close. Bulgarian." Except her Slavic accent was somewhat muted because her mother had taken her at age ten to Berlin when she accepted a position in the philosophy department at Humboldt University. "And you are from…Israel."

"Too easy."

"T-minus sixty and counting."

A nervous chuckle spread throughout the room at the leader's choice of words to hurry stragglers to their seats.

Mila scanned the hall to assess her rivals. She figured to be among the youngest. The selection committee had made clear the Mars mission was a one-way trip, and though they promised to consider applicants of all ages, the optimum range was late thirties–early forties. Her work was cut out to overcome their bias against youth, to convince them she would eagerly give up her life on Earth for the chance to colonize their neighboring planet.

In her introductory essay nearly a year ago—submitted along with her résumé, university transcripts and a brief questionnaire—she'd described her passion for space exploration, seeded firmly at age thirteen when US Air Force Major Jancey Beaumont set off on what was to be a two-year solo mission to test the potential for long-term survivability in space. Mila tracked her orbit through the NASA website and spent countless evenings on the rooftop of their Berlin apartment building with a telescope in hopes of spotting her spacecraft, *Guardian*, as it orbited Earth. The thrill of seeing it pass sparked her imagination of being inside—preferably with Major Beaumont, but she hadn't included that detail in her essay—and watching the world below.

The major's mission had been cut short in dramatic fashion at the start of her second year in orbit when an experimental Russian vessel lost power, leaving the two cosmonauts aboard only hours of life support. Using *Guardian*'s emergency thrusters for maneuverability, Beaumont left her assigned orbit to intercept the stricken craft and evacuate its occupants to safety as the world held its collective breath. With two extra souls aboard her tiny vessel, her only course of action was an immediate return to Earth.

It was upon the major's triumphant return that Mila decided she would study to become an astronaut. She was even more inspired when she read Internet rumors speculating that Beaumont was a lesbian, and while none were confirmed, they weren't denied either. Of course not. The major couldn't say for certain back then because of the American military's puritanical rules against gays. It only intensified Mila's interest, imagining her dashing idol having super-secret affairs with beautiful women.

Everything Mila had done since then—physical fitness training, a PhD in astronautical engineering from Delft University of Technology in the Netherlands, and keeping up-to-date on space programs—was in pursuit of her dream. And now she was on the brink of realizing it.

"T-minus thirty seconds."

With few exceptions, the other candidates appeared as strong and healthy as she. No surprise, since a medical exam was their third phase of preliminary testing. Mila had inherited her mother's thin frame, along with her genetic propensity toward low blood pressure, heart rate and cholesterol. No allergies, no digestive sensitivities, no disorders of any kind.

Where she'd held her breath was in the fourth phase of evaluation, the last one before being called to Hawaii for the competitive tests. That was the psych exam, an online multiple choice test in which she had to imagine working and living in close quarters with a fellow astronaut. For the rest of her life. Would she prefer to solve a problem this way or that? Was she a leader or follower? Did she read the directions or figure things out on her own?

She was by nature a loner, impatient with the very sort of chitchat Isaac had initiated, and mortified by conversations that required deeper engagement, especially those requiring her to share feelings or personal information. To make the cut for *Tenacity*, she'd guessed at what traits they were seeking. She had to convince the evaluator she was sufficiently easygoing to live and work harmoniously with someone else, but not so gregarious she would suffer from limited human contact.

At T-minus zero, the hall went completely dark, and in turn, silent. A low rumble emanated from the finely tuned sound system, growing louder as the towering screen brightened to reveal a space vessel clearly marked *Tenacity I* mounted above a massive rocket and quaking on a launch pad. The roll grew to a crackling roar and the rocket slowly climbed until a billow of orange-tinted smoke filled the screen.

Mila closed her eyes and rode the wave of thunder that reverberated off the walls and ceiling. As the roar gradually faded, it was replaced by a collective din of excitement, as though everyone in the room was as thrilled as she to be here. She blinked to find the room dark again.

"The extraordinary video you've just seen was taken three days ago at the Satish Dhawan Space Centre, a low altitude launch pad in India." A formal British accent belonging to a much older

man. "Tenacity I *is carrying a rover to Mars to prepare the site for a colony. Two years from now,* Tenacity II *will launch with equipment to construct a permanent habitat, laboratory and hydroponics garden, all underground and safe from radiation. And in four years,* Tenacity III *will take you and a colleague on an eight-month journey to establish permanent residence in that habitat. At one-year intervals following your launch, two more colonists will join you. That, ladies and gentlemen, is the Tenacity Project."*

A spotlight pierced the darkness on the stage below revealing a white-haired man, slightly paunchy with reading glasses perched at the end of his bulbous nose. He wore a dark three-piece business suit with a fat tie and matching handkerchief, and his cane hung from the edge of the podium. Mila recognized him at once. Sir Charles Boyd, the British multibillionaire space junkie behind the Tenacity Project. After selling the world's largest food conglomerate eleven years ago, he'd turned his attention toward fulfilling the boyhood fantasy of developing a new colony on a faraway planet. Now in his seventies, he acknowledged Mars as the only realistic option for a colony that might be established in his lifetime.

"Top of the morning to you all," he said as a slideshow began with an artist's rendering of a cylindrical vessel named *Tenacity III* approaching the Red Planet. "If you will, please examine your boarding pass. Should it say anything other than Mars, I'm afraid you are in the wrong departure lounge."

Mila's breath caught at the majestic image on the screen, her eyes drawn immediately to the structural features of the forward-most segment of the ship, the section that would land two astronauts on the surface of Mars. She'd learned of the Mars mission four years ago when Tenacity Project engineers came to Delft to discuss a paper she'd written for a Stockholm conference. It laid out theoretical plans for a hydrazine propulsion system that, once landed on the surface of a planet or asteroid, could be reconfigured to extract oxygen from water, and to route hydrogen to fuel cells. Such an apparatus on Mars, where ice fields were abundant, could sustain living conditions indefinitely.

"Tenacity." Sir Charles cleared his throat and allowed the word to momentarily stand on its own. "Determination. Persistence. Resolve. These are the human attributes that bring our universe within reach. If it can be done, it will be done."

Goose bumps rose on Mila's arms and chest as she absorbed his inspirational words.

Scientists laid the groundwork for travel to Mars over fifty years ago, and had built upon it with each successive program. By the turn of the century, technology had evolved that could transport astronauts across millions of kilometers of space and land their craft on the planet's surface. Since then, the principal barrier to a Mars mission had been funding.

The Tenacity Project was budgeted at forty-six billion dollars, two-thirds of which was provided personally by Sir Charles. He'd pooled his billions with several private corporations and a handful of wealthy donors who shared his fascination with space travel. Once the colony was established, they anticipated an influx of funding from governments, foundations and corporations all over the world to help it grow.

"Let me offer my congratulations for your achievement, not only for making it this far in the selection process, but also for the contributions many of you have already made in your specialized fields. Space alloys that protect from radiation. Propulsion systems that convert sheets of ice to energy and breathable air. Cloning technology that ensures a sustainable, healthy diet. All of these advancements and dozens of others were achieved by people in this room."

Mila glowed with pride at the special mention of her work. Surely that gave her the inside track, even if she was sitting at the top of the room. Who needed a yarmulke when she had a bullet point like that on her résumé?

"Indeed, you all are exemplary candidates for this remarkable expedition. I wish you the best of fortune as we determine the final four teams that will train for the *Tenacity* mission. The challenge before us requires many hands. Every person in this room possesses unique skills and expertise that can ultimately contribute to our success. Those of you who are not chosen to go shall be offered an opportunity to join the hundreds of engineers and scientists around the world already on board. It is my hope you will agree to stay on—perhaps even at our new project headquarters here in this island paradise—in order to help ensure the mission's success. And there shall be more opportunities to join the colony as the project grows."

Mila had left Berlin with the clear expectation of moving wherever the project took her, as the training facilities and technology centers were located all over the world—Germany, Japan, Russia and the US. If her youth worked against her this time, she would try again for a seat on a future launch. She possessed the ultimate quality of an astronaut—tenacity.

* * *

Jancey Beaumont, seated in her alphabetically-assigned seat near the front of the theater, had no intention of hanging around if she were cut from the candidate pool. Her backup plan was a cabin off the beaten path in Sedona. If she couldn't return to space, she might as well call it a career—at least when it came to working in someone else's lab. Her years at elite universities and on the speaker's circuit had paid well, leaving her plenty of money to get started toward self-sufficiency. It wasn't as if she needed a lot, since her life's work was a blueprint for survival on very few resources.

"The greatest challenge you'll face on Mars is an environment that is hostile to human life," Sir Charles continued, "with only one other person to share the workload and provide companionship—perhaps for all eternity."

Companionship...the last thing Jancey wanted. If she had her way, this would be a solo mission like *Guardian*. Nothing would please her more than to step alone aboard a ship bound for Mars knowing she'd never return. She'd proven long ago she could survive in space without company or replenishment of supplies. As a molecular biologist, she knew how to feed herself, especially given a plentiful water supply like the one on Mars. Coupled with the technical skills she'd gained from air force and NASA training, she was by far the most qualified to undertake this mission.

A glance around the hall confirmed her assumption that only a quarter of the candidates were women. The STEM fields—science, technology, engineering and mathematics—were notoriously biased in favor of men. Though she appreciated the project's emphasis on equal opportunity during the application phase, there were no guarantees a woman would make the final cut. She'd have liked her chances more had there not been forty-some married couples among the remaining contenders, including three with one already a trained astronaut. Couples had been encouraged to apply under the rationale that they were well suited to a long-term life in close quarters. Single candidates like her would have to pair with someone and then prove they could live and work together, something the couples had already done.

That meant Jancey had to take one of these dolts with her if she were chosen.

It wasn't fair to call them dolts, she conceded, not if they'd made it this far. Some, in fact, brought a lot to the party. An alloy that deflected radiation could add years to the lives of space travelers. Smart enough, but a metals expert was more useful in a laboratory on Earth than aboard a vessel, at least until the colony was established. The engineer who'd repurposed the propulsion system was far more serviceable. With her luck, she'd pair with him and he'd turn out to be a misogynistic jerk. Just what she needed for an eight-month trip in a mere seventeen cubic meters of living space.

The university science departments where she'd taught since leaving the space program were full of men who thought they were better, smarter and more deserving than any woman. Ditto for the air force. The one place she'd always felt respected was NASA, but it wasn't enough to save her from the budget cuts that gutted programs for long-term space flights. The ax had fallen on everyone.

Sir Charles flashed a cheesy slide of frontier settlers chopping down trees for their log cabin. "Two centuries ago, pioneers set out across the Great Plains of America to make a new life in a barren land. Their days were spent in tenacious pursuit of their very survival, whatever it took to feed their families, to shelter against the elements, to draw from nature and bend it to their will. This is the life that awaits our colonists."

By the looks of it, Jancey, at forty-three, was in the middle of the pack age-wise. Forty-seven at launch if she were chosen to go first. What she lacked in vigor—assuming she lacked anything—she made up for in experience. Plus she'd already proven her suitability, having spent an extended period in space with no ill effects.

That also was true for Colonel Marlon Quinn, an African-American from Detroit who'd logged five months at the International Space Station. Several other NASA alumni had made the cut for *Tenacity* as well, but only she and Marlon had long-term space experience. Besides the risk of exposure to increased levels of radiation, the biggest threat from living in zero gravity was intracranial pressure that could cause brain damage, loss of vision or pituitary problems. For whatever reason—genetics, metabolism, luck—she and Marlon had been unfazed. If she had to go with someone, it might as well be him.

Sir Charles glanced her way and smiled. "As I noted earlier, the Tenacity Project has already reached out to a number of experts across a variety of fields we deemed essential for success. Many of them sit among you, dignitaries in their own right. You'll meet some of them today, as we've asked them to share their expertise in our overview. The first shall discuss some of the nutritional issues that must be addressed in order to survive on Mars. She made her first and only trip to space fourteen years ago aboard *Guardian*, setting the endurance record for American astronauts as a mere lass of twenty-nine. It would have been longer had she not deviated from her mission to perform a daring rescue…"

As he droned on with his introduction, Jancey made her way to the stage, marching stiffly, a habit left over from her military days. From her speaking engagements, she was accustomed to public accolades, but humbled by the reception and eager to return to her seat. She'd never been comfortable in crowds. Yet another reason to go to Mars.

"It is my distinct pleasure to introduce Major Jancey Beaumont."

She acknowledged the applause with a small wave and adjusted the microphone to her five-foot-five frame. "Thank you, Sir Charles, not only for that gracious introduction, but for recognizing the colonization of Mars as an idea whose time has come. Your legacy for all time will be that of a visionary, the man who not only dreamed but made it happen."

She stepped back from the podium and joined the other candidates in prolonged applause. It didn't hurt to lavish praise on the man whose word likely carried more weight than any other.

"I've been asked to give a brief overview of some of the challenges our colonists will face. It's true that space travelers are like America's pioneers, but with far harsher conditions. It will take extraordinary effort to sustain life in a place where you cannot count on the soil. Where the water you drink and the air you breathe must be reconstituted at the molecular level. Where failure to maintain equipment can cost you your life in a matter of minutes."

On her cue, the slide changed to a small flat of seedlings underneath an LED grow light.

"When you entered the hall, you were given a newly developed tablet designed to boost energy levels. We'll be taking metabolic measures this afternoon to evaluate its effects."

A rustling of cellophane suggested more than a few had failed to follow instructions, so she gave them a moment to comply.

"Confession...those weren't really energy tablets. They were vitamins formulated at the cellular level from the parts of plants we don't generally eat—the pits, stems and rinds. The plants were grown in a lab using fertilizer made of human feces." She paused for a collective groan. "And as you may also have realized, you washed them down with recycled urine. There is no such thing as waste in space."

CHAPTER TWO

Jancey Beaumont!

Mila was bursting with excitement as she exited the lecture hall, craning her neck for a close-up glimpse. She'd just spent three hours in the same room with her all-time hero and hadn't even realized it until she took the stage. Not only was the major obviously in Sir Charles's inner circle, she also was a candidate for *Tenacity.*

How stupid of her not to realize sooner that the major would apply for the project. In every interview she'd ever granted—Mila had her name on a Google alert—she'd said her goal was to return to space. She was an expert in long-term space travel, probably the foremost expert in the world. A couple of Russians had stayed longer in space at the International Space Station, but not in a solo craft where they grew and prepared their own food. Jancey Beaumont was the perfect choice for a mission to Mars.

And Mila was the perfect choice to accompany her, or so she believed, since their skills were complementary. Beaumont was a molecular biologist. She could take the lead in food production while Mila handled the mechanical aspects—energy, life support systems and construction of the foundation for the colony. The perfect team.

From her seat at the top of the room, it took nearly ten minutes of her forty-minute lunch break to reach the exit. So much for getting a better glimpse of Beaumont.

"Mila...Mila! Wait up." It was Andi Toloti, her assigned roommate in the dormitory. Toloti had an impressive résumé, having completed a post-doc in organic chemistry at NASA. She was in her early thirties, compact and muscular with wavy blond hair, and according to her profile, gay. A Houston native whose father worked at Mission Control, she was obnoxiously confident of her chances of making the final cut. "Let's grab some chow before the line gets too long."

She'd noticed Toloti three seats down in the theater but deliberately ignored her in favor of Isaac so as not to be drawn into conversation. After only one night together in the dorm, it was clear the woman possessed most of the qualities Mila found supremely annoying in colleagues—she talked incessantly, waded too far into personal matters and seemed to think she was an authority on everything.

"No time," Mila answered. "There was an error on my profile sheet and I need to get it straightened out." It was an outright lie for which she felt no remorse.

"No shit? Lemme see what they did. Maybe I oughtta come along and help explain it in case they have trouble understanding ya."

Toloti had a distinctive drawl, and a tendency to drop both vowels and consonants. A southern US tendency, and one of the many dialects spoken among the candidates. Just because English was the international language of scientific literature didn't mean everyone spoke it with the same inflections.

"Why would they have trouble understanding me? I speak perfect English." She knew it as well as she did her native Bulgarian. Along with German and Dutch, and enough Russian to get by. "Do they speak something different in administration? Texan?"

Toloti laughed, oblivious to the fact she'd just been insulted. "Nah, I reckon you'll be okay. But just so you know…Texan's not a language."

Mila bloody well knew that, and the idea that Toloti thought she was stupid enough to believe otherwise made her want to scream. She'd pass on going to Mars if it meant sharing the rest of her life with such an idiot. No, she'd put up with her until it was too late to return to Earth and then push her out the airlock.

The Tenacity Project was temporarily headquartered at the University of Hawaii–Hilo. With most of the students gone for the summer, they had the run of the campus, including the cafeteria, for the two weeks needed to whittle the group down to thirty-two. Their first cut—to one-hundred-twenty-eight— would come in only three days.

Satisfied with her sinister plan, she detoured toward the administration office until she saw Toloti join another woman from their dormitory suite. Then she doubled back and got into the cafeteria line, which was moving quickly. The reason became clear when she reached the front and realized the menu wasn't à la carte—the food trays were prefilled by cafeteria workers in an assembly line. Everyone was given exactly the same lunch.

"Excuse me, what is this purple stuff?"

The Polynesian woman behind the food counter, wearing a white flower over her ear, smiled brightly. "It's called poi. Made from taro, a root vegetable. It's one of our favorite foods in Hawaii."

The woman was so obviously proud, Mila didn't have the heart to tell her she had no intention of putting something so gross-looking in her mouth.

Tray in hand, she scanned the room in search of Toloti— so she could sit as far away as possible. To her astonishment, there was an empty seat across from none other than Jancey Beaumont.

Did she dare? Of course she did. She might never have another chance to rub shoulders with someone so…so heroic. So iconic. So captivating. "May I join you?"

The major never stopped eating, just nodded toward the open seat.

Mila took it as a yes and sat, marveling at her luck. It would take all of her self-restraint not to blurt out how excited she was. That had it not been for the major's mission on *Guardian*, she might never have realized her passion for space.

Up close and in person, the major was stunning, especially her eyes, the deepest green Mila had ever seen. Her dark brown hair was cut short in variable lengths, giving it a ragged, carefree look, a perfect style for zero gravity.

Even more astonishing were her forearms. The bulging muscles were out of proportion to the rest of her slender body.

"I have to admit, Major, you got me with your energy tablet trick. For a minute there I think I even imagined myself feeling more vibrant."

"Good thing there wasn't an actual assessment afterward," the major said, the husky timbre of her voice sending a ripple up Mila's spine. "You might have been disqualified for your inability to provide accurate self-reports."

Taken aback by the no-nonsense response, Mila felt her face grow hot. The last thing she wanted was to appear incompetent to Jancey Beaumont, who was important enough that Sir Charles had invited her to speak during the introduction. What if she shared that stupid remark with the selection committee?

"I'm sure I could have performed a factual evaluation if I'd concentrated on the effects."

As a teenager embarking on a career in space science, she'd fantasized about a chance meeting like this with the woman who'd inspired her. They'd have a collegial discussion and the major would be impressed with her brilliance, so much that they'd become friends. Then someday the major would fall in love with her…since it was, after all, a fantasy.

None of it was playing out that way, she thought miserably as she downed her lunch. The sooner she finished and got out of there, the sooner she'd stop making a fool of herself.

The major peered across the table at her badge. "Todorov… Russian?"

"Bulgarian, but I grew up in Berlin. Studied in the Netherlands. Astronautical engineering." She was talking too much, just like Toloti.

"Delft, I assume. About the only decent option in Europe."

"That's right. I studied with—"

"Why not in the US? All the top programs are here. Stanford. MIT. Purdue."

Mila couldn't very well say she'd chosen Delft because it was close to home, not when she was competing for the chance to go to Mars. "Delft was the best place for me at the time. When I look back on my accomplishments there, it's difficult to think I could have been as successful anywhere else."

This was turning into a disaster. She should have sucked it up and eaten with Toloti where she belonged, instead of inviting herself to join one of the most accomplished space travelers in the world. It was depressing to recognize the gulf between candidates like Jancey Beaumont and common grunts like her. No way would she make the grade against competition of that caliber.

Suddenly self-conscious, she pushed back her chair and gripped her tray. "Thank you for letting me join you."

"You haven't eaten your poi."

Mila swallowed air, noting the major had cleaned her plate.

"Poi is nutrient-dense, Todorov. Very high in fluorine, which strengthens bones. You are aware that weightlessness causes bones to deteriorate?" From the major's tone, she might as well have added *you stupid idiot* at the end of her question.

With three quick bites and a focused effort not to gag, Mila polished off the pasty glob.

Beaumont nodded approvingly. "Good girl. Now have a nice day."

It was too late for that. The major had just ruined her day… her week…possibly her life.

* * *

Jancey had fond memories of her first day as an astronaut. Twenty-one years old, a prodigy already out of Princeton with a master's degree and—thanks to her ROTC scholarship— newly commissioned as a second lieutenant in the US Air

Force. With the eleven others in her astronaut group, she walked the hallowed halls of Johnson Space Center, home to America's space program. First they toured Mission Control, the heartbeat of every NASA space mission, but she had little interest in watching operations from the sidelines. For her, the most fascinating stops on the tour were the training simulators and buoyancy lab, a deep pool that allowed astronauts to practice extra-vehicular activities—EVAs—in weightlessness.

According to Sir Charles, they had only makeshift facilities here in Hawaii, sufficient for testing but not for training. The selection committee was looking for candidates with potential to handle the real challenges. The next two weeks should give her a chance to shine.

The materials they'd been given offered no clue as to who comprised the mysterious selection committee. She suspected Sir Charles sat at the top guiding a handful of department heads, the experts who'd gathered in Hawaii to help conduct the trials. On the other hand, they might simply be the conduits, reporting back to the board of directors who would make an objective evaluation based on test results. That's how she'd have handled it—by insulating the committee from lobbying by candidates.

They'd returned after lunch to the lecture hall for overviews of various aspects of the Tenacity Project. The presentations lacked the awe of the ones that had inspired her twenty-some years ago at the Space Center, but her feelings of uncertainty were the same. She'd been so eager to impress back then because the competition for flights was fierce. She had to be smarter, faster. More fit, more prepared. The pressure consumed her for two years of training before her efforts paid off with the assignment to *Guardian*.

Tenacity also had that element of a high-stakes competition. The difference was there were fewer missions, fewer slots. No telling how many molecular biologists and biochemists had made the cut so far, and every one of them was probably capable of farming on Mars. And how many were wunderkinds, poised to take their field to the next level?

"Ladies and gentlemen, if I could have your attention?" Moriya Ito, the Japanese director of instrumentation and communication, according to the program agenda.

The most obvious slide choice would have been a panoramic display of *Tenacity*'s proposed instrument panel, its colorful buttons and indicators a complex map of the vessel's inner workings. Ito's slide went one better, the cover removed to reveal a gnarly mass of wires, fuses and circuit boards. The Mars astronauts had four years to learn all there was to know about the ship's circuitry.

Jancey could have disassembled and rebuilt *Guardian* in her sleep. With training, she could do the same with the *Tenacity* vessel, even with the technological advancements of the last fifteen years.

As Ito presented his overview, she wondered how many of her fellow candidates were intimidated by the expectation of having to develop expertise in such complex disciplines as electrical engineering, medicine and biochemistry. Certainly those few whose backgrounds were outside the STEM fields were quaking in their boots.

What was Mila Todorov thinking right now? As an astronautical engineer, she likely was confident she could master instrumentation. Also propulsion, which was next on the agenda. Her freak-out might come in the third session— medical training. But even that could be learned by someone with a scientific foundation. Given her background, she had a decent chance of making the next cut.

No, Todorov's flameout would come when the practicum phase began. There was no room in space for a picky eater. For that matter, there was no room for preferences of any kind on a mission with limited resources. That was the whole point of her "energy tablet" exercise, and the fact Todorov had failed to grasp it made her candidacy tenuous.

Todorov probably had other "gifts" to share, however. Jancey had picked up a distinct vibe in the short conversation they'd shared over lunch, a vibe that said she'd be available should they find themselves with nothing to do for an afternoon. Quite young, but old enough to scratch that particular itch. And smart enough to make it this far, even if she went no further.

Ito wrapped up his presentation and yielded the floor to Svein Helland, a Norwegian physicist formerly with the European Space Agency.

Apparently Sir Charles had filled nearly all of the director jobs with men, an observation to be filed under *Things That Never Change*. If Jancey failed to make the final cut, she'd be offered a job working under Oliver Thomas, an Australian biochemist whose theories of sustainability rarely left the lab.

"*Tenacity* will employ a cutting edge design for propulsion, an engine that recycles the hydrogen byproduct into fuel cells for an efficiency increase of eleven percent. More important, the technology has been adapted also for the landing module. This represents a significant breakthrough, as once the vessel reaches Mars, it can then be modified…"

Jancey was particularly interested in this development, a critical advance in propulsion technology. It was genius to repurpose the equipment they'd no longer need once they reached Mars.

"For an overview on those modifications, I'll turn the presentation over to one of the engineers on the development team at Delft Technical University in the Netherlands, who also happens to be a candidate for the Tenacity Project. Dr. Mila Todorov."

"I'll be damned," Jancey muttered, loud enough to draw questioning looks from those sitting nearby.

So Todorov wasn't an idiot after all. She was clearly intelligent and entitled to feel proud of her work at Delft. Considering the importance of her work, the selection committee might already have her on the short list.

And Jancey would move her to that other list. *Potential Distractions.*

* * *

Jancey eased into the garage, careful not to bump her front grille against the block wall. She wasn't accustomed to driving such a luxurious car, especially one as long and sleek as the Jaguar coupe. The Range Rover would have been more to her liking but Grace was insistent she kick up her heels during her stay on the island.

The sprawling house was built in the long, low plantation style typical of Old Hawaii—white horizontal plank siding and a wide green roof, with several large porticos to cool the air before it blew inside. It was much larger than it appeared from the front, since its lower level opened onto a large patio and pool in the back. Beyond was a rugged cliff with the ocean below.

The front door opened to allow two Brittany spaniels to sprint across the courtyard. Duke and Sasha were the official welcoming committee, but Jancey didn't need them to feel at home. Their mistress did that, and she appeared right behind. A small woman of seventy-one years and dressed in a colorful wraparound dress and espadrilles, Grace Faraday clutched her hands with obvious delight. "I want to hear all about it, darling."

Darling was the friendly endearment Grace sprinkled throughout their conversations. Jancey could feel her delight at having her here in Hawaii, and shared it. True friends were the rarest of gems.

"Gracie, you make me feel like a first-grader stepping off the bus after my first day of school."

Besides being her longtime friend, Grace also was a big-spending political donor, always backing candidates who supported NASA's space program. An heiress to a telecom fortune, she had no heirs of her own and had jumped at the chance to join Sir Charles in his quest to colonize Mars. It was her generous gift to the University of Hawaii that opened the doors for their competition on the Big Island.

Shortly after returning from space, Jancey had found herself seated next to Grace at a black-tie banquet in Washington DC. Just when she thought she couldn't take another minute of self-serving platitudes from politicians, Grace whispered that she had a driver waiting at the curb. The two of them bolted and spent the evening on a tour of the monuments talking about the mysteries of the universe.

"Konani made us chi-chis. Yours without the vodka, of course, and mine with a little extra." Her smile made her blue eyes sparkle.

With Duke and Sasha on their heels, they walked inside and down the wide teak staircase to the lower level. Their drinks were on a cocktail table poolside.

"Give me a minute to change. Something tells me I'm going to be sick of these clothes after the next ten weeks."

A mulch-covered walkway shrouded in native palms led past the pool to a guest house built in the same Hawaiian style, but obscured from view by the soaring vegetation. It was small but private—a living room-kitchenette combo and a bedroom with bath attached. Much better than a college dormitory with potluck for a roommate.

In under a minute, she traded her T-shirt and bra for a tropical shirt, and her khakis for a very old pair of cutoff jeans. If she made it to Mars, these two items would go with her.

She returned to the pool with her grip exerciser and collapsed next to Grace in a chaise. Three hundred squeezes a day kept her hands and forearms strong for twisting, turning and pulling, the tasks most often performed by astronauts. The rest of her body was toned by a thirty-minute uphill jog on the treadmill every morning.

"How bad was it?" Grace asked.

"What makes you think it was bad?"

"Because that little girl getting off the bus should have been excited. She should have smiled and started jabbering about all the things she learned and the interesting people she met. She most certainly shouldn't have scowled as though she dreaded going back tomorrow."

Since Grace knew her better than anyone, it was no use trying to hide her feelings. "If you must know, I'm a little worried about the competition. There were twelve of us in my astronaut class and enough missions on the board to feel good about our chances to fly. We helped each other...shared what we knew so the others would be better prepared."

"I'm sure there were hundreds of others trying to get into the astronaut program when you did. The only difference is now you know what some of them look like because they brought in two-hundred-fifty-six of them instead of just the final twelve."

"Why did they do that? They could have cut this list down a couple more rounds." She was asking the right person, since Grace was on Tenacity's board of directors and privy to inside information on their decisions.

"You know how Charles is." Grace sipped her drink, closed her eyes and licked her lips. "Konani makes the perfect chi-chi."

Not all of Sir Charles's decisions made sense. This one struck her as a waste of precious dollars that could be spent on equipment, testing or training. "Is it PR?"

"No, I think his primary reason is recruitment. He argued for doing this so it would bring the top talent in space science here to our headquarters. The board wants to get them excited about it. They get a chance to meet some of the other people behind the project and see for themselves what we've done. And yes, it's good PR. Having so many people here from all over the world expands our footprint. Their hometowns, their home countries...they all get a piece of the dream too because they have someone to root for."

Prying scientists away from their labs and classrooms for a practical mission ought to be easier now that *Tenacity I* had lifted off with the rover. This project was happening, and a *real* scientist should be eager to join up and make history.

"What worries me is how smart they are," Jancey said. "How young and strong. How up-to-date on new technology. I thought walking in there this morning I was the odds-on favorite, but I'm not so sure anymore."

Grace didn't comment, but Jancey recognized her contorted face as a sign her brain was spinning.

"I know what you're thinking and the answer is no. Don't go pulling any strings or putting any bugs in Sir Charles's ear. I need to do this on my own." Rather, she *wanted* to do it on her own. Should she feel the opportunity slipping away, she might not be able to resist asking Grace to pull out a trump card and buy her one more round to prove herself.

"Lana used to say youth was overrated." Grace spoke wistfully of her late partner, a common effect of the alcohol warming her within. Soon she would also drop the formal cadence characteristic of her billionaire station.

"She was younger than you by what? Eighteen years?"

"I used to worry out loud about being too old for her, but she wouldn't have it. She never minded our age difference, but if one of us could have changed, she would have wanted to be older like me."

"She would have aged gracefully," Jancey said. "Forty-six was way too young for someone so full of life."

Lana was the reason Grace had settled in Hawaii, and also the impetus for her involvement in funding for space missions. An astronomer, she worked at the NASA Infrared Telescope Facility atop Mauna Kea. After her death from breast cancer seven years ago, Jancey had gone to the summit with Grace to scatter her ashes.

"Too bad sh-she didn't live to see the Tenacity Project," Grace went on, stumbling over her words as she often did after a double vodka. "Then again, she'd have wanted to apply and we'd have fought the war to end all wars. It's all I can do to let go of you."

"Space is bigger than any of us, Gracie. It's a fight you can't win. The pull is so strong it sometimes makes me ache. I never told anyone this, but I used to wonder if I'd gotten the chance to fly again at NASA...I might have been tempted not to come back. That's what makes Tenacity so enticing. It's designed that way. A whole new life on another planet, and I get to leave the mess on this one behind."

"Is this life really so bad that you feel you have to run away?"

Jancey groaned. "It's not bad. It's that it's...let's just say if I run away to Mars, it solves the number one reason I can't keep a girlfriend." She ticked them off mentally—Monica, Lindsay, Jill. All three had broken up with her because she was obsessed with her space career at the expense of everything else. Each time she'd mourned the loss of intimacy, tenderness and companionship, all the while relishing her newfound freedom from the guilt over always choosing her own goals. "Nobody wants to invest in a long-term relationship with someone who wants more than anything to leave."

"It wasn't only that," Grace murmured, firmly in the throes of melancholy. She always seemed to mourn Jancey's broken romances more than Jancey. "Jill called me after you two broke up. She told me she'd have been willing to take a chance on you anyway. She'd have followed you from one university or space agency to another, wherever you felt you needed to be for your best shot at getting back to space. And she'd have stayed with you right up until the moment you blasted off. The problem back then was there weren't any opportunities. So you were unhappy all the time and there wasn't anything she could do about it. It's hard to watch the person you love suffer like that."

"But I wasn't unhappy with her. If I couldn't fly again, a life with Jill would have been a decent alternative." Even as the words left her lips, she knew it was a feeble and selfish way to express her feelings. "At least with Tenacity, I'm guaranteed to get a partner for life, whoever it is. Neither of us can leave. Isn't that what you always wanted for me?"

"Not if it's a man, you doofus!"

Jancey smiled. Still, it was sobering to note Grace Faraday was possibly the only person on Earth who would miss her if she went away forever. But no matter how much she missed having someone special in her life, she'd never put anyone in front of the chance to fly again.

CHAPTER THREE

The campus library opened each day at seven a.m. Only a handful of summer students milled about, probably desperate to complete last-minute reading assignments. Mila took advantage of the quiet time—her only free window for the next six days now that the testing phase was officially underway—to video chat with Vio Vanderwulp, her best friend from university. Vio lived in Rotterdam, where it was early evening.

"You aren't going to believe who I had lunch with yesterday," Mila said, ducking low into the computer carrel for privacy. "Jancey Beaumont, my all-time hero. Remember me telling you about her?"

"Yeah, the one who saved the world with one hand tied behind her back."

"Close enough." Apparently, she'd raved a little too much about the major. "Anyway, she's trying out for Tenacity too, which probably means the rest of us don't have a chance. Except I made a complete idiot of myself."

"That's good. Now you won't get picked, and I won't have to go looking for someone else to play *BattleStorm*."

It wasn't worth scolding Vio over her wrongheaded wishes. Even if she kept them to herself, they'd both know they were there.

It was a battle Mila fought on other fronts too. Her mother, her grandmother. They were proud of her achievements but had no desire to see her leave this world. Their idea of a suitable career was teaching at a top university in Europe. Specifically, Humboldt in Berlin or Sofia in Bulgaria. No matter how many times she tried to explain her lifelong dream, they just couldn't understand the allure of going into space.

"I figured out why so many Americans have guns," Mila said. "Because it's full of people like my roommate. You wouldn't believe what she did this morning. She used my hairbrush!"

"Does she have lice?"

"How should I know? I asked her very nicely not to do that anymore, and you know what she said? That I should get used to sharing things with someone else if I wanted to go to Mars because there wouldn't be room for two of everything." Just thinking about it made her shudder with disgust. "I'd shave my head before I'd share a hairbrush with her."

Vio shrugged. "Meh. It's no big deal."

"It's repulsive." Vio drove her crazy sometimes and it was best not to encourage her. "Forget it. They're breaking us up into groups today. I'm Blue. We're supposed to have three days of baseline tests before they make the first cut. Concentration, comprehension and physical fitness. All starting in about"—she checked her watch, an expensive Sinn from her mother that would be useless on Mars because the days were forty minutes longer—"eighteen minutes."

"That's enough for one round of *BattleStorm*."

"I don't have a joystick. You'd kill me in about three seconds if all I had was a keyboard. Besides, I don't think these people would appreciate hearing me get my ass blown up while they're trying to study."

"Guess who finally showed up online this morning?" Vio asked.

"This morning?"

"This morning here, like twelve hours ago when I got up."

"I hope you're not going to say that BattleStud creep. I thought he'd get lost after the whipping we gave him last time."

"No, not BattleStud. JanSolo. He came in when we were at Level Nine and still managed to catch up and take us all out. I lasted to Level Thirteen."

Mila had never actually seen JanSolo online, just his scores. The top four of all time. "So he's real. I kind of figured he was fake to make people keep playing so they could try to beat him. Was he really that good?"

"Hell, yeah. We could take him together though. Hop on when you get done today. I should be out of bed by then."

"No joystick, remember? Anyway, my brain will be wiped by tonight." The minutes were ticking away and she hadn't yet eaten breakfast. "Time to go. I'll catch you later in the week."

They'd been divided into four color-coded groups—Blue, Green, Red and Orange—sixty-four candidates per group. On her way to their check-in station in the computer lab, Mila downed an energy bar and a carton of orange juice, the latter from a vending machine.

Everyone inside was dressed in the cargo pants and T-shirts they'd worn the day before. Not clean ones—the very same ones. Three days before they could change, according to the handbook. Their clothes would probably be filthy by then, but at least they were allowed to shower every day and put on clean underwear. For now, anyway. If she made it as far as the analog trial, they'd have to simulate conditions in space, where doing laundry was a major ordeal.

To Mila's extreme displeasure, Toloti was also Blue. No escaping her for the next few days.

"Hey, Mila. Nice hair."

The urge to pummel her impish grin was almost overwhelming. Instead, Mila ignored her and proceeded to the check-in table for her blue wristband and schedule. First up were tests in the computer lab to measure concentration and memory.

She hung back to give Toloti time to claim a seat, and then settled into a computer carrel far away on the back row.

"Is this seat taken?"

The familiar husky voice sent a thrill to her core. An uncontrollable thrill. A stupid, inexplicable, uncontrollable thrill. "It's yours."

How was she supposed to concentrate with Jancey Beaumont sitting beside her?

"Good morning." A diminutive man—from his dark features and sing-song accent, she assumed he was Indian—rose from behind the control console at the front of the room. He wore dark slacks and a yellow polo shirt, which Mila now recognized as the staff uniform. "My name is Dr. Chet Viswanathan. Dr.V if you prefer. We'll begin today's exercises with…"

An introductory page appeared on each monitor that allowed everyone to follow along as he described the procedures. The entire test was computerized and scored individually, and the sample questions were straightforward. The object was to assess short-term memory and the ability to concentrate.

Seemed easy enough to Mila, even with Jancey Beaumont distracting her from the next seat.

The test began with a series of triangles. At rapid fire speed, she indicated with her computer mouse if the triangle was pointed up, down, left or right. About ten slides in all, she guessed.

Effortless.

The next set of triangles had dots inside. One, two, three or four. She had about four seconds to choose the correct answer. Two left? Three down? Two down? Three right?

More challenging, but manageable.

Then the triangles were different colors. Four down green? Three right green? Four down red? Four right red?

She survived the triangle array only to see it replaced by four colored rectangles with a number inside. What color was four? What number was yellow?

Eight rectangles on the screen. Sum of the yellow. Product of the red.

After each set of tests, Mila waited for…hoped for…would have killed for a break, but the problems kept coming. Always the same pattern. An easy one with each new grouping but increasing in complexity at each step. A peek at her watch—forty-eight minutes—cost her a question, and nearly the whole grouping. On a space mission, a lapse in concentration like that could be deadly.

At one hour, the screen went blank and Dr. V stood from his platform again. "That completes Part One. In a moment you'll see your score, along with how you ranked in the Blue group. Your concentration and memory scores will be averaged with those from comprehension. Those who score in the top half and also pass the physical fitness test will proceed to the second round."

As if she weren't anxious enough. She rubbed her eyes furiously and rolled her head in a circle on her shoulders. Others in the room stood and stretched, talking with their neighbors to decompress.

After a few seconds, her score appeared. She'd missed only seven of nearly four hundred problems, for a score of ninety-eight percent.

Awesome. Concentration was one of her strengths. She'd proven that in her work at Delft when she waded through massive computer programs to find errors as small as four decimal points. No one on their team was better with details.

Then her group rank appeared: five.

Bloody hell! Four people in the room missed fewer than seven over a span of an hour. How was that even possible? Maybe because there were at least that many trained astronauts in the Blue group. If she was fifth in her group, she'd be twentieth overall after the other groups tested. Good enough to make the next cut, but not the finals. And this was supposed to be one of her strong suits!

"How'd you do?" Beaumont peered around the carrel to peek at her screen. "Seven. Not bad for the first try, but you'll need to get better."

When the major leaned back in her chair, Mila took the liberty of peeking at her score. Perfect.

Perfect!

"For those of you worried about your score, I have good news," Dr. V said. "Over the next three days, your test will be divided into six segments, with the lowest score dropped from your average. Now that you are acclimated to the structure and format, you should perform better. However, the remaining segments will be longer and more difficult. We'll begin Part Two in T-minus three…two…one."

She'd so hoped for a bathroom break.

The test started out like the first segment—sets of problems increasing in complexity—but this time, the visual displayed for only three seconds, followed occasionally by a screen from which she had to select the correct response based on memory. As the test wore on, the display time seemed to decrease, as did the time she had to mark her answer.

Mila tuned everything else out, refusing to glance away from the screen even for an instant. She played *BattleStorm* the same way and some of her sessions with Vio lasted hours. By her estimate, this segment was already twice as long as Part One, but still she focused, even ignoring the fly that began buzzing around her head.

Finally—*finally!*—the screen went blank and the room let out a collective groan. Even Jancey Beaumont flopped against the back of her chair.

"Still perfect?" Mila had to ask.

"We'll see. That damn fly was a pain in the ass. I never had to deal with flies in space."

Mila checked her watch. The test had lasted two hours, forty-five minutes. After what the major had endured on *Guardian*, it was clear why long periods of concentration were important. An article in *Scientific American* from twelve years ago—which Mila had saved and read dozens of times—detailed the extraordinary efforts Beaumont had made to guide her vessel into an adjacent orbit with the crippled Russian ship and complete a docking procedure. The entire episode had spanned seven hours and required continuous adjustments and monitoring. Only a well trained, highly disciplined astronaut could have accomplished such a feat.

The last line of that article stuck with Mila to this day. It was a quote from the major dismissing her own heroics. *I did what I was trained to do.*

Her new score flashed on the screen. Perfect. And tied with two others for first.

"Better?" Beaumont didn't wait for her answer, leaning around the carrel to peek. "There might be hope for you yet, Todorov."

* * *

The gymnasium was partitioned into eight fitness stations, each staffed by a pair of training assistants wearing yellow polo shirts. The Blue group was subdivided into teams of eight, one team at each station.

Jancey had hoped to find herself with Todorov, the poi-hating, forward-thinking engineer with the focus needed to make the next cut. It would have been nice to see if that brain was matched by enough physical capability to handle the rest of their training. A lot of the brainiacs she'd known at NASA were out of their element in a gym.

The director of fitness training was a Canadian, Danielle Zion, dressed in dark blue warm-up pants and the yellow staff shirt. According to her bio, she was fifty-two years old, but that had to be a misprint.

Fifty-two! Jancey considered herself fit and healthy for forty-three, but she paled next to Zion, a model of athleticism with finely sculpted muscles and short bleached-blond hair that stood at attention. A drill sergeant in sneakers.

"You've seen the schedule," Zion barked from the center of the gym. "You're mine until five o'clock. The fitness test is not a competition. Repeat. Not a competition. It's an elimination test with minimum requirements. You don't get extra points for running the fastest, lifting the most or stretching the farthest. You'll work with a partner from your group. We have three days together. You'll be tested at every station on the last day. You fail even one of them—you're out."

Most of the candidates appeared to be in decent shape. Not surprising, since they knew the minimum requirements and had months to prepare. Nonetheless, it was still possible a handful would come up short.

"I have one rule: Don't hurt yourself."

Jancey didn't have to be reminded. Pulling a muscle or spraining a joint would mean certain disqualification.

From her own experience in space, she was well aware of how hard it was to maintain muscle tone in zero gravity. It was one of the reasons she'd been chosen for the extended mission instead of a man, since NASA researchers felt she'd have an easier time staying fit than someone with more bulk. She hoped the Tenacity committee would come to the same conclusion, especially since she'd proven those researchers correct.

Her team started at the sit-up station, which was equipped with mats and stopwatches. A placard indicated the required baseline—forty sit-ups in one minute—along with instructions to complete at least three timed trials before moving to the next station.

The group consisted of four men, two women and one ready-made team, a married couple from Japan. The men paired up immediately, leaving Jancey to team with the other woman. She was a few years older with a mass of curly red hair breaking free from a tie. From the looks of it, she hadn't spent quite as much time in the gym as the others.

"I believe you need a partner," the woman said, extending her hand. "Shel Montgomery, Helena, Montana. Freelance space journalist."

Jancey introduced herself.

"You're kidding, right? Everyone knows who you are. Hell, I bet you're the reason half of these younger people are here."

"Now you're making me feel old."

"Age is a state of mind. Show them how it's done."

Since Shel was already holding the stopwatch, Jancey went first. Sit-ups were part of her regular routine, and she easily reeled off sixty-four in one minute.

"I think I'm screwed," Shel said, swapping positions so Jancey could hold her feet. "I've been trying to work out ever since I got word to come to Hawaii, but I have a lot of neglect to make up for. I hadn't done sit-ups since high school."

Unfortunately for Shel, it showed. Thirty-one, and during the last five, her face was as red as her hair.

"You can do this, Shel. There's a trick. I'll show you." In slow motion, she demonstrated an abbreviated crunch, lifting only six inches off the floor. "It's all about the abs. You don't need to involve those other muscles. Pick a spot on the ceiling and focus on it. That'll keep you from losing your form."

On her next try, Shel managed thirty-six.

"That's it. You'll easily get to forty by Wednesday. I guarantee it." As much as Jancey hated to admit it, helping and encouraging someone else was intrinsically rewarding. She might not have been so generous had it been Mila Todorov, who had the potential to be a significant rival. Her perfect score on the concentration test was nothing to take lightly, especially since she'd never gone through formal astronaut training. Plus she had special knowledge of propulsion systems.

Over at the next station, Todorov was climbing a knotted rope to the rafters as smoothly as if it were a ladder. As her arm stretched upward, her T-shirt rose to reveal the rippling muscles of her torso.

Jancey wasn't the only one to notice. Zion watched from directly below, her face fixed in a look of admiration. Or was it something else? Todorov was definitely worth a second look with her taut body and exotic eyes.

But not worth the distraction. Jancey needed every single synapse trained on her goal of getting to the round of one-twenty-eight. It would be foolish to assume she'd make the first cut just because she was Jancey Beaumont. The new blood around her was fit, young and smart, and there might even be some among them who were as hungry as she to go. It wouldn't do to let someone like Mila Todorov distract her, even for an instant.

* * *

"Push it up from your chest, not your shoulders," Toloti said. She stood behind Mila to spot the thirty-pound barbell.

It wasn't the way she usually pressed, but admittedly, it took the strain off her triceps and transferred it to her pectorals. Despite the benefits, she hated taking direction from Toloti.

No matter what Zion had said about only needing to pass the baseline scores, as long as the invisible hand that controlled them kept pairing her with Toloti, there would be competition to see who was stronger, faster and could do more reps. The cynic in Mila considered she might be a plant to see if she would break under psychological torture. The secret to controlling her fury was closing her eyes and imagining she were pushing the barbell into the bridge of Toloti's nose.

"Nineteen…twenty. That's it. My turn."

Toloti's presses looked effortless, not a single grimace or even a slowing of pace as she ticked off twenty reps. *Showoff.*

The most challenging task Mila had faced during her PhD program and postdoc was dealing with the personalities of her colleagues, especially when her fellow graduate students bonded socially and brought their Happy Hour atmosphere to the propulsion lab. If she could have done the project on her own, it wouldn't have mattered. Instead she'd been forced to adapt.

Adapt and persist. What astronauts were trained to do.

She looked admiringly across the gym at Jancey Beaumont, whose face was streaming with sweat from her agility drills. A fine specimen at forty-three years. A fine specimen at any age. She had the whole package—fitness, intellect and a mental focus unmatched by anyone in the room.

The major picked that moment to look up, catching Mila in her gaze.

Toloti punched her arm lightly. "You having a nice nap?"

Mila settled onto the bench and gripped the bar. As she pressed upward, she inhaled, a voice in her head clearly enunciating, "Screw." On her exhale, that same voice said, "Toloti."

Screw. Toloti.

CHAPTER FOUR

Mila liked her chances for surviving the first cut. She'd sailed through the fitness test while turning in top scores in concentration and comprehension. None of that meant she'd sleep peacefully, since the results were to be posted the next morning. She was as anxious as anyone.

The cafeteria line offered a buffet for dinner, one with a variety of choices rather than the same plate as everyone else. As she'd done every night so far, she went to the pasta bar, loading up on shells, pesto and crumbled feta cheese, with a simple salad. On principle, she also took a scoop of poi.

The sight of Toloti eating alone gave her pause. Toloti, Toloti. She was trying to get into the habit of using her first name, Andi. The selection committee would expect them to be friends by this time.

It was reasonable to want some downtime alone to decompress from their rigorous testing schedule, but she couldn't escape thinking they all were under observation. No one knew who was on the selection committee. Perhaps the woman checking meal cards or the man wiping tables. Virtually anyone could be writing reports and slipping them into their files for consideration. She had to prove she could get along as a member of a team.

"Okay if I sit down?"

"Sure thing." By her typically bubbly demeanor, Andi was extremely pleased. "Ew, I cain't believe you're eating that poi crap. That stuff is gross."

Mila's initial reaction was to bristle at the notion that it was any of Andi's business what she ate. Saying so, however, would defeat the purpose of sitting with her. Besides, she happened to be correct. "It's very high in fluorine, which is good for bone density."

Andi lifted a forkful of baked beans. "So are beans, 'cept they don't taste like Elmer's Glue."

"No, but they cause flatulence, and as your roommate, I'd prefer you ate poi."

"Cain't argue with ya there." Andi leaned back and rolled her shoulders. "I'm gonna be sore tomorrow. I pushed it too hard climbing that rope today without using my legs."

Otherwise known as showing off.

"I nearly puked after the cardio this morning," Mila confessed. "I've never run two miles in twelve minutes in my whole life." The baseline fitness level needed to earn a passing grade was sixteen minutes, but she wanted to excel.

"You think we'll make the first cut?" Andi's voice was somber, a marked change in her usual cockiness.

Everyone was nervous about what the morning would bring. Half would go to the next level while the others either joined the ranks of the support team or went home.

"I'm pretty sure I will. You?"

Andi shook her head. "No idea. The concentration tests killed me. I'm not used to having to do things so fast. I'm a biochemist, not a jet pilot. We take our time in the lab, double-checking, triple-checking. My scores came up a little after the first day, but so did everybody else's, so my rank is stuck around the midtwenties. That might not be good enough."

If Andi got cut, she'd get a new roommate. Maybe someone worse. Better the devil she knew.

"They're puttin' all of us in teams for the next round, you know," Andi went on. "I heard one of the assistants say they'd probably pair us up with our roommates, since we were already matched by computer as a good fit. You think we are?"

"For our skills, yes. For our specialties, yes. For our personalities, no."

"Aw, come on. We get along just fine. I bet one of the reasons they put us together was because we're both gay. Maybe they figure we'll hit it off."

The thought alone was enough to make her choke without the oh-so-confident flirtatious smile Andi threw in to see if she'd bite. Mila snapped back, "We will most certainly not hit it off. You are so far from my type, you might as well be another species."

"Lemme guess. You like your girls in high heels, short skirts, painted faces."

"I like women, not girls. And I don't care what they wear as long as they're intelligent, independent,"—she ticked off the words on her fingers—"enjoy the tango, and don't mind being worshipped, because that's what I do when I find a woman who is worthy of my affections."

All in all, it was the perfect description of Frederica, with whom she'd had an off and on relationship for the past nine years. Twenty-one years older, her mother's colleague from the university. And mother of a ten-year-old boy who drove Mila insane with his incessant neediness. Frederica's problem was that she didn't enjoy being worshipped publicly, at least not by another woman. Always hiding. Always pretending. Even around her son, which made having a relationship with her more challenging than the Tenacity trials.

"The tango? Are you seriously from this planet?"

"Hopefully not. I'd like very much to be from another one soon."

* * *

Jancey patted her stomach after finishing the last bite of a delicious grilled mahi-mahi with mango sauce, served poolside by Konani. "Too bad Konani didn't apply for Tenacity. I'd love to take her to Mars."

"Over my dead body," Grace said. "Lana hired her, you know. She was a janitor at the telescope center and got laid off. Lana sent her to culinary school and after three months we both had to go on a diet. I don't know what I'd do without her."

And vice versa. Jancey had been a visitor to the seaside home for a dozen years and knew Konani was far more than just a live-in cook and housekeeper. She also was Grace's personal assistant and trusted companion, and Jancey liked knowing she was there, especially after Lana died.

"That goes for you too," Grace said. "I don't know what I'll do without you once you go to Mars."

Jancey sipped her Frangelico, one of the few indulgences she allowed herself, knowing it would help her sleep. "Don't count your chickens. I may not be going anywhere, especially now that I know if I stay here, I can eat like that."

"Where do you think you stand?"

"I should be okay for this round. We'll find out tomorrow morning, seven o'clock. Then it's back to the lecture hall all day to talk about teamwork." Jancey refused to worry about surviving the first cut. She'd hardly felt challenged so far, logging nearly perfect scores on every test. "Next they'll pair us with someone at random to see how we work as a team. I have to manage not to kill my partner for six whole days."

"You should be able to last that long...I think."

"We'll see. Depends on who they give me. I have a suspicion it'll be Shel Montgomery, since we were teamed together for the fitness tests."

"Is that good or bad?"

"The jury's still out. She's a science writer. I looked up some of her work. It's good. Logical, original. She did great on the concentration and comprehension tests. Top ten percent. I'll be surprised if she makes it much further though. Not hands-on enough. I wish they'd let us pick our own partner."

"They will once you're down to sixteen. That's the group that goes up on Mauna Kea for six weeks. In the meantime, they're doing all the pairings within your color group."

Grace had enough inside information on the assessment process for Jancey to speculate she was part of the selection committee, but sworn to secrecy. There were three or four others who'd kicked in major funds too. They probably had a say in the outcome as well.

"I'm thinking about asking Marlon Quinn if he wants to pair up. With our training and experience, we ought to be unbeatable."

Her main concern with Marlon was the committee disregarding objective criteria in favor of making a public relations splash. Choosing a pair of NASA-trained astronauts to go to Mars was hardly outside the box. They might be tempted to choose one of the married couples, who were allowed to partner with one another throughout the competition. Or someone famous, like one of the athletes or politicians. If they opted for a safe choice, it most likely would be a pair of men. Straight men, not the gay couple from Norway, even though one was an astronaut from the European Space Agency.

"Do you think you could live out your years with Marlon Quinn?"

"Sure, why not? He wants to go as badly as I do, so we'd make it work. He's a good guy. We respect each other. That counts for a lot."

"I'm thinking more about what happens at the end of the day. That's a lot of time to while away with someone who doesn't sing from your choir book."

Grace offered to pour another Frangelico, but Jancey waved it away. It was an unspoken ritual that Grace would have three drinks over the course of each day. Never less, rarely more. An afternoon cocktail, a glass of wine with dinner and an after-dinner cordial. A longstanding habit that honored her years with Lana.

"You can do better than Marlon, you know. You just have to know where to look."

"Where to look? Trust me, I know exactly where to look. My hormones are still clicking enough that I still notice an interesting woman when she walks by. One in particular, in fact, and I'd lay you odds she sings from our choir book."

"Do tell."

"A little on the green side. A lot on the green side, actually, but smart. Very smart. You show her something once and she's got it. A propulsion engineer." She recalled her impression the day Mila sat down across from her in the cafeteria. "There's something about her eyes. I can't put my finger on it, but they're different...interesting. And that Eastern European accent with the hard R's. Like a spy from the Cold War."

"So why in the world would you pick Marlon Quinn when you could have someone like that?"

Jancey laughed. "She's just a baby. Twenty-seven years old. She'll probably make it to Mars eventually but not for another ten years."

"Lana was twenty-seven when we met. And I was forty-five. If I'd turned her down because I thought she was a child, I'd have lived a lonely life."

"The difference is you didn't want to be alone. Apparently I do. Monica, Lindsay, Jill...they had me pegged. I only want what's important to me, and to hell with everyone else." The last she added with no small dose of agitation. Just because it was true didn't mean she liked it. Anyone as selfish as she deserved to be alone.

"That's not even relevant in this case. You have to go with someone. If she's made it this far in the selection process, she wants to go to Mars just as much as you do. That makes you the perfect pair...even if you aren't chosen to go." Ignoring her protestations, Grace poured another inch of liqueur into her snifter. "To help you sleep. Just promise me, Jancey...if it doesn't work out, think about staying on with the program. Teach them what they need to know to live on Mars. You can even get in line to try again, but better yet...find someone who shares your passion for the stars and settle down. Let someone in there."

It was a promise Jancey couldn't make. Sticking around to watch others steal her dream was more than she could bear.

* * *

"I didn't sleep at all," Andi said as they approached the growing crowd gathered around the electronic billboard at the computer center.

Mila knew for a fact that wasn't true because she'd been forced in the night to put in her earplugs to muffle Andi's snoring. "A bunch of people failed the physical fitness test. That makes our odds better."

"Go up there and look for me. I cain't do it."

It was an emotional scene before her. Jubilation and heartbreak, cheers and tears. Mila wedged herself through the crowd until she was close enough to see the board. The names of the candidates who made the cut were listed in alphabetical order, and in parentheses was the name of their assigned partner for the next round of assessment, and their group.

Joy and misery hit her at once: *Todorov (Toloti) (Blue)*, and immediately below, *Toloti (Todorov) (Blue)*.

She scanned the board for familiar names. *Beaumont (Montgomery) (Blue)*. Montgomery was the journalist who'd been paired with Jancey during the physical fitness tests.

As expected, all of the astronauts were still in the running. So too the scientists and experts who'd given presentations during the overview. The robotics expert who'd helped design the rovers, and his wife, the NASA astronaut. The bacteriologist on the spacesuit team. The married couple who'd written the systems software. All were formidable candidates.

Isaac Tobias and his yarmulke had missed the cut. So had the Blaskos, the married couple in her fitness group. In fact, she and Andi were the only two from their group of eight to make it.

"We made it. They teamed us up for the next round."

Before she could get out of the way, Andi leaped onto her chest, wrapping her arms and legs around her. "That's so awesome, Mila! You and me. We're gonna rule."

"Get off me, please," Mila said dryly. "If you break my back, I'll be disqualified."

She grudgingly admitted to herself they made a competent team. Provided, of course, they could overcome Andi's lapses in concentration. And Mila's urge to kill her.

* * *

The selection committee hadn't bothered to pair candidates according to their skills, which suggested they weren't planning to assess on any of the specific elements related to the mission. This was about teamwork, and it was apparent they'd preserved a number of the teams from the physical fitness test.

Jancey felt certain she could work with Shel Montgomery, but it was difficult to imagine Shel moving on after this round. An astronaut couldn't rely only on her brain, or even her brawn. She needed finer skills, such as dexterity and good reaction time, something you didn't get from years at a keyboard. That said, Shel had earned her respect by pushing herself hard on the fitness test.

Inside the lecture hall, candidates buzzed with excitement over making the cut.

Shel slid into the seat next to her. "Sorry they saddled you with this old albatross again. Between you and me, I was surprised to see my name on the list."

"I'm sure they were impressed by how much you improved after only three days in the gym."

"It felt more like six. I went in there every night after dinner. I had to do something or it was lights out."

Jancey was even more inspired. "You show that kind of dedication over the next couple of weeks, you just might find yourself on the short list."

"Don't let my wife hear you say that. The only reason she let me come was because I convinced her I didn't have a snowball's chance in hell. She thinks I'm here working on a story."

"Your wife?" Jancey's gaydar was obviously broken. "You'd actually leave her if you got chosen?"

"Tough call. This is Mars we're talking about."

If anyone understood that, it was Jancey, though Shel's jovial tone suggested she had no real intention of following through, nor the expectation that she had a legitimate shot.

"I wonder how many of these people have a wife or husband at home. Can you imagine the ruckus when they said they wanted to go to Mars?"

Shel huffed. "I don't have to imagine it. Pat thought I was crazy."

"You are. We all are."

CHAPTER FIVE

Throughout the first round of testing, Mila had gone to sleep each night hearing Danielle Zion's booming voice in her head. *Lift more, run faster, climb higher*. She'd expected a break now that the fitness testing was finished. No such luck.

No matter what the activity, if it took place in her gym, Zion was in charge. Here she was again, pacing the hardwood floor like the lord of her castle.

Now on their third day of testing with partners, Mila was optimistic about surviving yet another round. Her reaction time scores were superb, thanks to thousands of hours of playing *BattleStorm*. High enough in fact to carry Andi, who wasn't as quick.

Moriya Ito, who headed up the instrumentation team, had put them through an exhaustive battery of dexterity tests, all of which required teamwork. Sorting nails and screws, assembling pins and washers, pushing pegs into holes of various shapes and sizes. Simple stuff until the second round, when they'd been given bulky work gloves and glasses that limited their field of vision.

Only one more afternoon of tests before tomorrow's cut, which would take them down to sixty-four.

Zion split them into groups of eight, with one observer in a yellow staff shirt assigned to each group to keep track of scores and take notes on individual performances. Notes for the mysterious selection committee, no doubt.

Mila was intrinsically motivated to do well, but having Major Beaumont and her partner in her group brought out her best effort.

Just call me Jancey.

That was hard to do, especially since Jancey not only called her Todorov, she made it sound as if it came from a barking bulldog. Toloti's name was even worse, like a throat-clearing.

Also in the group were the Fagans, Brandon and Libby, both MIT grads. Brandon was the robotics engineer whose company had built the Mars rover that launched a couple of weeks ago aboard *Tenacity I*. His wife was a NASA astronaut with a PhD in botany, but she'd never flown a mission. Still, their complementary skills made them a sure bet to advance.

Rounding out their group were Guillermo Rojas and Wei Chai. Throughout the morning, the two had provided comic relief trying to communicate with each other, one with a heavy Spanish accent and the other, Chinese.

"I want all groups lined up behind the cones," Zion yelled. "On your butts, side by side with your partner."

Mila's mind flashed back to the games she'd played in primary school. Many of the Tenacity exercises they'd done as partners were quite similar to children's games, but here the stakes were much higher.

It was undeniable she and Andi made an effective team. Only once had she really, really wanted to kill her. That was when Andi made a joke to the others about Mila eating poi with every meal. *It's high in fluorine*, she'd mocked in a high, squeaky voice. Jancey had laughed. Snorted, actually. Mila wanted to crawl under a rock.

At the front of each line, Zion had placed several small wooden blocks of varying shapes. Toddler toys, the kind they stacked into castles, cars or monsters.

"Imagine you're in space and your vessel suffers external damage. One of you has to put on the spacesuit and go outside to fix it. The other has to stay inside and read the instructions aloud. That's what we're doing here. First team in the line, come up to the front and have a seat back to back. One partner gets the blocks, the other gets the envelope. Inside is a picture of a structure using all the pieces. You'll have two minutes to describe to your partner how to build the structure you see."

A staff observer stood by to supervise the activity and record scores. And no doubt to keep anyone from turning around to sneak a peek at the photograph.

Mila and Andi were first in their line, and Mila got the envelope.

"Let's make this a bit more realistic, shall we?" Zion handed out two pairs of gloves, one made of stiff rubber, and the other bulky canvas. "Put the rubber ones on first."

"I feel like an idiot," Andi said as she wiggled her fingers open and shut. "And don't you dare say what you're thinking."

"Questions?" Zion allowed less than two seconds to respond. "Proceed."

Mila ripped open the envelope. "This would be so much easier if I spoke Texan."

"Or if I spoke Bulgarian gibberish."

"Oops, I've loosened your tether. There you go…drifting away." She rotated the photo until she was sure she had it upright. "Start with the rhomboid. Lay it flat on the floor with the smaller angle on the lower left side. Next, stand the trapezoid upright with the widest side as the base, bisecting the center of the rhomboid with the ends at two o'clock and eight. Now take the triangle…" Using precise angles and measures, they were able to reconstruct the sculpture with relative ease well before time ran out.

She bumped Andi's fist in celebration as their team's observer recorded their success on a score sheet.

Next came the Fagans, whose envelope contained a different photo. They got the pieces in the right order, but Brandon failed to specify the proper rotation of the base. Nearly perfect, but not.

"You didn't listen," he snapped.

"I did. You never told me the rectangle was supposed to be vertical."

"You should have asked instead of assuming. One little mistake like that could knock us out of contention."

Mila traded awkward looks with Andi as the couple squabbled, but she didn't dare turn around. It wasn't any of her business if Libby was willing to put up with being bullied by her husband. It probably threatened his masculinity that she, as an astronaut, was already in one of the world's most elite clubs and he wasn't.

Guillermo and Wei took their turn, talking hopelessly past one another. It would be a miracle if either of them advanced to the next round.

Zion clapped. "Last team. You're up!"

By this time, Mila and Andi had moved back to the front of the line, close enough to hear Jancey and Shel struggling with the task. Shel confused the trapezoid with the rhomboid, and had trouble estimating degrees and centimeters.

"This is impossible," Shel said. "We should have switched sides so I'd get the envelope. I'm no good on this end."

"You have to focus," Jancey told her firmly as the clock ticked. "You heard what Zion said. If this is an exercise in space, failure isn't an option. Now pay attention. We've got less than a minute left."

"I'm serious, Jancey. I can't do it this way. The harder I try, the more confusing it gets." Shel staggered to her feet, gripping her head with both hands. Her eyes were squeezed shut and her face was twisted in a look of pain.

"What's happening?" Jancey rushed to her side, as did Zion and their team's observer.

"That ringing…can't you hear it?"

Mila jumped up also, moving closer in case Shel stumbled.

"Easy does it," Zion said. "It's probably just some pressure built up in the inner ear. Take her outside and walk her around." She gestured for Mila and Andi to go along.

A blast of hot, humid air enveloped the four women as they stepped outside in the afternoon sun. Mila supported one of

Shel's elbows while Andi held the other. They guided her to a bench where she collapsed, still holding her head.

"I'm fine, ladies. Just trying to make it look good."

Jancey checked her forehead, obviously worried. "What the hell are you talking about?"

"I was killing you, Jancey. That guy in the yellow shirt…our observer. I saw him write something in his notebook when I was trying to make sense of what you were saying. He checked *your* badge, not mine. I don't want to be known as the idiot who got Jancey Beaumont bounced out of the Tenacity Project."

"Are you insane? You can't just give up like that. One little test doesn't mean anything. We train like this for a reason."

Shel looked at Mila with pleading eyes. "Tell her. You saw the guy."

Mila felt her stomach drop as she came under Jancey's fiery gaze. "I did. He checked your badge and then made a mark on his clipboard."

"So freaking what? He should have been writing that I remained calm. That I was clear and persistent."

"I don't think so." It took nerve for Mila to disagree with Jancey, but this was important. "He frowned and shook his head. Whatever he wrote, it wasn't good."

"He frowned and shook his head," Shel repeated pointedly. "The only reason I got this far was because all the tests have been visual up to now. I've had a problem with auditory directions ever since I was a kid. I have to record everything and transcribe it to make sense of it. I can't even use a talking GPS in my car. It's been a good run, but this is the end of the line for me. If I don't pull out right now, your scores are going in the toilet."

Jancey threw her hands up. "That's it? How can you just give up like that? This is Mars we're talking about. Do you know how many people would kill to be where you are?"

"And we both know I don't stand a chance of getting there. It's not even a real test because there's no way you'd ever get sent to Mars with a journalist, not when half the people left are astronaut material. Do you want to risk losing your shot?"

"She's right, Jancey," Andi said. "You can't take a chance on this. There's too much at stake."

The veins in Jancey's neck rippled as she clenched her jaw. "If this is how you're going to deal with adversity in space, I sure hope none of you end up going with me. Where's your tenacity? Your persistence? Your determination?"

"She's just being logical," Mila said. She felt bad for Shel, who'd just fallen on her sword to save Jancey's chances. "When you're faced with a situation where one of you *might* succeed or both of you will *probably* fail, there's only one rational choice. I'd have done the same thing Shel did, Jancey. At least for you. Not for Shel or Andi though. The stronger one must survive."

Andi smacked her on the upper arm. "You think you're stronger than me?"

"It's *stronger than I*, and yes. Maybe not physically, but I can improve that during training. I don't believe any amount of training will bring your concentration or spatial acuity up to my level. On a mission to Mars, those skills will be far more important than physical strength."

It hadn't been her intention to insult Andi. She only meant to dispel the tension between Shel and Jancey, and apparently she'd done that. Both of them were looking away and whistling innocently as if trying not to witness Andi's humiliation.

"I'm not saying you aren't smart enough to make the cut. Organic chemistry is very important in a long-term space project."

"Damn right it is. Without me you'd starve to death, so don't go thinking you're going to cut my tether and let me drift off into space."

Mila could have argued that she expected to be trained in the science of growing food and cloning protein, and that she was fully capable of learning it. Something in Andi's red face told her she'd already said more than enough.

* * *

As much as Jancey hated to admit it, her chances for moving on were notably improved now that Shel had withdrawn. Not only was she free from the consequences of her auditory learning problems, she was reaping a clear advantage from being grouped with Mila and Andi for the rest of the afternoon. They were smart and capable, and took their tasks seriously.

They also were competitive with one another, and it made both of them better.

Mila in particular seemed to grasp how the small details added up to the big picture. She was confident of her strengths and determined to overcome her weaknesses. Logical, systematic, unexcitable. Perfect qualities for an astronaut.

The observers scurried around the gym passing out pencils and index cards.

"Something a little different this time," Zion yelled from the center of the gym. "Not a test…just something to get you thinking about life on Mars. You may launch with three personal items. Assume that all of your scientific needs are met, as are your basic necessities of food and hygiene. I'm talking about personal items for leisure and comfort. Be reasonable. That means no bicycles or grand pianos. Write down which three things you'll take."

Thanks to her year-long mission, Jancey knew exactly what she'd take to Mars. A tablet computer so she could read or watch video without having to sit at the command console. She expected Mission Control to supply her with a steady stream of science articles so she could keep up with her field, though once she left for Mars, the scientific discoveries on Earth would have less consequence for her. Her work—her experiments and observations—would constitute a new subfield of molecular biology, one that depended solely on her dedication to sharing her newfound knowledge.

The other two items were critical to keeping her sane— her clarinet and a box of reeds that would last until supplies could be replenished within a couple of years by the next wave of colonists. There would be little time for leisure, but she understood after her year alone in space how important it was to make time for relaxation.

"I'll go first," Andi said. "I want my noise-canceling headphones. And I want an iPod that holds every piece of music I like. And third, I want my neck pillow, the one I use on airplanes."

Mila nodded slowly. "Those are very good choices."

"You're going to say something smartass now, aren't you?"

"You might consider it smartass, but I'm sincere in saying how much I appreciate that you included headphones so I wouldn't be impacted by your desire to listen to music I don't enjoy."

"It's better than that crap you listen to…Bulgarian choirs. They sound like elephants at a funeral."

"I'll have you know Bulgarian choral music is a centuries-old style that contains complex diaphony and dissonant harmony, all of which are culturally conditioned. It takes a trained ear to appreciate it. A trained Bulgarian ear. Whereas your music… what is it they say? It has a nice beat and you can dance to it."

"Girls, girls." Jancey was both impressed and entertained by Mila's precision takedown, but with the observers wandering around taking notes, it mattered more to show they could work as a team without bickering. "I'll go next."

She listed her items, explaining their importance during her time aboard *Guardian*. When she mentioned her clarinet, she glowered at Andi, daring her to call it crap.

"I would take a Rubik's Cube, a five-by-five," Mila said. "I've only solved it once, and it took me weeks. If I had the time to concentrate, I'd try to figure out the algorithms so I could get my time down to under an hour. And I'm very interested in reading, so a tablet computer would be a good idea, especially since I could also use it to watch video and listen to music. Including tango music. I would enjoy very much teaching my partner the tango."

Andi rolled her eyes dramatically and addressed Jancey, "Are you hearing this crap?"

Not only was Jancey hearing it, she was keenly aware that Mila appeared to be directing her comments to her and not Andi. That took chutzpah.

"And third…I have noise-canceling headphones on my list too. That way, my partner can do whatever she wants and it won't disturb me."

"Next exercise," Zion bellowed. "Name one item you'll take for your partner, the other person in your crew."

"Andi needs her own tablet," Mila said without hesitation. "Music's fine, but it doesn't stimulate as much as reading or watching video."

"Who says I wanna be stimulated? The way I see it, we could be working fifteen hours a day. That's enough stimulation for me. Besides, we can trade back and forth, my iPod for your tablet. That way you can listen to your *dissonant harmonies.*"

Jancey heard an undertone of grudging camaraderie between the two, but hoped for Mila's sake she ended up with someone else if she were chosen to go. She needed a partner who was committed to her success, not one needling her at every turn. "I agree with Mila. I'd take along a tablet for you. If you never used it, I'd have an extra when mine wore out."

"Fine, then I'd take an iPod for Mila. I can't take one for you though because you won't have any headphones."

"Of course I will," Jancey said. "The ones that come with our comm system are far superior to anything you can buy commercially."

Mila scrunched her nose and nodded, clearly conceding she'd wasted a pick. "Jancey, I'd take along another box of reeds for your clarinet so you wouldn't have to worry about running out."

Thoughtful and selfless. Exactly the way a partner should be. "Thank you. Except I'd probably run out anyway, because I'd take a second clarinet for you. I'd teach you to play, and perhaps you'd train my ear in the Bulgarian tradition. It sounds very challenging, like something we could work on together for years."

She held Mila's look for several conspicuous seconds, biting her tongue to keep from adding that she'd love learning the tango.

Andi scoffed, breaking their gaze. "Thank God you didn't pick a clarinet for me. I'd take a tablet over that any day."

Jancey shook her head as she snapped their gaze, scolding herself. She didn't need a distraction like Mila, not when both of them were fighting for a seat on *Tenacity*. Grace Faraday would say otherwise, that Mila was the perfect partner for a lifelong trip to a hostile planet. They had to get there first, and that wouldn't happen if she didn't focus.

CHAPTER SIX

On the video screen, Mila's grandmother sat at her kitchen table in Sofia. "Who will take care of me if you go to Mars?"

"The same person who will take care of you if I don't—you. You take care of yourself better than anyone else can." She'd learned from her classmates at Delft that the guttural sounds and harsh cadence of Bulgarian made her sound angry. Those in the library at this early hour likely thought the same thing. "Mother promised to come see you more often, and you could always go to Berlin for a visit."

"Fine, go to Mars. You don't care about me."

She shouldn't have been surprised by her grandmother's sullen reaction to her news that she'd survived another cut. Vio had responded exactly the same way. "I do care, Grandmother. I love you."

"I love you too, Milanka."

Mila cringed at the cutesy nickname. Why couldn't her mother have chosen a stronger name that couldn't be cutesy-fied? Like Gergana or Genoveva. Those names commanded respect.

The Blue group had been divided into two teams for today's test. According to the schedule, her team was to report to the pool. The word alone was enough to convince her to skip breakfast. She was a fair swimmer—good enough not to drown—but she hated being submersed. Her older cousins in Bulgaria had made a game of holding her underwater as she thrashed, laughing cruelly when she coughed up half the river.

She would know today if she had what it took to be an astronaut. Much of their training would be conducted underwater to simulate weightlessness. If she couldn't beat back her anxiety, she had no business going further.

Andi and Libby Fagan were coming out of the women's locker room in their swimsuits when she arrived.

"Hustle up, Mila," Andi said. "If you're late, I'm gonna kick your ass."

"Is that Texan for please?"

She found a locker with her name on it and removed a swimsuit and towel. Getting naked out in the open was disconcerting but she didn't have time to go searching for a stall, not at the risk of being late. She'd stripped down to nothing when the door opened and Jancey came in.

"Ready for your big swim?"

Mila fumbled with her suit and finally stretched it into place. Of all the people in the world to walk in on her naked, it had to be Jancey Beaumont.

Jancey wasted no time peeling down to her underwear.

"Ready as I'll ever be." If she waited five more seconds, she'd have a glorious vision burned into her memory to last for all of eternity. Her face was already on fire at the thought of being caught staring. Without even stashing her clothes in the locker, she blew past Jancey and out the door.

The rest of their group was waiting on the pool deck, where Mila got her first look at the day's exercise. A cube-shaped scaffold about three meters across had been lowered by a boom to the bottom of the diving well. An etching along the side noted its depth at five meters. Judging from the equipment on the pool deck—scuba tanks, diving masks and bulky gloves—their job was to construct something underwater. That something was in a fishnet bag, but she couldn't make out what it was.

The new Blue group looked a lot like the old one with Jancey and the Fagans. Guillermo and Wei were gone, replaced by Gunther Hardig, a German chemist, and Jerry Huffstetler, a NASA alum from Huntsville, Alabama, who talked a lot like Andi. One thing was clear: the remaining candidates represented serious competition.

Mila and Andi had continued to work well as a team. They'd breezed through the puzzles, peg boards and pin sorting by establishing a pattern of helping. Both were capable of completing each task individually, but they worked faster when one assumed leadership and the other served as support.

Irrespective of the task, the greatest challenge today was the water.

As Jancey exited the locker room, Mila's eyes were drawn to the subtle ripples in her thighs. She was perfectly proportioned. Only her forearms were outsized, and Jancey had let them in on why. Astronauts used their hands more than anything else—twisting, winding, turning. Not only was it a waste of effort to overdevelop larger muscles all over her body, it was counterproductive, since those muscles would lose mass in zero gravity.

Mila looked down to realize she'd begun opening and closing her fists. Starting tonight in the gym, she'd focus more of her workout on her hands and forearms.

The last person to arrive poolside was Marlon Quinn, the African-American astronaut who'd spent months at the International Space Station. Mila had seen his name next to Jancey's this morning on the partners list. The rumor mill yesterday afternoon had it that his former partner, a Scottish RAF pilot, had left the project unexpectedly after learning his ex-girlfriend was pregnant with his child. *Oops.*

Jancey and Marlon. The top two candidates in the whole program, and now they were paired together. No one else stood a chance.

Danielle Zion emerged from an office near the diving platform. "In case you're wondering, the only way to get away from me is to go to Mars." Her voice echoed off the tile walls.

"Wanna bet?" Andi whispered. "She'll probably be on an exercise hologram."

Zion shook out the contents of one of the fishnet bags onto the pool deck. "Today's task is worth twenty points to your team. Each bag contains two plastic water jugs with screw caps, four of these plastic zip ties,"—she waved them in the air—"one rubber hose with couplings on each end, and two washers that fit into those couplings. Your job is to use the zip ties to mount these two jugs on the crossbars of the scaffold. Then you take off the caps and connect them to each other with this hose. Easy-peasey, right?"

That sounded simple. Too simple.

"I forgot to mention…we don't want any water in these jugs. How are you going to do that?"

"Keep them level with the opening down," Marlon said.

"Correct. This is a precision exercise. If you tilt your jug even a little with the cap off, it'll fill up with water. If that happens, you need to get it out. Bring it back up and empty it if you have to…whatever it takes. But you'll lose a point every time you break the surface. That includes chasing down any floating pieces that get away from you. You also lose a point for every half-liter of water I drain out of your assembly when we raise the scaffold. Questions?"

One second…two seconds…

"Each tank has approximately ten minutes of air, give or take a few minutes. Don't assume your partner has the same amount as you."

With the air tank strapped on her back, Mila followed the rest of the team into the water to check the seal on her mask. According to the air gauges, she had more minutes than Andi.

I can do this. I have to do this.

Zion tossed their fishnet bags into the water, where they floated on top.

Andi said, "First thing we do is secure this bag to the scaffold so it doesn't float up."

"I have more air than you, so if one of us needs to go to the top, I'll do it."

"Works for me."

As Zion finished passing out their equipment, Mila visualized completing their task. "I've got this figured out, Andi. Just follow my lead."

"What if you're wrong?"

"I'm not. Just do this one thing without arguing, and I'll… I'll let you be in charge next time. Deal?"

Zion yelled, "Good luck, mateys! Down you go."

It took both of them kicking furiously to get the air-filled jugs to the bottom of the pool, where they tied the bag to the scaffold. With her foot hooked on the lower crossbar to control her buoyancy, Mila loosened the opening of the bag and snaked her hand inside to grab the zip ties, which she looped through the belt on Andi's air tank for easy access.

One of the washers escaped while they were removing the first jug, but Mila was able to snatch it before it floated out of reach. To keep that from happening again, she grabbed the other washer and placed both of them in Andi's glove for safekeeping.

The pressure against her ears made her head hurt, but her typical anxiety about being underwater was allayed by having something urgent to do. This wasn't about the water. She had plenty of air. No one was holding her down.

It also eased her nerves to see everyone else absorbed in the task. On their right, the Fagans were working together in similar fashion with Brandon taking the lead and Libby assisting. Jancey and Marlon were side by side, each strapping a jug in place. Theirs was a different kind of teamwork, where they trusted one another to work independently. Impressive.

With Andi holding the first jug in place, Mila strapped it vertically to the crossbar, leaving just enough play to tighten it later in case it wasn't level. They repeated that procedure with the second jug.

The next part was trickier, but first she took a moment to check Andi's air supply. Down half. They'd be lucky to get one end of the hose in place before she had to bail.

Ever so carefully, Mila unscrewed the cap on the first jug, watching closely for air bubbles. None appeared, confirming they'd gotten it level. She carefully tightened the zip ties to hold it firm.

As she began to unscrew the cap from the second jug, Libby Fagan kicked the scaffold on her way up to the surface to retrieve something that had floated away. The wobble caused their open jug to take on about ten centimeters of water. That would cost them three or four points unless they got it out.

Andi pointed up but Mila doubted there was time to unstrap it and get it to the surface.

After a deep breath, she removed her mouthpiece and pressed the air hose against the opening of the jug. Though most of the bubbles escaped to the surface, the water level inside rapidly fell until it was nearly even with the opening—just in time for her to return the mouthpiece and take a much needed gasp of air.

The second jug was slightly off-kilter and took on water as soon as she removed the cap. With Andi holding it straight, Mila tightened the straps and repeated her trick with the air hose to restore the water level.

The hose was a different animal, open on both ends and already filled with water. She took another deep breath and blew through one end until she felt no resistance, then quickly pinched each end of the hose to seal it.

This was where she needed Andi most, but her air tank was nearly empty. She stayed long enough to place one of the washers in the coupling and the other in Mila's hand.

Mila needed one extra hand to hold the jug steady while she screwed in the coupling. Out of options, she loosened her grip on the hose and allowed it to fill up again. One last coupling to go, and her own air supply was dangerously low.

Directly across from her, Jerry too was working alone. The Fagans were swimming up, while Jancey and Marlon were already out of the pool.

She placed the final washer and pulled out her mouthpiece to suck on the hose. Suck, pinch the hose, spit, breathe. Suck, pinch, spit, breathe. Suck, pinch, spit, breathe.

Breathe, breathe. Her air was gone.

Suddenly it was worse than all the times her cousins had held her under water. Fighting a powerful urge to inhale, she screwed the coupling into place. Then she pushed against the floor of the pool and rocketed to the surface.

* * *

Marlon stretched across the table and tapped his water glass to Jancey's. "You've still got it, Major. I've been hoping we'd get paired together."

Between them, they'd probably logged four hundred hours of underwater training at the EVA lab in Houston, dressed in heavy spacesuits with bulky gloves. Unsurprisingly, they'd earned all twenty points in their pool exercise, which qualified them for the round of thirty-two.

"It hardly seems fair." She dragged her breaded fish filet through the puddle of poi and took a bite. Foul, foul stuff, that poi. Rich in fluorine…good for bones. "From the looks of things, they put a little more thought into the pairings for this round. I noticed a lot of shifts."

"Me too. I guarantee you all the rookies thought that pool exercise was hard. They have no idea what kind of abuse they're in for when the real training starts. Remember the Vomit Comet?"

That was their name for the aircraft that took them through parabolic maneuvers to simulate weightlessness. Everyone—Jancey included—had gotten nauseated.

"Ugh. Let's not talk about that while we eat," Jancey said. "I have to hand it to Sir Charles and his team though. They've put together a pretty good series of tests on a low budget. Precision skills matter when it's time to step outside and put on a new heat shield. Anyone who mucks it up or gets rattled in an exercise like this doesn't belong in space."

"You like our chances, Jancey?"

She thought about it all the time, alternately whipping herself into an indignant frenzy that the selection committee might pick someone else versus assuring herself she was the only logical choice. That went double now that she was paired with Marlon.

"That depends. If they choose based on science, reason and test scores, I don't see how either of us could lose. We've both proven we can live in space without a brain bleed. That ought to be a primary consideration. Competition-wise, I'm most concerned about the married couples. If just one of them proves mildly competent, Sir Charles might be inclined to pick them just for the PR splash."

Marlon was nodding along, his lips fixed in a scowl. "If you're free this weekend, maybe we should go get married."

A bizarre suggestion that she momentarily entertained. "Seriously?"

"I know you like women, but—"

"Thanks to the *National Enquirer*, the whole world knows I like women. And because of that, I have a feeling our funders would question our integrity."

"Probably...but it says a lot about both of us that we're willing to put the mission in front of our personal lives." Marlon had always kept his private life private. Probably because the gossip at NASA was that his longtime girlfriend was a certain *Playboy* Playmate of the Year. "What do you think of the Fagans?"

"They're smart, and I wouldn't rule out anyone with robotics experience. Their skills are complementary. They seem to work well together but he's kind of an asshole to Libby when he thinks nobody's listening."

"No kidding. He snapped at her when Zion gave them eighteen points. Hell, I thought that was pretty good considering he'd never had any underwater training. And those two girls...I forget their names."

She pointed her fork at him. "Todorov and Toloti...and once they reach the age of eighteen, they're called *women*."

"Sorry, women. Twenty points. I expected twelve, fifteen at the most."

"Todorov—she's the one who worked on the modifications to the propulsion system—she's smart. And she aced the concentration tests."

"Still…she's just a kid."

"Twenty-seven. I joined NASA at twenty-one and went up seven years later." She leaned across the table and lowered her voice. "By the way, I heard a rumor. They've put all the top candidates so far in the Blue and Green groups. That's all of us. Everybody from NASA, plus two from the European Space Agency and two from Japan. The astronaut from India landed in the Red group. Shows what they think of India's space program. Anyway, I figure as long as we stay ahead of everyone in our group, we should be good for the analog trial."

It was more than a rumor. She'd gotten inside information from Grace, and knew for a fact the committee considered everyone in the Blue and Green groups to be viable contenders. Once they got down to sixteen, the married couples would be paired together automatically, while the remaining candidates would choose partners for the final test, the analog trial. Six weeks on Mauna Kea in conditions meant to simulate Mars.

"I'm not worried," Marlon said, shaking his head. "Jerry's a tough competitor but Gunther's a little on the quirky side. Even if they both got through this round, I don't see Jerry choosing him for the analog. He'll have to break in somebody new. And let's face it—there's no way the committee's going with two women, so we don't have to worry about Todorov and Toloti."

The cynic in her hated to admit he probably was right. "I'd like to think I've helped disprove the sexist trope that women aren't as capable as men."

"Can't argue with that, Jancey. Why do you think I was so glad when I saw my name next to yours on the board this morning?"

"Instead of Jerry? You two would have made quite a team."

"Jerry might have been my first choice for a short-term mission, but not for this. He's a test pilot. What good would it be to build a whole city on Mars if the people who lived there starved to death? One of the people on that ship needs to make sure there's enough food to thrive, and I can't think of anyone I'd trust to do that more than you."

Marlon was right. The best team would be an engineer and someone with the skills to cultivate food. No matter what sort of PR splash the committee wanted to make, the future of the Tenacity Project depended on the success of its first pair of colonists. They'd be foolish to choose a team without those essential competencies.

"I'm inclined to agree," she said. "I get the feeling Sir Charles and his friends see it that way too. Look how they've paired us. Gunther's a chemist, Jerry's a test pilot. Toloti is a chemist too, and Todorov's an engineer. Libby Fagan's a botanist, and—"

"And her husband is an asshole."

* * *

Mila straddled two of the study carrels, logged into both computers at once. *BattleStorm* filled the screen on the right, a game she could only observe since she had no joystick. Vio was on the left, also juggling two monitors, and doing her best not to get killed by JanSolo.

"If I had a stick, I'd blow him away," Mila said.

"No, you wouldn't. You can't even kill Toloti."

"Did you have say that name? I deserve at least five minutes of the day where I don't have to think about her."

Vio winced and ducked sideways as if to dodge an actual laser shot. "What did she do this time?"

"She drew breath. Isn't that enough?" Mila shuddered at the memory of finding her razor in Andi's toiletries bin. "She acts like we're married or something."

"Hold on, I'm about to be killed." In a hail of laser pings, Vio's avatar retreated from the battle scene only to be pursued by JanSolo, who finished her off. "Unbelievable. That's the most points I've ever scored and I'm still dead."

"I have to go so I can rest up for whatever terrible fate The Powers That Be have planned for me tomorrow. Let's hope they don't try to drown me again."

With a wave to the media specialist, she exited through the glass door into a light rain that felt as warm as bath water. When she first arrived in Hawaii, she'd found the heat and humidity oppressive. While her opinion hadn't changed, her attitude had. It was ridiculous to complain—even to herself—about anything unpleasant on Earth while she was vying to go to a far bleaker planet and a life filled with hardship. Someday she would surely miss the warmth and the smell of fresh rain.

"Todorov!" The voice belonged to a man wearing a hooded rain jacket. As he walked closer, she recognized him as Brandon Fagan.

"Yes?"

"What you did today...I bet you thought you got away with it, but I saw you."

"What the hell are you talking about?"

"Go ahead. Play dumb like you don't know. My wife and I know, and don't think we won't report it."

Her mind raced back to their underwater exercise. "I have no idea what you saw or what you think you saw. If you have a problem with something I did, take it to Zion."

She stormed off toward the dormitory, furious at his accusations. At the same time, it bothered her to think she might have broken the rules during the underwater exercise. Was it cheating to use her air hose the way she had? It couldn't have been. *Whatever it takes.* Those were Zion's exact words.

Besides, they wouldn't have had a problem in the first place had Libby not kicked the scaffold. If anything was cheating, it was that. Sabotaging their opponents.

Andi was already sacked out when she reached the room.

As quietly as she could, Mila readied for bed, still fuming about Brandon Fagan. Maybe she should be proactive about it. Take the matter to Zion, explain what she did and that she might have misunderstood the directions. It could cost her and Andi several points, but the committee would value her integrity. Unless Fagan went behind her and told them he'd pressured her to come clean.

Or she could ignore it for now. Explain herself only if confronted. That would bolster her contention that she didn't think she'd done anything wrong.

Even with her clean conscience, she tossed and turned. Not good, since tomorrow's exercise was rumored to be the toughest yet. By four o'clock, only sixteen candidates would remain. Eight teams set to compete in the analog trial.

She needed rest and she wasn't getting it.

Brandon Fagan had probably done that just to get under her skin. Such an asshole.

CHAPTER SEVEN

Jancey was the first of her group to arrive in the library's conference room. Already uneasy about the day's exercise, she bypassed the coffeepot and poured herself a glass of water. The last test before the analog on Mauna Kea. Grace had warned her it was a doozy.

Marlon was next to enter, and he took the adjacent chair. "Missed you at breakfast. Oh, I forgot. You're staying in some cliffside mansion with one of the funders. I bet you had Eggs Benedict out by the pool."

"Hardly. It was a poached egg over steamed spinach. And we ate on the veranda. Makes it easier to keep the eggs warm."

"Of course." He rolled his eyes. "I heard some grumbling at breakfast about this test. Only one of the teams from the Red group passed. Nobody from the Orange. Must be a killer."

"We just need to stay focused and not make any stupid mistakes." That's all it would take to end their chances. Their NASA training had instilled an urgency about even the smallest detail. They couldn't think about the last cut at four o'clock until they got this test behind them.

The team of Toloti and Todorov arrived next, with the latter taking the seat on Jancey's other side. Her dark eyes were outlined in red, with puffy bags underneath.

"Excuse my French, but *tu regardes comme de la merde*."

"I feel like shit too. Can I ask you a question?" She was clearly worried about something. Toloti too, apparently, since she leaned closer to listen. "Yesterday in the pool, Libby Fagan kicked the scaffold and we got water in one of our jugs."

"I saw that. We still had both of our caps on or we would have taken on water too."

"Yeah, we took on half a liter at least. We'd already strapped our jugs in place, so instead of taking it up to dump it, I took off my air hose and blew it out. Was that cheating?"

Just when Jancey thought it was time to give Todorov and Toloti their due, they did something to underscore their youth and naiveté. "If you were in space and got water where it wasn't supposed to be, would you leave it there and take your lumps or get it out?"

"I'd get it out."

"And that's exactly what you did, so why are you second-guessing yourself?"

Toloti smacked Todorov on the shoulder. "I told you."

Todorov slumped back in her chair and rubbed her face with both hands. "He was messing with me and I let him."

As Jancey heard the story of Brandon's confrontation, the Fagans came in and sat at the far end of the conference table. Their scornful looks and whispering made it clear they were still talking about the incident. Apparently they felt threatened by the competition, but it would surprise her if Libby had kicked the scaffold on purpose. Not the sort of thing a NASA astronaut should do.

"Let it go," she said sternly. "Astronauts are trained to think ahead, not behind. If you do X and it causes Y, then you do A. If you do X and it causes Z, then you do B. Always know your next step, and don't dwell on your last one."

Gunther and Jerry were the last of their group at the table, followed by Moriya Ito, the head of instrumentation.

"I am sure you are all eager to get this last test over with. I believe you will find it to be the most challenging. Yesterday's groups did not fare so well...only one of the teams passed. The Green team is being tested as we speak."

The Green and Blue teams should do better, Jancey thought, because their skills were better across the board.

"We've tried to design exercises to see how our candidates will perform as a team under pressure. Obviously, we do not have sophisticated equipment here, so we do what we expect of astronauts—we adapt. Our friends at the Oceanographic Institute were kind enough to lend us one of their submersibles to use as a testing module."

He passed out training pamphlets and used a slideshow to explain the exercise. Teams were to remove the instrument panel and install the vessel's onboard SONAR, a simple task that required connecting three sets of color-coded wires. Next was to calibrate the Fathometer to zero, since the vessel was in dry dock. When both instruments were functioning properly, they were to replace the panel and exit the module.

"You will have six minutes to complete this task. During that time, you will notice a gradual drop in available oxygen. You may become disoriented or experience difficulty concentrating. One person yesterday reported hallucinations. Several passed out. Your first duty is to preserve the integrity of the vessel. Without it, you cannot survive. Imagine if you will...this is not a SONAR on a submersible in dry dock. It is a life support system on a spaceship a hundred million miles from Earth. If *Tenacity* fails, you die."

Ito's speech brought back vivid memories of the cosmonauts she'd rescued thirteen years ago. If *Tenacity* failed on its way to Mars, there would be no one coming to the rescue.

"Your second obligation is to survive. If you suffer debilitating symptoms and stay too long, you will pass out. In space, we call that dying. An ideal candidate does whatever it takes not to die."

* * *

On the bus ride to the marina, Mila and Andi studied their training pamphlet and planned their approach.

"When we get the panel off," Mila said, "I'll hook up the SONAR while you calibrate the Fathometer."

Andi shook her head. "Screw you. I'm in charge today. That was our deal. I'll do the Fathometer and you do the SONAR."

"That's what I said," she hissed through gritted teeth.

"It is not. You said it the other way around."

"Whatever." There were moments in life she wished she'd been wearing Google Glass to record every word, but knowing Toloti, she'd have argued anyway.

Several staff members were patrolling the dock in their yellow polo shirts, but the ones who stood out to Mila were the emergency medical technicians. When she stepped off the bus, she spotted their ambulance nearby.

"Bloody hell," she murmured, prompting a chuckle from Jancey.

Two by two, they toured the submersible, a compartment barely six cubic meters with a glass dome. Mila and Andi made note of every detail—how to turn the power off and on, how to remove the panel, and how to activate the airflow in case of emergency.

"For emergency air, turn the lever toward the green," the technician explained. "If you turn it the other way—the red—all the oxygen is drawn out."

"Try not to kill us, Mila," Andi said on her way out of the hatch.

"I'd never kill both of us. Remember what I said? The strongest one must survive."

Jancey and Marlon volunteered to go first. When they emerged after five minutes, both bent over on the dock gasping for breath.

"Bloody hell," Andi repeated. "We're gonna die down there."

Jerry persuaded Gunther they should go next. Unlike the pair before them, they used the whole clock. Instead of bursting out of the module when the air ran out, they apparently pushed the lever for emergency air. One of the EMTs entered the hatch and stayed several minutes. By the time the men emerged, they'd recovered.

"I'm guessin' they didn't finish," Andi said.

"You know what I just realized? This is just one test, Andi, and from the looks of it, there might not be eight teams that pass. Maybe it's like Jancey says. We just need to be logical about it. Plan what we're supposed to do next. Even if we don't finish, we have to make the right decision at the last second."

While the staff reset the module, the Fagans pushed past them and started down the dock.

"I want to beat those two," Mila muttered. "I want to pulverize them and grind them into the dirt."

She followed along on her watch. As the six-minute mark approached, one of the EMTs climbed onto the dome and peered inside, flashing the thumbs-up signal. Moments later the couple emerged. Like the others, they were spent and needed oxygen right away.

"Guess it's us now," Andi said.

It was several minutes before the staff waved them over.

Jancey stood as they walked by and held out her hand for a fist bump. "Good luck."

The technician met them on the dock with tools—pliers, channel locks, a hammer and two flashlights—and the SONAR they were to install. "Don't forget. Green means air. Red means dead. Clock starts when the hatch closes."

Their dockside preparation paid off. In a matter of seconds, they had the panel off and had located the wires needed to connect the device.

"Kill the power," Mila said, not caring who was supposed to be in charge. With the butt end of the flashlight in her mouth, she went to work loosening the caps and twisting the wires together. By the time she finished the second one, her head was pounding. Only one more to go. Gripping the light with her teeth, she sucked in deeper breaths in an effort to clear the fog. "You okay?"

Andi panted and shook her head wildly. "Barely."

"Focus. We're almost done." She wrapped the last wire and pushed the SONAR into place. The beam on her light confirmed the Fathometer was calibrated. "That's it. Power on."

With the flip of the switch, the console lit up. All that was left was to replace the panel.

A loud pop on Andi's side was followed by a stream of sparks, and suddenly, a fire around the power switch. An acrid smoke filled the cabin.

"Fuck! We gotta get out of here." Andi reached for the hatch.

"No!" Mila grabbed the collar of her T-shirt and hurled her to the floor. "Hold your breath."

With smoke already in their lungs, it was nearly impossible not to cough. Fighting the urge to inhale, she tumbled on top of Andi and pushed the air lever to red.

The smoke stung her eyes, but she focused long enough to see the flame expire. Then with what felt like her dying breath, she swung the lever back to green.

* * *

"What the hell is that?" Jancey jumped to her feet as a plume of smoke spilled out of the submersible.

EMTs and staff converged on the dock where the technicians had dragged Todorov and Toloti out.

Ito motioned for the other candidates to stay put, but Jancey ignored him. When she reached the dock, both women were sitting up taking oxygen.

The technician emerged from the hatch. "Looks like a faulty power switch. The whole thing fried."

Todorov removed her mask and scowled at him. "Are you telling me that wasn't part of the test?"

"Are you kidding me? You're lucky to be alive, and so is everybody who was down here on the dock. With the oxygen level that low, it would have blown sky high if you'd opened that hatch. That was some heads-up thinking to kill the air supply and put it out."

Jancey shuddered to think of what could have happened. Everyone at NASA knew—the Apollo 1 fire had killed three astronauts on the launch pad during a systems test.

It could have happened to any of them. If she and Marlon had been inside, their training would have kicked in and they'd have shut off the oxygen. Same with Jerry and Gunther, or the Fagans, because Jerry and Libby were trained to deal with fire emergencies. It said a lot about Todorov and Toloti that they held it together and did the right thing intuitively.

The two of them…they deserved a shot at Mars as much as anyone here.

* * *

Andi Toloti was shaken. Her usually confident voice creaked with uncertainty and she wouldn't look at Mila.

Detective Kevin Onakea of the Hawaii Police Department had assured them his interview was merely a formality, something he was required to do because the incident involved damage to public property. "Is there anything else you'd like to add, Ms. Toloti?"

She shook her head. "No…just that I'd be dead right now if it hadn't been for Mila."

That probably was true but Mila didn't want to dwell on it. It was five thirty and she was itching to get to the computer science building to see if they'd made the cut. Even though the fire wasn't a part of the test, they'd failed to complete their assignment.

"That wraps it up then. If I need anything else, I'll follow up with…"—he flipped through his notes—"Sir Charles Boyd."

With her hands in her pockets, Andi's head hung low as she exited the administration building. "It's true what I said. I'd be dead if you hadn't knocked me down."

"I don't want to talk about it. It didn't happen." Mila expected to have nightmares, especially if she missed the cut.

Andi turned toward the dormitory.

"Where are you going? Let's go check the list."

"I'll save you the trip, Mila. You made the cut. Moriya Ito told me this afternoon while you were in the exam room. So did I, but I…I told him to drop me. I don't have it."

"What do you mean you don't have it? You're one of the top candidates left."

"And I nearly got you killed today. My head is"—she gripped her scalp with both hands—"I cain't focus like you do. I don't think as fast. You said it yourself the other day but you were bein' an asshole about it. I might be able to improve a little if I practice, but there's a ceilin' on how far I can go. I wanna be part of the project, but that needs to be here on the ground. As long as I can take my time and think things through, I'm real good at what I do."

Mila was admittedly relieved. Even though they made a good team for testing purposes, she couldn't stand the thought of having to work closely with Andi for the next four years while they trained. Going with her to Mars forever would be purgatory.

And at the same time, she was oddly disappointed. Of all the candidates, she and Andi were the closest in experience and expertise in their respective fields. If Andi didn't have what it took, maybe she didn't either. What if Sir Charles was keeping her on for analog testing only out of pity? It wasn't her fault the switch caught fire. The selection committee wouldn't want it to look like she didn't get a fair shake.

"I'm gonna get started packing up," Andi went on. "They'll probably want me outta the dorm within a couple of days. If you wanna wish me luck, maybe they'll set up the organic chemistry lab here in Hawaii. I could get used to living in a place like this."

A different person might have offered a comforting hug, but Mila wasn't a gratuitous hugger. Family and very close friends only. Certainly not for Andi. The woman drove her insane.

Nonetheless, when Andi stepped closer and held out her arms, she quietly complied. It wouldn't kill her to be nice.

The lobby of the computer science building was empty. Half of this morning's candidates were somewhere celebrating while the others, like Andi, were packing up, their dreams dashed.

The list of finalists was alphabetical with Jancey Beaumont on top. Four married couples, each of which included one trained astronaut. The Fagans. The Clarkes, from Britain. Knut and Henrik, the gay couple from Norway. The Hatsus, from Japan. Marlon, Jerry, plus a Frenchman she recognized from the European Space Agency. Three other men she didn't know, including the only survivors from the Red group.

Out of sixteen, nine were trained astronauts. Five women total. She and Jancey were the only women not married.

At least with Andi in the mix, Mila had known who her partner would be. Of the fifteen left, eight were already partnered with a spouse. That left seven potential partners. Far and away, her first choice was Jancey, but she apparently had already paired with Marlon. Her best shot at winning a seat was probably with Jerry or one of the other space agency alums.

It was up to her to sell herself. Her background and accomplishments so far in the competition stood on their own. Her challenge would be finding someone she could live with. Or who could live with her. There weren't many people in the whole world who fit either side of that bill.

At the bottom of the list was a message.

Enjoy your Friday, a well-deserved day off!

You are cordially invited to a Hawaiian luau at the home of Grace Faraday.

Get to know some of our funders, staff and your fellow explorers in a relaxed atmosphere filled with fun, food and traditional Hawaiian dance.

Shuttle bus leaves at 5:30.

p.s. See Alani in Admin for your tropical shirt!

CHAPTER EIGHT

Jancey stood before the mirror with her hands on her hips. Yellow capris hugged her thighs and the tropical shirt dipped low enough to show a little cleavage.

"You look lovely," Grace said, clapping softly to show her enthusiasm. She was dressed for the luau in a long floral dress, with a plumeria blossom tucked behind her left ear. She'd tried to get Jancey to wear one too—on the right side to indicate she was available.

"I'd just as soon wear a space helmet."

For most of her adult life, she'd worn either a uniform or a pantsuit suitable for business. If the occasion called for something finer than that, she tried very hard to get out of going.

She'd seen Grace's stylist that morning for a super-short cut in anticipation of six weeks on Mauna Kea. "I hope I can train Marlon to cut hair."

"So you've decided on *Marlon*?" Grace's voice lilted to show her disappointment.

"We make a good team. There's a lot that can go wrong in space and you don't want to have to worry about how your partner's going to handle it."

Grace pursed her lips and cocked her head to one side. Itching to say something, and she eventually did. "What about Mila Todorov? I looked over her application. She's family, you know."

Jancey rolled her eyes. If Grace had gone so far as to pull her file, she was planning a hard sell.

"Moriya Ito said she was quite heroic yesterday. Kept her cool under the most trying circumstances. He seemed to think the selection committee liked her quite a lot."

Funny how she always referred to the committee in third person, as if purposely denying she was on it. She had too much access and insider information to be on the outside looking in.

"Of course they liked her. She dazzled everyone with how she handled herself. She's a propulsion engineer. She knew very well what would happen if that door opened. Marlon and I would have done the same thing she did, and so would all the others who went through NASA training. The only difference is Todorov got a chance to prove it."

"Do I detect a hint of envy?"

Jancey sighed and slumped into an antique parlor chair. "It's not envy. It's…call it concern. I was there by the dock yesterday when all that smoke poured out of the hatch, and it scared the life out of me. I've never been so glad to see two people get up and walk away. The other one, Andi Toloti…she had the sense to drop out. I hate to see someone with so much potential as Mila bite off more than she can chew before she's ready. This is dangerous work and I don't think she's mature enough to handle it."

"Remind me again how old you were when you went up on *Guardian*."

Twenty-eight. "I was very level-headed for my age. Besides, it's a moot point. You and I both know the committee won't select two women."

"Don't be so sure. What the committee cares about most is success, and the science tells us women live just as well in space as men. Maybe even better. If anyone should know that, it's you."

"What I know is there are a million things that could go wrong on a trip to Mars. The lander could come down on a boulder. The life support system could malfunction and poison us with carbon monoxide. The modified atmosphere could reject our crops or the water could be tainted with radiation. No matter what the cause, you know as well as I do exactly what they'd say if the mission failed. *We never should have sent two women.* That's a conversation no one wants to have."

The arguments were as endless as they were exhausting, but it was clear Grace wasn't buying them for a minute.

"They could have said all those things when you were chosen for *Guardian.* They weren't true then and they aren't now."

"I hear you, Grace. But here's the bottom line. I like my chances better with Marlon. He's capable and he's proven."

"And you'll be giving up the chance to have an actual life instead of just a lifelong space mission."

"Is that what this is about?" Jancey began to pace the bedroom. "You should have listened to Jill, Grace. She had me pegged. I care only about myself and what I want. It's a fact. I accept it. I want to go to Mars, not find everlasting love. Marlon will help get me there."

"But—"

"Period." She crossed her arms defiantly and gave Grace her most exaggerated glower. Miraculously, it worked.

* * *

Mila's plan to approach Jerry on the eighteen-mile ride up the coast fizzled when she boarded the bus and found him already seated with Wade Hackett, a payload specialist from San Diego who had flown one shuttle mission to the International Space Station several years earlier. If those two hooked up, that left her by default with Jean-Paul Robillard, from the European Space Agency. Perhaps they'd bond over their European heritage. That was a great plan...except for the fact that he was French and probably wouldn't give her the time of day.

As they pulled into a large circular drive, she grasped immediately why Jancey had declined quarters in the student dormitory. Anyone who had access to a home like Grace Faraday's would be crazy to choose a twin bed, a snoring roommate and a communal shower with strangers.

All of that would change in two days when they moved their operations up to the small cluster of buildings four thousand feet below the summit of Mauna Kea. There they'd be paired with their partners for classroom training while materials were transported to the slope for their analog trial.

A graceful woman, small and gray-haired, smiled down at them from the wide porch. Grace Faraday, aptly named. Billionaire space fan. "Welcome! Please come in. Follow your nose down the stairs and out on the patio. Makoa is your bartender and he can't wait to make you an island delight."

An island delight probably contained pineapple juice, which didn't delight Mila at all. "Do you happen to have any German beer?"

"You're in luck," he said, producing a Spaten lager.

She didn't care much for dark beer, but Makoa was smiling with inordinate pride so she felt obligated to drink it.

The pool area was decorated with tiki torches, palms and flowers. On the lawn were four large round tables covered in white linen with elaborate place settings. It wasn't at all what she'd expected at a luau. In the corner of the lawn, four young men hoisted a large net from the ground. A roasted pig, she realized as its intact head slumped to the side.

At an umbrella table at the far end of the pool, Jancey was engaged in what appeared to be amiable conversation with Sir Charles. Everyone sucked up to Sir Charles and with good reason.

He met Mila's eye and waved her over. "Please tell me you're better today. No ill after-effects, I trust."

His formal British accent was starkly different from Andi's Texas drawl. Far more animated and authoritative. It was easy to see how he'd charmed so many people into opening their bank accounts to help fulfill his dream.

"I'm fine, thank you. Just a little coughing immediately after the fact. We wouldn't even have gone to the hospital if Dr. Ito hadn't insisted."

Mila smiled at Jancey, noticing at once her very short hair. Normally she preferred a different look. Long wavy hair with lots of body that she could bury her face into. Jancey gave her plenty of reason to think again.

"Mila." Jancey nodded toward the chair Sir Charles was holding for her.

"Oh, thank you." She consciously turned away to gaze at the ocean instead of Jancey, acutely aware it was the very first time the woman had used her first name.

Sir Charles continued, "We all were very concerned after yesterday's incident. Fluttered the dovecotes, it did."

She had no idea what that meant, but from his admiring smile, he was pleased. "The very best tests are the ones that simulate actual conditions, especially emergencies. That exercise was very challenging, as was the underwater test. I hope never to be in a situation where I'm running low on oxygen, but learning to keep my head may save my life."

With two red spaniels on her heels, Grace Faraday crossed the patio to their table and extended her hand. Her beauty and regal posture personified radiance. "You must be Mila Todorov. What an adventure you had yesterday!"

Mila stood and took her hand. "Thank you so much for sharing your lovely home with us. I'm honored to be here."

"You're so very welcome. We must make time to talk." She turned to Jancey, who was sipping a glass of white wine. "Jancey, be sure to save me a chair near this young lady." Then to Sir Charles. "My dear, could I get your opinion on the seating arrangements?"

He and the dogs followed her to the lawn, leaving Mila alone with Jancey.

"I hope Grace is serving poi, don't you, Mila?" She looked away innocently, her tongue planted firmly in her cheek.

"I'll have you know it's good for my bones."

Major Jancey Beaumont had a lovely smile when she dared to let it show.

"The truth, Todorov. Are you really all right after yesterday? That wasn't an ordinary training accident. You and Toloti could have been seriously injured…or worse."

"I'm okay, but Andi didn't handle it well. She's all right physically but she decided a mission to Mars wasn't for her."

"And you? I bet you came away with a few doubts too."

Mila shook her head. "Not at all. I'm even more convinced than ever that I'm right for this mission."

"Oh, for Pete's sake. Forget all that drivel you just laid on Sir Charles. He's never been up there so he has no idea what it's like. These tests don't come close to real emergencies in space. And there aren't going to be three EMTs waiting outside the door to save your ass." She took a gulp of wine and turned away, mumbling, "You're like one of those space cowboys. You had a big thrill and now all of a sudden you think you're the most qualified one here."

Taken aback by the harsh tone, Mila considered for a moment whether it might be best to find another place to sit. Instead, she decided to stand her ground. "No, I don't think that at all. You're the most qualified and everyone here knows it. The only way I'd be chosen is if I were paired with you. That's the only way *anyone* will be chosen."

She'd tried to keep her voice level and respectful. It was crazy that she'd finally gotten the chance to meet the woman whose photos had decorated her adolescent bedroom, and instead of using the opportunity to say how Jancey had inspired her, she was defending herself against an accusation of hubris.

"Look, Major. When I said I was right for this mission, I meant I was the right person to go with *you*. You and Marlon Quinn…you're great together. He's awesome, and if you go with him, you can count on his expertise, his training and his—for lack of a better word—leadership." Men always assumed they were in charge. "If you go with me, you'll be the leader. I promise to learn everything there is to know about the ship and the mission. I'll train seriously until I can handle every last detail with my eyes closed and one hand tied behind my back. And I'll give you the authority you deserve, that you've earned. You'd be the commander of the mission. I'd support you completely. But I'll be more than capable to take command if it becomes necessary."

Jancey's face had softened a bit from the steely glare that punctuated her accusation. More important, she didn't push back against Mila's presumption that the Mars mission required a command structure, or that a partnership between Jancey and Marlon would evolve naturally to him assuming command.

"They're calling us to dinner," Jancey said, nodding in the direction of the lawn. "You're to sit next to Grace."

In fact, placards were already in place and Mila found herself between Grace and Jancey. Also at the table were Marlon, Jerry, the gay couple, and Svein Helland, the Norwegian physicist who had introduced Mila during their orientation in the lecture hall.

Marlon toyed with the placards before sitting down, swapping his with Mila's. "I should sit next to you, Jancey. We need to get used to being with each other twenty-four-seven."

She chuckled and switched them back. "All the more reason to avoid it while we can."

Grace arrived and prompted everyone to introduce themselves with their name, hometown, area of expertise and a single word they'd used to describe their nature. "I'll start. Grace Faraday, born in San Francisco. I first heard of astronomy back when scientists still believed the sun revolved around the earth, but my real area of expertise is living well. My word is curious."

She turned to Knut on her left for the next response, meaning Mila would be last. Next was his husband Henrik, followed by Svein.

"Marlon Quinn, Detroit. Mechanical engineering. My word would be…confident."

Jancey glanced at Mila ever so briefly, as though acknowledging how Marlon's "confidence" could be construed as a sign he would take over a two-person mission.

"Jerry Huffstetler, Huntsville, Alabama. Navy test pilot. My word is tenacity." He grinned at the chorus of groans for his too-obvious choice.

"Jancey Beaumont, Charlottesville, Virginia. My expertise is long-term sustainability in space. My word is survivor."

Mila took note of how she'd worded her expertise, tailored perfectly to the mission. "I'm Mila Todorov. Born in Sofia, Bulgaria. I'm an astronautical engineer who thinks in terms of how we can get the most out of the resources at hand. My word is persistent."

"My goodness!" Grace proclaimed. "I'd go with any of you tomorrow. Let me make a toast…good luck and Godspeed."

Servers made the rounds with pork, fried rice with mixed vegetables, and something called pohole salad, which was tomatoes and onions on what looked like clumps of lawn grass. And of course, poi.

"She likes that," Jancey said to the server, "but she's too shy to ask for extra."

Mila quietly endured Grace's delight and Jancey's snickering, knowing she'd have to eat every bite to satisfy her hostess. On a trip to Mars, Jancey would likely terrorize her by breeding grub worms and insects for their evening meal, but she was determined to prove her promise—if Jancey commanded it, it would be done.

* * *

No luau was complete without the obligatory parade of half-naked native islanders, most of whom were female, dancing to the rapid beat of tom-toms. Jancey found it exploitive, though Grace insisted it was perfectly acceptable as an honor to Hawaiian culture. Marlon, Jerry and even Sir Charles had moved their chairs as close as possible to the dancers in order to "honor Hawaiian culture."

Mila stood in the back talking to Jean-Paul Robillard. If she had hopes of persuading him to join her, she was in for disappointment. Frenchmen were notoriously sexist in the workplace. The only way she'd be paired with him—or anyone, probably—was by default, since it was unlikely any of the men would choose her, despite the ingenuity she'd shown the day before.

Jancey watched her break for the house and rushed across the pool deck to catch up. "Leaving so soon?"

"I was looking for a restroom. I find beer to be, how should I say...temporary."

"I'll show you." To put distance between her head and the pounding tom-toms, she bypassed the guest bath on the lower level and led Mila upstairs to the powder room off the foyer. While she waited, she poured out her chi-chi in favor of ice water with fresh lemon.

"Grace Faraday is your friend, I take it," Mila said when she returned to the kitchen. Her blue and yellow Hawaiian shirt hung loosely from her thin frame, so much so that she appeared the most relaxed of anyone at the luau. "It shows in the way you smile at each other."

"She's someone I care about very much...like family. If it weren't for Grace, I might have disappeared into the desert for good the minute NASA terminated the long-term space program. She'd been brainstorming with Sir Charles for years about a possible mission to Mars and convinced me to bide my time teaching at a university until the opportunity arose."

She prepared a second glass of ice water and offered it to Mila, who appeared to be in no hurry to return to the party. The granite island in the kitchen became their bar table, a place to anchor them while they talked.

Mila rested her elbows on the counter, causing the neckline of her shirt to drape so low Jancey could see her sports bra. "What do you find so appealing about disappearing into the desert?"

"Are you interviewing me, Todorov? I saw you talking to Robillard. I'm guessing he wasn't cooperative."

"He wasn't. He wants to hook up with Jerry or Wade. Like it or not, one of those three will end up with me as a consolation prize."

While Jancey respected both Jerry and Wade, she wouldn't choose to fly with either. Jerry was too sociable for her tastes, always joking about this or that. Wade was the opposite, with the personality of a potato. Still, both of them were preferable to Jean-Paul, who was an unknown entity.

"What do you think, Mila? Will you be able to live and work alongside a man? What if your partner suggests…let's call them benefits?"

"That sort of thing has never been much of a problem for me. If the men are intelligent, they realize I'm not interested. If they aren't intelligent, they're usually intimidated by the fact that I am."

Jancey had never thought of it quite that way, but it made perfect sense. Men didn't hit on her either probably for the same reasons.

"But just because I can work with men," Mila continued, "doesn't mean I want to. I want to work with you."

"And I want to go to Mars—more than anything I've ever wanted in my whole life. Surely you know what it's like to have a dream like that. My very best chance to make that come true is to partner with Marlon Quinn. He's proven he can survive in space long-term."

"Maybe so, but I'll make a better partner for you than Marlon Quinn. Far better. I'm certain of it."

This was not the same timid woman who'd joined her in the cafeteria on their first day. The tests she'd mastered, the challenges she'd conquered, her harrowing escape the day before. All had given her fanatical confidence. Arguably, well-earned. She would make someone an excellent partner.

"You're going to do great, Mila. But we both need to pair up with one of the men. You know as well as I do the committee will never pick two women for this mission. Look at the bias we face in the science fields. We're interlopers in the boys' club."

"What makes you think the committee will pick two Americans? Half the finalists are from other countries. Sir Charles is British, and all of the *Tenacity* ships are launching from India. Have you seen the training sites? Germany, China, Russia and the US. And what about our corporate sponsors? The biggest ones are in Germany and Japan. Did I happen to mention that I currently live in Germany?"

Jancey had no answer for that. In fact, it was quite a good point. If two Americans were chosen, the project might lose its global appeal. "I believe they'll pick the team that's going to give them the best chance for success, no matter where they're from. You heard the plan. They'll send the second group a year after the first. That's how they'll keep the other countries engaged. I'm telling you, they won't pick two women."

Mila scowled and stared at the floor like a teenager getting a lecture.

"Your own words, Mila. If it's likely both will fail but there's a chance one will succeed, there's only one logical choice."

"Your logic is flawed because I don't think it's at all likely we'll fail. If you team up with Marlon, I'm sure it will be fine. But if you team up with me, it will be perfect. You and I would do everything better. Everything."

Voices grew louder as the luau guests ambled upstairs en masse. Jancey ignored them as long as she could, holding Mila's stare until Marlon called her name.

"Major Beaumont, you'd better enjoy this while you can. I hear the crew quarters on Mauna Kea leave a lot to be desired. I'm calling top rack."

"See what I mean?" Mila whispered.

Indeed she did.

* * *

Mila passed the open seat beside Wade to sit alone in the back of the bus.

It will be perfect. Of all the pompous, conceited, Toloti-like things she could have said, why that?

Because it would have been perfect...for her. Had Andi still been in play—annoying, know-it-all Andi who used her hairbrush and razor—Mila would have chosen her over any of the men, even those who weren't annoying know-it-alls.

How Jancey could choose to live forever with a man instead of a woman who'd practically promised to worship her was difficult to comprehend. The only way it made sense was if Jancey didn't see her as capable.

Maybe she'd been fooling herself all along. Her test scores were good, but without training, she'd never measure up to any of the NASA astronauts. They were an exclusive club. Loyal and willing to place their lives in each other's hands. Mila had done nothing to prove herself worthy of that.

CHAPTER NINE

The residential buildings above the visitors center at Mauna Kea were designed for visiting astronomers who worked at one of the twelve telescopes located at the summit. Situated at nine thousand feet, they allowed staff to "sleep low," which made it easier for them to handle the higher altitude when they were working above.

That also was why the Tenacity crew, consisting of the finalists and a few of the staff, had moved up from the dormitory at the university. Five days of seminars and sleeping at nine thousand feet would help them acclimate to their analog habitats two thousand feet higher on the eastern slope.

Jancey had toured the facility years ago with Grace, never imagining she would someday stay there.

The four married couples were assigned to the suites in Building B, leaving Building C to Jancey and her group, who hadn't yet formally chosen their partners.

"Not exactly a seaside palace, is it?" Marlon said as he looked around. A common area with a small kitchen, two bathrooms and four bedrooms.

Tonight, she'd be sharing one of those bedrooms with Marlon. She fully expected it to be awkward but only at first. They both were professionals after all. Male and female astronauts had been sharing close quarters at the International Space Station for years without problems. Privacy was nearly nonexistent there, but everyone sucked it up and did their jobs.

Someone else would be sharing her room with a man tonight, Jancey realized as she heard Mila introducing herself to the two men from the Red group.

"Hello, I'm Mila Todorov." Amiable and eager to please.

Kamal Sidhu from India and David Pillay from South Africa already planned on teaming up together. That left Mila with Jerry, Wade or Jean-Paul. Most likely the latter, because the two NASA astronauts would naturally choose one another. Not necessarily a good idea in light of what Mila had said about the committee perhaps being reluctant to send two Americans.

That wouldn't affect her and Marlon. Not only were their scores better across the board, they also had proven their qualifications for long-term space missions. The committee would be pleased to choose an African-American, and also to have someone of her notoriety. The ideal team.

The day had brought a change of uniform. Gone were her thin T-shirt and khakis, replaced by a dark blue one-piece flight suit bearing her name over her chest pocket and the Tenacity Project patch on both sleeves. It was fashioned from durable material designed to be worn over thermal layers if necessary. If her experience at NASA was any indication, the suit would become a second skin as they trained over the next four years.

"Good afternoon." A new face—another man, natch—entered the residence carrying a worn brown leather briefcase. He looked to be in his sixties, with wavy gray hair, and eyebrows that curled upward sharply. "I'm Dr. Edwin Calloway from the University of Hawaii. Please call me Cal. I'll be leading a discussion on teamwork to help prepare everyone here to select a partner."

Jancey asserted herself, gesturing for Jerry to scoot toward the center of the sofa next to Wade so she could have the end. The others pulled in chairs to make a circle.

Cal commandeered the only armchair and began flipping through a yellow legal pad. "Since arriving here on the island, you've had an opportunity to get to know some of your fellow candidates, but perhaps not in a personal way. Our objective here today is to open up with one another so you can get a glimpse of traits that draw you to someone, or conversely, that might be difficult to reconcile with your own. By the time our session ends today, I hope you'll have enough information to choose the one person from this group who would make the best partner for this mission. The concept may seem foreign to some of you, but your partnership in the Tenacity Project is very much like a marriage, and if you're selected to go, your wedding is today. For better or worse, as long as you both shall live."

Jancey noted his wedding ring and wondered what his wife was like. Had she been drawn to his studious intellect, or was she taken in by his soft-spoken manner? According to their handbook, he was a professor in the department of psychology. Likely an independent contractor, though it wouldn't be unreasonable to have a psychologist on staff.

Despite his overall pleasant demeanor, she wasn't interested in his touchy-feely exercises. She'd made her decision about a partner, and had based it on logic.

"I'd like to begin with a series of questions. We'll go around the room and give each person time to respond. It's perfectly all right to give the same answer as someone else, but I ask each of you to be as truthful as possible. Don't tailor your remarks based on what you think others want to hear."

Mila had pulled one of the dining chairs over to the circle. With her long legs stretched out and her arms folded across her chest, she looked disengaged. Not a wise move should Dr. Cal report her lack of interest. She could be bored without looking it.

"How will you spend your free time on Mars?"

Starting on his left with Wade, they reeled off top of mind replies. Reading spy novels. Working out.

Marlon huffed. "I don't expect to have any free time on Mars."

Writing notes to friends and family on Earth.

"I enjoy playing the clarinet," Jancey said.

Sleeping. Sketching.

"I'm not exactly sure," Mila said. "Something that doesn't disturb my companion."

Cal shook his head. "Remember what I said. The truth. Not the answers you think people want to hear."

"It is the truth. I wouldn't do something that annoyed someone else, especially if there was nowhere they could go to get away from it. That would make me feel bad and I wouldn't enjoy it. I'll find quiet things to do, like reading or working a Rubik's Cube, something to keep my brain engaged."

It was a good answer, Jancey conceded. Mila struck her as someone who could entertain herself. More power to her if she did so without disturbing those around her.

For more than two hours, Cal pelted them with questions. Pet peeves, things that make you sad, happiest childhood memory. From the answers, they were to glean enough insight to know what life would be like with each person in the group.

Jerry would keep things light with jokes and wisecracks. Marlon was mission-oriented to a fault. Wade was "utterly fascinated" by the space science, and couldn't wait for the chance to gather data and send it back to Earth. Jancey could easily work with someone like that.

Apparently Mila could too, since she'd listened intently as he spoke. Wade showed interest in her as well, nodding along as she talked of her obsession with engineering systems. They might make a decent team.

"What is your most important consideration in choosing a partner?" Cal asked.

One after another, candidates answered with various synonyms for professionalism. A partner who could do the job.

But not Mila. "Normally, I would say competence, but I expect all of us to be well-trained. The most important thing to me is compatibility. Who would be the best companion?"

Jancey found her insight irritating. Not because it was simple or naïve, but because it was spot-on. No one among them would skate through training and emerge incapable of performing the required duties. Their biggest challenge was establishing a comfortable rapport, something the married couples had already done. Mila could have been channeling Grace.

"All right, last exercise. I'm assuming by this time you've narrowed your choices. It's your turn now. One question you can pose to three people. This is your chance to cover anything I missed. Let's start with Jerry."

"One question…one question. Do you snore?" He'd narrowed his choices to Wade, Jean-Paul and Marlon.

Marlon asked which was best, sharing all the work equally or dividing it according to capabilities.

Jancey answered, "As Mila pointed out, I expect to be capable of everything. That said, a division of labor seems like a good idea for those tasks we particularly enjoy. No one, however, should think I'm going to do all the cooking just because my expertise is growing food." She bolstered that with a narrowing of the eyes directed at Marlon.

He threw up his hands in mock surrender. "I hear you loud and clear."

As they continued around the room, no one posed a question to Mila, proof she wasn't on anyone's shortlist. She likely was correct that her partner would be chosen by default.

It was painful for Jancey to see someone with obvious capabilities and a demonstrated sense of staying cool under pressure be overlooked. She'd always believed the men of NASA would place respect for those things above inherent gender bias, but clearly that wasn't the case, since she too had been snubbed by everyone but Marlon. As the only one in the room with expertise in food production, she'd expected more of them to express interest in partnering with her.

When her turn came, she used her question to help Mila decide who would accept her, who would respect her.

"My question is for Marlon, Jean-Paul and Wade." She'd ruled out Jerry in fear his antics would turn hostile if he were teamed with someone he considered inferior. "Be honest here. How would you treat me—or any woman—as a partner on Mars?"

Marlon started. "Don't take this the wrong way, Jancey, but I don't see you as a woman. I mean, I do…but I don't. You're an accomplished astronaut, a scientist and a major in the US Air Force. I couldn't possibly respect you more than I do. You're my equal in every sense."

Not bad, but there was no way Marlon would see Mila in the same light. "Jean-Paul?"

"Asking a Frenchman not to notice a woman is like asking a rooster to ignore the sunrise. It does not mean I would not respect you as a colleague, but I would be dishonest to pretend you weren't a woman. I would treat you as a gentleman should."

She appreciated his candor and suspected he wasn't alone in his ingrained chivalry. While it wasn't threatening, it was condescending for someone who didn't wish to be coddled because of her sex. Mila would find it infuriating. "And Wade."

"My first question of anyone is going to be, 'What are you working on?' It doesn't matter to me if you're a woman, a man or a space alien. I want to learn everything you know. I want to pick your brain on my work too. We should build on that together. That's the whole reason we want to go to Mars—to expand our knowledge of the universe."

She had grossly misjudged him, thinking him dull and dry. He actually was an ordinary science geek—socially awkward but someone Mila probably would enjoy working with.

Predictably, Wade used his opportunity to ask his question directly of Jerry first, then Jean-Paul. In a mild surprise, his third potential candidate was Jancey. Perhaps he'd thought she was entertaining a possible pairing because of her question to him.

"Let's see…what will I be working on?" she said, stroking her chin pensively. "In addition to training for this mission, I expect to spend the next few years working on ways to grow food on Mars. Something tells me I'll still be doing that when I get there."

Jerry chucked Wade's shoulder. "Sorry, bro. I've changed my mind. I'm picking Jancey."

When Mila's turn finally came, she leaned forward in her chair with her fingertips pressed together, her mouth twisted with doubt. "I couldn't help but notice no one seems to have me in mind as a partner. Someone will get me though, so I guess I need to know how hard you'll work to be selected if you know it means working in tight quarters with me forever."

Under the circumstances, it was the best question she could have asked, Jancey thought.

Jean-Paul answered first, smiling wryly. "I very much want to go to Mars. I'd go with the Beast of Gévaudan if it was my only way to get there. I want a partner I can work with. All you have to do is show me you can be that person."

Not exactly a ringing endorsement. The underlying message was that Mila had something to prove, while he did not. She'd be expected to shape her work around his directives. Not acceptable.

"Kind of what Jean-Paul said," Wade answered. "Going to Mars would be the biggest thrill I could imagine, no matter who I went with. If I end up being your partner, all I care about is whether or not you can hold up your end."

At best, it was a lukewarm response. Neither had shown even a trace of enthusiasm at the idea of being paired with Mila. Nor had they spoken of working *with* her, certainly not as an equal partner. She'd be choosing the lesser of two evils, both of whom were set to blame their possible failure on her perceived shortcomings.

"And Jancey."

She needed to show them Mila was someone they'd be lucky to get as a partner, someone who possibly had more upside potential than anyone in the room. "How hard would I work if you and I were partners? As hard as I'd work with anyone. After seeing your propulsion design, I'd like our chances a lot, since it's obvious you're a gifted engineer."

The doctor put his notes away and passed out a stack of forms and pencils. "That wraps up our questions. Your last task is to choose a partner. Circle your name on this list and rank all the others, with one being the most desirable, seven being the least. I just got a text that your lunch has arrived. While you're eating, the committee will review your selections and announce the pairings."

The pairings. From three dozen questions and a handful of structured interactions, they were supposed to select a lifetime partner. At least she had a history with Marlon. Poor Mila was left to choose based on little more than she'd get from an online dating site. Except instead of dinner and a movie, it was a wedding.

* * *

"Lunch" turned out to be a soy concoction blended with sweet potatoes and cinnamon. It was supposed to be indicative of a quick meal they might have on Mars when their work kept them from preparing something more conventional.

Mila noticed right away the men's shakes were nearly twice as large as hers and Jancey's. Metabolically balanced. Yet another reason they'd be the perfect choice.

The morning session had shed little light on the question of who besides Jancey she'd want as a partner. It probably was a moot point. Marlon and Jancey, David and Kamal. From the answers Jerry and Wade had given, they were likely to team up. That left only Jean-Paul.

It would be interesting to hear of his experience with the European Space Agency. She'd applied two years ago but made it only to the second level. In their thirty-year history of human space flight, only three women had been selected for the program, and only one had ever flown a mission.

Jean-Paul had designed one of the crew modules for the ISS and flown on a *Soyuz* mission to install it. Over the past four years, he'd worked with engineering teams on the blueprints for *Tenacity*'s living space aboard the vessel and also in the planet habitat. A space architect. From a practical standpoint, that was a useless skill, since their quarters were already designed. Even after four years of identical training in food production, he'd probably expect her to serve him dinner every night on Mars. In return, he'd behave "like a gentleman."

Jean-Paul, David and Kamal were clustered at the counter talking about working in weightlessness. Jancey and the others—the four NASA astronauts—were seated in a grouping around the sofa. It was Mila's own fault she wasn't accepted by anyone in the group, not only here today but throughout her time in Hawaii. She'd fooled the psychologists into believing she could work cooperatively when all she'd done was complain about Andi and try to undermine Jancey and Marlon.

She needed a reset. Accept her assignment with Jean-Paul and set out to make him glad the dice had rolled their way.

During a pause in their conversation, she wedged herself between Jean-Paul and David. "Tell me more about this Beast of Gévaudan."

His welcoming hand on her shoulder felt genuine, as though he too recognized their fates were intertwined. "The hybrid wolf. We should take along one silver bullet."

Several staffers entered carrying canvas duffel bags, each with a name stamped on the side. Their analog gear, no doubt. Mila spotted hers between Jean-Paul's and Wade's...if that meant anything.

Danielle Zion, wearing a dark blue sweater atop her yellow polo shirt, followed and waved a single piece of paper. "I have your assignments. When you hear your name, collect your gear and stow it in one of the bedrooms with your partner. Then proceed to Building A for Dr. V's afternoon seminar. He'll provide an overview of the analog trials...what your quarters will be like, communications with Mission Control, the experiments you'll be running. Also, very important—how you'll be evaluated. That begins in fifteen minutes."

Mila drew a deep breath through her teeth and did her best imitation of an actual smile. *Just get on with it!*

"Most of you got your top choice. These are the teams— Pillay and Sidhu, Huffstetler and Hackett, Beaumont and Todorov, Quinn and Robillard. Everybody get that?"

Beaumont and Todorov. Her heart pounded as she played it back in her head. Had she heard it right, or was her mind playing tricks on her?

Before she could react, Jancey tossed a duffel at her feet and muttered, "Go put our bags away."

"What the hell?" Marlon exclaimed. "There has to be a mistake."

With her insides doing cartwheels, Mila lifted both bags and shuffled across the room, straining to hear the conversation.

"I'm sorry, Marlon. I decided it was better for me to go with Mila."

David and Kamal had already ventured into their room, but the other astronauts were frozen in their tracks to hear what Jancey would say, making the moment even more awkward than it already was.

"I don't understand." His face a mask of hurt and confusion, he looked over his shoulder at Mila and back at Jancey. "Is it… because you're both gay?"

Jancey panned the faces of the other men, finishing with a brief glance toward Mila. "You're kidding, right? Let's talk about this later."

Mila whirled around and continued toward the room with Jancey right behind her. She felt guilty for eavesdropping, but not enough to dampen her elation. Never in her wildest dreams did she think Jancey would choose her.

"You'll never be sorry, Jancey. We're going to win this competition. I can feel it."

"Feeling's not enough," she snapped. "Right now one of my best friends thinks I've lost my mind and he might be right. If we want this, we're going to have to work harder and smarter than everyone here. The committee doesn't want to pick two women for this mission. We have to make them." She poked a finger in Mila's chest for emphasis. "Whatever they ask us to do, we do more. We do better. No slacking off, not even for a minute."

The harshness of her voice didn't faze Mila because she agreed with every word. "This has been my dream since I was thirteen years old. I will not let you down."

Left unsaid was that her dream had always included Major Jancey Beaumont.

CHAPTER TEN

"It wasn't about you, Marlon. But it wasn't about her either... not the way you might think."

They were standing outside Building A, huddled against a wall that blocked the wind. Even in July, the air at nine thousand feet was chilly.

"I don't understand, Jancey. Ever since we got here, we planned this together."

She'd thought all along she'd team with Marlon, but never had she actually promised to do so. "I've been watching her. She got a perfect score in concentration. Sailed through the dexterity tests. Nailed the underwater exercise and then kept six people from being killed down on the dock."

"I did all those things too. Not the incident on the dock, but you know I would have handled it the right way."

"I know. All of us would have because we were trained that way at NASA. She did it without the training. And the propulsion system we'll use to get to Mars—that's her design."

He shook his head, clearly not buying any of it.

"Look, Marlon. You asked me if it was because she was a lesbian. The answer's no. But the fact that she's a woman…that mattered to me more than I thought. When it came down to finally having to choose, it was about more than teamwork. It was about living with somebody for the rest of my life. I had to go with what made me comfortable."

A staffer poked her head out the door to signal them. "We're getting ready to start."

Marlon tightened his lips and sighed. "I hear you, Jancey. I thought we had the best shot."

"You and Jean-Paul will be tough to beat. And Mila mentioned something that made a lot of sense—the committee's more likely to choose an international team. I expect all four of us to make it to Mars one day."

The common area in Building A had been configured classroom style with four long tables angled to face a podium and screen. Jancey took the open seat on the back row next to Mila, whom she now looked at in a whole new light. Intelligent, capable, determined.

Intriguing.

Do not go there. There was work to do.

Eight teams. Sixteen finalists down from over forty thousand. From the day she'd sent in her application, she always knew deep down she'd be sitting here. She'd never imagined it would be with a twenty-seven-year-old woman with zero space experience. A foolish move? Time would tell. Six weeks to be exact. Probably sooner, since Mila would show her mettle as soon as they began their preparations. Dreams weren't enough. She'd have to put them aside and focus on the task at hand. Jancey would see that she did.

Dr. V paced the floor at the front of the room as he spoke. "The analog trial isn't only a test of survivability. It's a test of prosperity. After all, that is the objective of colonization—to prosper. Which team is likely to grow the most crops? Produce the most energy? Successfully complete all the experiments that will help us prepare for future colonization?"

Beyond the performance of those duties, the selection committee also would look for signs of cooperation and effective teamwork. Did your partner lose weight or muscle mass? Were the workloads balanced? Were there any signs of discord? They would show up quickly in an isolated habitat.

Success on Mars would take an all-out effort and that's what the committee wanted to see in the analog trial. Six exhausting weeks that would prove which team deserved the first two seats on *Tenacity*.

"More than anyplace on Earth, the barren slopes of Mauna Kea are uniquely suited to Mars analog training. The soil—if you can call it that—is rich in volcanic mineral deposits, but none that are amenable to plant life, so all of our crops must be grown indoors with hydroponics."

They'd have to use grow lights, which would draw heavily on their limited power supply, to say nothing of their water.

"At eleven thousand feet, you can expect thirty percent less oxygen. Temperatures range from a balmy ten degrees Celsius during the day to below freezing at night. However, atmosphere and temperature will be irrelevant on Mars, since all of your extravehicular activities will require a spacesuit. To simulate that on Mauna Kea, you'll be required to don one of those every time you exit the habitat. It will not be pressurized or temperature controlled, so dress accordingly underneath."

Jancey had never practiced planetary EVAs. Like most NASA astronauts, the bulk of her training had taken place in the Neutral Buoyancy Lab, underwater for up to eight hours a stretch working on simulated repairs in space.

"As you know," Dr. V continued, "communications from Mars must travel hundreds of millions of miles through space. Accordingly, your questions—no matter how critical—will require a minimum of twenty minutes for a response. You will find the same delays in your Internet usage, so do not allow yourself to get sucked into click-bait. You'll receive a daily newsletter apprising you of world events—this world, that is— which will allow you to keep up with the Kardashians."

Jerry laughed. "That's the main reason I want to go to Mars—to get away from those people."

His quip was worth a chuckle, but it resonated with Jancey in a decidedly serious way. The world was a mess. Global war, economic and social inequality worldwide. An abuse of nature that threatened to drown its cities and turn out the lights forever. The Tenacity Project wasn't only about venturing into space. It would lay the foundation for how Earth's inhabitants might have to live in the future, their air unbreathable and their resources depleted.

Dr. V commenced a slideshow with an artist's rendering of the Mars colony, and asked everyone to follow along in their training manual. "This is a repeat of the presentation you saw on the first day of orientation, but now the details will come together."

They reviewed the timetable. Two launches of equipment and life support systems, one of which was already en route. Robotic construction of an underground habitat. Manned flights at one-year intervals.

"If everything goes as planned, you will arrive on Mars to find your underground home already built. It will be up to you to secure the proper seals and connections that will allow you to maintain life support throughout the structure, and to activate your power and water supply."

Nothing ever went as planned but that's why they trained— to overcome equipment failures. Maintenance of the life support units was their top priority, another reason she'd be glad to have Mila on her team.

"You remember this slide." *Tenacity* en route to Mars, the first illustration they were shown on orientation day. Using a laser pointer, he described the various segments of the vessel. "During launch and landing on Mars, you will occupy this cone-shaped module. If you look closely, you'll see that it's identical to the life-support units that will already be operational on Mars, and in fact, that's what it is. It isn't designed for long-term occupancy. It's quite small, containing two ergonomic seats around an instrument panel. Those seats, by the way, will be detachable so you can use them in your living area on Mars."

"Don't expect to hit the ground running," Jancey offered. "After eight months in zero gravity, just expect to hit the ground."

"Absolutely right," Marlon said. "It took me three days to walk on Earth again after being on the ISS for five months."

It pleased her to hear him speak up in response to something she said, and she turned to see a hint of a smile that made her both happy and sad. She shouldn't have blindsided him like that, but her decision to go with Mila had come at the last second. Besides, she hadn't been sure it would even happen. If Mila had given up on her and named someone else first, Jancey would have ended up with Marlon as her second choice.

"During your eight-month trip to Mars, you will live inside this second segment, which we'll call the travel habitat. Practically speaking, it's only a bit larger than your average cargo van. One of your fellow finalists, Jean-Paul Robillard, helped us create a design that maximized our usable space. As you can see, that space includes a sleeping chamber large enough for two"—the slideshow continued with sketches of the interior design—"a lavatory, exercise equipment, a galley and a very small common area for laboratory experiments and leisure. The sleeping chamber doubles as a radiation shelter in the event of a solar flare, which you can expect periodically throughout your trip."

Missing from the neat illustrations were the dozens of Velcro patches needed to keep their hand tools and implements from floating around in zero gravity. It had taken Jancey a year after returning from her mission to break her habit of wanting to stick everything to the wall.

She eyed the rendering with relief, increasingly convinced she and Mila were ideal for this mission. They were fifty pounds lighter than any other team, took up less space and required fewer calories to maintain their muscle mass. Of the final teams, only two others—the Norwegians and the Fagans—contained both an engineer and an expert on food production. There was no better combination of skills for laying the foundation of a colony. All they had to do was prove they were more capable than anyone else.

"By this time, I'm sure you're ready for me to shut up about Mars and tell you what you're in for on Mauna Kea. The reason

I've taken the time to go over these points is because we've melded some of the elements of your eight-month travel with your duties upon reaching the planet. Over the next few days, you and your partner will construct your habitat on the eastern slope, a geodesic dome approximately the same size as the travel habitat on *Tenacity*, and with many of the same features. Tall enough that you can stand in the center, and just barely large enough to hold everything you need."

The slideshow advanced to an actual photograph of one of the domes, and then to its interior, where one of the staffers sat at the worktable to illustrate just how tiny the habitat was. More than anything, it underscored the significance for Jancey of choosing the right teammate for the mission. Sharing such a small space with Mila would be difficult. Sharing it with Marlon would have been impossible.

"After putting your dome kit together, you'll stock it with food sufficient for six weeks and a week's ration of water, which will be replenished by staff at regular intervals. On the day you begin the trial, staff will deliver outside each habitat the assembly kits for solar panels and hydroponic food production. You're to set those up immediately and put them to use. We'll have a workshop tomorrow on how that's done."

There had to be more to it than that. It wasn't feasible to limit their air supply, but none of the other tests had been as straightforward as this.

All around her, the other candidates were exchanging curious looks, as though waiting for the other shoe to drop.

"Ah, yes…there's always a catch," he added with a chuckle. "Do not be surprised to arrive and discover some of your equipment is not working as it should. Or that part of your food supply is tainted. Expect a solar flare. Or two. Or ten. The message for the next six weeks is to be prepared for anything. Monitor and maintain your equipment as though your life depended on it. Once you leave this earth, it will."

* * *

OMG !!! OMG !!!!! OMG !!!!!!! JANCEY BEAUMONT PICKED ME!!!!!!!!!!!!!!!!!! :-D

In one brief message, Mila had managed to violate all four of Vio's email peeves by using an Internet acronym, all caps, excessive exclamation points and an emoticon. A video chat was out of the question, since their project-issued tablet computers were now programmed to delay Internet activity for twenty minutes.

Five days of training and construction followed by six weeks in a tiny freezing bubble with hardly any oxygen. I CAN'T W8 !!!!!!!!!!!!!!!!!!!!!

Jancey had barely spoken to her since the selection, opting to sit with the other NASA astronauts during dinner, which was real food for a change. Roasted pork, potatoes, peas and pineapple. Four P's that didn't include poi. Only fitting, since they probably were still drinking recycled pee.

The bedroom door opened and Mila hit the Send key on her message. In the same instant, she swung her feet off the desk and sat up straight as if at attention.

"Why haven't you put your things away?" Jancey asked. By her exasperated tone, she might as well have added *you lazy twit.*

"I was waiting to see which side of the room you wanted."

Jancey launched into an elaborate display of incredulity complete with an eye roll, head shaking and deep, indulgent sigh. "For the love of the Big Banger himself, Todorov. Which of these two identical sides should I choose?"

"It depends on your preference," Mila said evenly, hoping Jancey would appreciate her attention to detail. "That side has an extra power outlet, plus the thermostat and the drawstrings for the blinds. I would have given you those automatically, except the mattress on the other bed appears to be new."

With a snort, Jancey tossed her belongings onto the newer mattress. "I don't care about the outlet or the thermostat. Leave the blinds closed."

Mila wasn't sure how much freedom she had to talk, or how casual she was allowed to be. Jancey was single-mindedly dedicated to the analog trial and so was she, but that was no reason not to be friendly. On the other hand, Jancey might view an attempt at conversation as an invasion of privacy, or worse, a sign that she was more interested in socializing than in preparing for their trial. A better use of her time was reviewing the technical materials for the solar panels and hydroponic gardens.

"Those probably won't do us much good," Jancey said. "We won't have all the pieces, or the pieces won't fit, or everything will fit but nothing works."

"Did you find that to be true on *Guardian*?"

"Yes and no. NASA tests all the equipment a million times and they're meticulous about packing everything you need in a repair kit. But what if the only wrench that fits goes drifting off out of reach? Then you have to improvise. When I had that emergency with the Russians...I was able to reach their vessel, but we couldn't dock because both of us had male ports. Ended up using my robotic arm as a lasso and then I had to escort them into my airlock."

"I know. Trust me, I read every word that was ever written about that, including the congressional report. It was amazing. What you did...you really were a hero." Despite her intention of talking only when necessary, Mila couldn't stop her feelings from spilling out. "I've looked up to you ever since I was thirteen years old. If it weren't for you, I'd probably still be in Europe teaching physics at some university. I don't know what made you change your mind about me, but I'm glad you did, because going to Mars with you will be the greatest privilege of my life."

Her fears were realized when Jancey scowled and shook her head. "I don't want to be your idol, or your commander either. Don't sit there and wait for me to tell you what to do. Learn your job and do it."

"I will." *Shit.* That wasn't at all the impression she'd wanted to make. "I didn't mean for you to think I wanted to be your little helper. I only wanted to make sure no one else would try to turn either of us into theirs. I've worked with mostly men ever since I started college and that's what they do. Every time they're with women, they feel entitled to take over. Even when they're total idiots."

"Especially if they're total idiots." Jancey softened a little around the eyes. "I've seen it too, especially at the universities where I taught after NASA killed the long-term space program. Marlon and those guys...they're not as bad as the men in academia, but that's because our jobs at NASA were compartmentalized. Each of us trained for very specific tasks. That's one of the things I like about Tenacity. Everyone is expected to do it all. You and I"—she wagged her finger between them—"we need to be interchangeable."

"Exactly. That's another reason I wanted to be your partner. You're one of the world's leading experts on making food out of thin air. I want to learn that from the best."

When Jancey dumped the contents of her duffel on the bed, Mila did the same. A basic toiletry kit. Tightly rolled underwear and socks. Three sets of thermal underwear. Lightweight T-shirts and microfiber shorts for exercising or sleeping. Another flight suit like the one she was wearing. A thermal coat, cap and gloves.

As she stowed her clothing, she noticed someone had already stamped her initials inside each piece. The label on her thermal coat was marked LF. "Uh-oh, it looks like I have Libby Fagan's jacket. I hope she has mine."

As she turned to show the label to Jancey, she was startled to find her naked from the waist up with her back turned as she slipped into a T-shirt for sleeping. Mila quickly spun back around, trembling with...*damn it*...trembling with excitement. Very not good. She had to rein that in now.

"You and Libby are about the same size. At least they didn't give you Marlon's."

"I'll see about trading with her tomorrow." With her back to Jancey, she too changed into a T-shirt and knit shorts, all the while conscious of being watched.

"We'll need to get our rhythms sorted out for the analog," Jancey said. "When to sleep, when to eat. Our exercise schedule. And we'll have to set aside several hours a day to work together. I usually like to work out first thing in the morning, but two hours at this altitude...I may have to split it up."

Mila had gone to the exercise room in Building A immediately following the afternoon seminar but had managed to complete only half of her workout before her muscles became fatigued for lack of oxygen.

"Spreading out the workouts might be better anyway," Mila replied. "According to the handbook, our biggest challenge will be boredom. Other than maintaining our habitat and keeping the logs, we don't have much actual work to stay busy."

"That's kind of the point of the analog—to see how we'll handle long periods of not having anything to do." Jancey removed her new tablet from the backpack. "So what have they loaded on this thing?"

"All the training materials are there. Communications software. Interface plug-ins for the equipment we'll be using… the solar panels and the water meter. Duty logs, exercise logs, food logs, sleeping logs. There's probably one there for peeing and pooping too," she added sarcastically.

"You'd better believe it. The whole time I was on *Guardian*, everyone in Houston knew when I got my period. There's no such thing as privacy." Jancey propped against her pillow and stretched her legs out on the bed with the tablet in her lap. "Any external apps on here?"

"There's an Internet browser but it has a built-in delay so everything you try to access takes twenty minutes. Works fine for email though. A few solitaire games. And there's a gaming app that looks like it's set up to network with nearby tablets. We'll probably have time to check that out in…oh, about six or seven years."

"No *BattleStorm*, huh? Too bad."

"Are you serious? You play *BattleStorm*?"

"Of course. All of us do. Anything with a joystick keeps you sharp, but *BattleStorm* is better than most. Even if you're playing by yourself, there's enough with all the built-in layers and levels to test your reaction time and dexterity. When you add in other players, you get that human variability that really makes you have to concentrate. You have to study everyone's patterns so you can guess their next move."

Mila envisioned Jancey sitting alone in her office at a gaming console, the only light from a gigantic monitor. From her captain's chair, she—

"Oh, my God." *Jancey* Beaumont. A *solo* space mission. "You're JanSolo. You have the top four all-time scores."

"Five, counting last night. And you are?"

"I go by The General. One night I had an amazing game and took over the top score. Then I went to bed, and six hours later, there you were in first place again. You didn't even let me enjoy it a whole day."

"The General...I remember seeing your name. How come we never played against each other?"

"Different time zones, I guess. I haven't played since I got here, but Vio—that's my friend in Rotterdam. She goes by Second in Command. She saw you online when you got to Hawaii. It's a twelve-hour time difference. You must have been playing when you were staying with Grace Faraday."

"Affirmative."

"But your avatar is male."

"It's an avatar," she said sarcastically. "Gamer boys don't like to play with women."

"Tell me about it. That's why Vio and I have to crash everyone else's game. I want them to know it's a woman kicking their ass."

"Which is exactly why you can't get a higher score. Those boys aren't going to stick around for an ass-kicking by a woman. The reason you don't get to vanquish them is because they drop out before that happens."

Mila fumed to realize she was right. She rarely got the chance to put her opponent away in glorious battle fashion because they simply bowed out. "Those chickenshit, mouth-breathing knuckle-draggers."

"Change your avatar. Tell your friend too. We'll take them on together sometime." Jancey set her tablet aside and flipped off the light above her bed.

Mila could have stayed up and talked all night. How was she supposed to sleep when everything was so awesome?

CHAPTER ELEVEN

Dressed in a freshly laundered flight suit, Jancey stood at ease alongside her fellow finalists on a makeshift stage in the parking lot in front of Building A. Sir Charles spoke from a podium to a small audience of staff and press who had come to cover the start of their analog trial.

"I can't begin to tell you how inspired I am by these sixteen candidates, and how much I envy the task before them. Over a year ago, we began our selection process with an open call for those keen on being among the first of humankind to colonize Mars. We received over forty thousand applications from all over the world. That alone should tell you how extraordinary these sixteen people are. It's obvious from looking at them they're in superb physical condition, but that's only a very small piece of what they offer. They are intelligent, curious, quick-thinking. They met all of our challenges and refused to take no for an answer. I expect them to sail through the next six weeks with the same perseverance they've already shown."

In the last half hour, the wind had picked up, sending temperatures on the mountain into the single digits, the low forties in Fahrenheit. Photographers and reporters huddled in their coats while staff shivered in their pullover sweaters. Jancey tried to ignore the chill, focusing instead on the afternoon ahead, when she and the others would be dropped off at their habitats. By the end of the day, she'd be tired and hungry, this ceremony a distant memory.

"At the conclusion of our trial, the Tenacity Project selection committee will choose four of these eight teams you see behind me for continued training. What they don't know"—he turned and looked over his shoulder, smiling broadly—"is that just this morning the committee agreed we must take advantage of this exemplary slate of candidates rather than call for new applicants and repeat the selection process. Therefore all four teams who perform best on the analog will be slated for a mission to Mars. One of them will launch four years from now to establish the colony. The other three teams will follow at one-year intervals."

That was a bombshell. Half of them would get a definitive assignment to go to Mars at the end of the analog. Jancey still wanted to be first, but it took a lot of pressure off to know she wouldn't have to go through the selection process again if they finished lower. Given their skills, it was ridiculous to think she and Mila wouldn't be among the top four teams. Furthermore, the committee wouldn't dare cut the only team of women.

Mila too seemed to realize the significance of his statement. She was grinning openly and even winked when she caught Jancey looking her way.

The last few days had left Jancey feeling encouraged—and relieved—about her decision to choose Mila as a partner. They'd worked together methodically to assemble their habitat on the slope, where Mila's engineering expertise was immediately obvious. Even more impressive was her demeanor. Quietly confident, thanks to the time she spent each night preparing for the next day's work. If her goal had been to impress, she'd done it so far.

It didn't hurt that Grace's disembodied voice had been whispering encouragement in her ear the whole time they worked. Mila could very well turn out to be more than a workmate, and even more than an interesting companion.

But only when Jancey decided the timing was right. She had no intention of losing control just because they were alone together. In a small space. With little else to do. No matter how tempting it might be.

"With that, I know you join me in wishing them well. We'll be serving refreshments in Building A, where you'll have a chance to question each of these teams before they depart."

Once she'd moved inside and poured herself a cup of water, Jancey migrated to a corner well away from the microphones and throng of reporters. Publicity was one part of the job she didn't enjoy at all.

A familiar face squeezed through the crowd and joined her.

"Well, if it isn't Shel Montgomery. Are you here to ask if you can share our little round hut?"

"No way in hell. I can hardly breathe up here as it is." She flipped open a reporter's steno pad. "Turns out Sir Charles was serious about letting all of us stay on with the project. Guess who's Number Two in the media relations department? That's gainful employment for at least the next fifteen years. My mother will be so proud."

Jancey laughed. "And all this time I thought you dropped out because you were unselfish. Now I see you had an ulterior motive."

"Damn right. I'll take a cushy life right here on Earth as long as I have a meal ticket." She studied the questions on her pad and held out a small digital recorder. "I'm putting together an official press release on all of the finalist teams. Something for the average newspaper reader, like hometown, hobbies, why you want to go to Mars. Got any juicy quotes for me?"

Before her *Guardian* mission, Jancey had received very little attention from the press beyond her hometown newspaper and TV stations. That changed after her dramatic return, when she was swamped by interview requests from all over the world. Those interviews continued for years as part of the publicity campaign for her speaking engagements around the country. They were all the same. Boilerplate questions, boilerplate answers.

"I've got to tell you, Jancey. I was blown away when I saw you were paired with Mila Todorov. I thought you and Marlon Quinn were teaming up. What happened with that?"

Jancey looked around to make sure no one was within earshot. "Off the record, okay? I don't know a better astronaut than Marlon, but I started having some doubts about how we'd live together. *Personal* doubts."

"I get it. So you went with Mila because she's a lesbian?"

"No!" The last thing Jancey wanted was another tabloid rumor. "She happens to be quite good. Like I said, Marlon's top-notch, but I've watched Mila work too. She'll be *at least* that good once she's gone through training. Maybe even better. That you can print. This part, no, because I don't want tongues wagging over my personal life. My decision to team with her had absolutely nothing to do with her being a lesbian. But yes, I chose her because I came to realize how difficult it would be for me to live with a man. It just isn't in my DNA."

Shel tipped her head toward Mila, who was standing alone behind the refreshment table as though hiding from reporters. "You have to admit she'll make an interesting companion."

"Oh, please. I have socks older than her." After the sacrifice Shel had made to save her chances, Jancey doubted she'd take advantage of her confidence for a sensational story. "You're jerking me around, right? You aren't seriously going to write a story like that."

"You're safe. My audience is PG. But don't be surprised to learn your partner has other ideas. There's something about the way she looks at you."

"What the hell are you talking about?" Try as she might, Jancey couldn't hold back an embarrassed smile.

"I noticed it that first day we were in the gym. She couldn't take her eyes off you."

"That's ridiculous. She was starstruck, thanks to you and your friends in the press. I was just doing my job on *Guardian* and you guys turned me into some kind of media sensation." Mila had admitted as much with her claim that Jancey had inspired her to study space engineering.

"Just look at her…quite a package. What's not to like? And no, I'm not writing any of this down. I write about science, not gossip. But from a personal standpoint, it would be kind of nice to think you're both going off on a grand adventure where you get to do something besides work every day."

And now Shel was channeling Grace.

Jancey kept telling herself that wasn't her plan. At least not her conscious plan. Her whole argument had been that Mila would be easier to live with than Marlon. But would she have chosen Libby Fagan for the same reason? Doubtful, even though she too was a trained astronaut. She'd chosen Mila for Mila, and it had more to do with their chemistry than she was willing to admit.

"Let me call her over so I can interview both of you together."

"No surprises?"

Shel shook her head and gave her a reassuring pat on the shoulder. With a wave of her hand, she invited Mila into the corner. "Jancey's been singing your praises. How does that make you feel?"

"It's gratifying to know I have my partner's confidence. She certainly has mine."

"Tell me your story, Mila. Why are you here?"

"I'm here to be part of something extraordinary." Her voice was low and even, with no trace of self-aggrandizement. "From the time I was a little girl growing up in Sofia, I've been fascinated by space exploration. I dreamed of blasting off someday in a rocket ship, and I set out to make that dream come true. What I learned through my studies is that space exploration is so much more than a personal quest. It's a gift to all of humanity, and my job is to help unwrap it. All of us who study space want to make contributions to our knowledge of the universe. I would be honored if the colonization of Mars was mine."

Jancey was impressed by her well-articulated response and thoughtful demeanor. For someone who'd never been in the limelight, she had a remarkable media presence.

"I agree with every word," she said, "but I'd like to add one more thing. With the honor bestowed upon us for the Mars colonization comes an obligation. This is not a part-time job, nor does it end at sixty-five with a gold watch and a party. It requires a relentless dedication to the mission. All the funders, scientists, engineers and support staff...they're going with us. Our success is theirs."

"Whoa, that's about six money quotes from just one question," Shel said. "Something tells me you two are going to make a great team."

"Working with Jancey will be like nonstop training. It's phenomenal how much she knows, how sharp her instincts are. As long as she's around, I won't ever stop learning."

Jancey didn't want anyone to come away thinking she'd chosen a partner who wasn't capable of holding up her end. "Don't listen to her. I've learned to get out of her way when it comes to building something. She gets so wrapped up in the challenge, she doesn't even know I'm there."

Mila blushed so quickly, so deeply, it was hard not to be amused.

"Seriously, Shel. When you're mired in a mission of this magnitude with so many working parts, you have to be willing to put your fate in other people's hands. On this project, the most important person is your partner. I feel confident Mila Todorov is one hundred percent capable not only of doing what's required of her, but of going well beyond her mission. She's going to make a great astronaut, and I trust her to be there for me."

"That's good to know." Shel looked over her shoulder and lowered her voice. "I'm going to let you both in on a little secret. The rumor mill's already churning. Sir Charles likes you two a lot. He likes Marlon Quinn and Jean-Paul Robillard too."

"The international pairs," Mila said, with a nod toward Jancey. Exactly as she'd predicted.

"Bingo. They like the idea of a married couple too, and since Libby Fagan came out of NASA and Brandon has all that expertise in robotics, they probably have the inside track on that front. I'd bet anything you guys will be the top three teams... unless one of you screws up." She peered around again as if to make sure no one had overheard. "I probably should make an attempt to talk to someone else…at least look like I'm working. Good luck, you two. We'll do this again in six weeks—with champagne."

Armed with Shel's tidbit of inside information, Jancey checked off the competition. Nothing she'd learned was particularly surprising, except perhaps to know Sir Charles and the committee were already discussing favorites. If that were true, then Shel was absolutely right—all they had to do was get through the analog trial without a major screw-up.

* * *

Danielle Zion stood at the front of the bus facing the passengers, bracing herself as the rugged service road caused her to jostle from side to side. "Two hours each. That's all you have outside your habitat every day, and only in your spacesuit. Don't forget to record your in and out."

After three days working on the slope to build their habitat, Mila hardly noticed the thin air anymore. Her workouts were back to normal, and she had no signs of headache or stomach upset from the altitude. Two hours of physical labor outside ought to be easy, but Jancey had warned her about tiring sooner in a full suit.

"Your power pack should be good for at least twenty-four hours, depending on how much you use. Top priority is communications. Your comm should be active at all times."

They'd been over the guidelines several times already. Everything was to be managed for maximum efficiency of time and resources. They were advised to anticipate failures—damaged equipment, spoiled food, inadequate supplies, communications outage—and emergencies. Solar flares could happen at any time.

"In the event of a real emergency—and by that I mean something outside of the analog, such as a life-threatening sickness or injury—your trial will be temporarily suspended. If you're able to return quickly, you will not be penalized. Bear in mind that altitude sickness can come on at any time, so if you have chest pains or a severe headache, the only cure is to descend immediately. Use your head. The trial is not important enough to cost anyone their life."

Mila could see Kamal was anxious. He and Phillip Clarke had struggled with the altitude, so much that they'd been forced to descend the first night to six thousand feet to sleep in an RV.

The bus stopped to allow David and Kamal to exit at their site. "Your trial starts when you reach your habitat. Good luck."

The eight habitats were situated along the slope at fifty-meter intervals. Mila and Jancey were next to last to step off. Their nearest neighbors were the Fagans on one side and the Clarkes at the end.

When they reached their hut, Mila held the door and allowed Jancey to enter first. A quick glance around the perimeter outside confirmed their equipment had been delivered—solar panels, water supply and a hydroponics kit. With a deep breath, she ducked her head and entered, their analog now officially underway.

"Home sweet shoebox," Jancey said.

The dome was two and a half meters in diameter and only a few centimeters higher than Mila around the edges. Someone as tall as Marlon couldn't move comfortably inside unless he was standing in the middle. Advantage Mila and Jancey.

On one side was a sleeping platform, waist-high with a plywood enclosure meant to simulate a radiation chamber. Two people could sleep comfortably inside, and even sit up in bed, but the men would never consider such a thing. It was "gay." They probably would sleep in shifts. Mila would leave it up to Jancey to decide their schedule. As long as they left their communication channel open, it wasn't necessary to have someone awake monitoring it at all times.

Beneath the platform was storage space for food lockers, supplies, and their personal belongings, which included their clunky spacesuits. The other side held a drop-down table with two low chairs, a small galley and a hydraulic stair climber with exercise bands attached. Directly opposite the door was a closet that jutted out from the back of the dome, closed off with an accordion curtain, and a window that opened to the outside—the compost lavatory. The only empty space, less than a square meter beside the door, was reserved for the hydroponics garden.

Over the last three days, they had constructed the dome themselves inside and out from a kit, and stocked it with equipment and six weeks' worth of supplies.

"So far it looks like everything's still where we left it yesterday," Mila said.

"Don't celebrate yet. We don't know if any of it works."

They had scripted every step the night before to make the best use of the two hours they could spend outside. The first task was to confirm their water tank had been filled. It was mounted on the exterior of the dome and insulated to keep it from freezing, and had a valve inside from which they could draw what they needed. One hundred liters per week was their ration. Jancey assured her they could make do with less. Much less. Mila was afraid to ask if that had anything to do with urine.

The most complicated job was to mount the solar panels on their roof so they could begin charging their other two power packs. Once that was done, they'd move back inside to assemble the hydroponics garden and get their seedlings started.

Jancey went to work unpacking her spacesuit, which wasn't a spacesuit at all. Actual EMUs—extravehicular mobility units—were multimillion-dollar individual life support units designed to maintain body temperature and air flow, and deflect bullet-like particles that floated through orbit. Their analog suits were bulky and restrictive to simulate the difficulties of EVAs in space, but had none of the technology.

"I'll get changed and go start on the solar panels," Jancey said. "You check out what's in the widget box and I'll let you know what we need."

The widget box looked as though it had been assembled by sweeping the floor in a hardware store. Spare parts, specialty tools. Duct tape, plastic tubing, sealant. Twine, razor blades, binder clips. Pipe fittings, conduits, wire connectors.

"Uh-oh," Mila said, holding up a spool of electrical wire. "What do you want to bet the connectors have been stripped out of the solar panels?"

"I'm worried about the water caddy too. We should put a seal around the valve just in case, and check the bottom for cracks."

It was all Mila could do to keep her eyes on the widget box when she realized Jancey had stripped off her clothes to put on a moisture-wicking layer underneath her spacesuit. After four nights together in close quarters at the residence, they'd surrendered all sense of modesty, but seeing her naked still had the same effect on Mila as the first night. She'd lain awake for hours fighting to erase the vision and then fighting to bring it back.

Jancey was gorgeous. A real woman, not one of those waifs from the fashion rags. Sculpted nipples sitting high upon her rounded breasts. A dark triangle of reddish-brown hair at the top of her curvy thighs. A stubborn paunch below her navel, the only extra fat she carried. In a word, perfect.

She dressed methodically, pulling the bulky leggings over her shoes. A stiff vest encased her torso like a cage beneath an overstuffed jacket. Once everything was in place, she put on a wide belt that snapped it all together at the waist. It looked vaguely like a spacesuit. Or more accurately, like a spacesuit costume one might wear on Halloween.

The one piece that was close to authentic was the communications cap—the comm cap—which had a built-in headset and microphone that worked wirelessly off an ordinary smartphone in her chest pocket. It was imperative they stay in constant communication outside the habitat.

"Here I go. Log me out."

Mila entered the data into their primary tablet computer, the one linked to project headquarters. As promised, there were data logs for practically everything—EVAs, exercise routines, menus. She logged Jancey out and slipped on headphones that connected her to both Mission Control and Jancey.

As Jancey called out the materials she needed, Mila placed them in a canvas bag by the door.

"See any Martians out there?"

A crackle came through the headset as Jancey chuckled. "The Clarkes are out together. They dragged their widget box outside. Something tells me they don't quite understand the objectives."

As Mila waited inside for further instructions, she meticulously inspected their indoor equipment. "The plug on our stove appears to be French. *La* stove."

"Is there an adapter in the widget box?"

"Of course not. I'll have to adapt another adapter."

The friendly banter between them had been slow to emerge. For the first couple of days after their pairing, Jancey had seemed almost resentful, as though already second-guessing her decision. That changed once they went to work on their habitat. Using her natural gift for spatial relations, Mila took over the construction inside and out with Jancey following her lead. The result was a structure completed more than an hour before any of the other teams.

That's what Jancey had bragged about to Shel. She trusted Mila to take charge and wasn't afraid to admit it. None of the men would have deferred to either of them on something related to construction. They would have taken over and relegated them to holding the ladder or handing them tools.

They were perfect together. And they were going to Mars.

CHAPTER TWELVE

Jancey squeezed her grips, fifty reps. It was the only exercise she could do without making noise. The only *anything*. Even though it was nearly two hours past her own bedtime, she didn't want to wake Mila, who had struggled to sleep their first three nights in the habitat.

Presumably, all of the married couples slept together, probably from ten to six just as they'd always done. Jancey had considered asking to share the bunk with Mila so they could get on a normal schedule. They'd have to do that anyway if Mission Control announced a solar flare because it doubled as a radiation chamber. Plenty of room for both of them to stretch out without touching.

So why hadn't they? Jancey had told herself when she was drafting their timetable the first day that sleeping at the same time meant she'd never have a moment alone. A split schedule gave her seven hours of privacy while Mila was sleeping.

Except Mila hadn't slept that long until tonight. She usually flopped around for a couple of hours before falling asleep and then woke well before midnight. That wasn't enough to function effectively, or to maintain her attention level throughout the day. Now exhausted and running on fumes, she'd crashed completely, sleeping like a teenager on the weekend.

Jancey had spent the last four hours reading but her brain needed a break. Her favorite way to unwind was to turn out all the lights and play her clarinet, but that was out of the question with Mila sleeping. Mendelssohn, Mozart, Strauss. She'd told Mila if they went to Mars together, she'd take along an extra clarinet and teach her to play. It was too bad she hadn't packed it for the analog. Then she would have had an excuse to suggest sleeping together so they'd have time to play in the evening.

What was she afraid of?

Losing control. Giving someone else power over her. Those were the obvious.

Mila had the very sort of sex appeal Jancey had always been powerless to ignore. It began with smart. A physical spark couldn't happen without it, and Mila had it in abundance. She also had a tantalizing body. Smooth-looking skin and long, lean hands only a lesbian could truly appreciate. Add to those things her sensitivity and easygoing manner, and she definitely was a woman Jancey could fall for.

No, her greatest fear at this point was growing close enough to discover something about Mila she didn't like. Something that would unravel the possibility of having a near-perfect life with a partner on a world far away. Better she remained a mystery for now.

* * *

Mila blinked herself awake and stared at the arched ceiling only a meter above her head. A sliver of light from Jancey's headlamp pierced the corner of the sleeping enclosure like a saber. Even through her earplugs, she could hear fingertips tapping on the tablet's keyboard.

After four nights on the slope, she still hadn't adjusted to her new sleep schedule, four to midnight. Admittedly, the lack of sleep was wearing on her but the bigger issue was how bad it looked on their log that she was averaging only a few hours a night.

It was nervous energy, she decided, along with the shift in her schedule that had her in bed at four in the afternoon. Plus the excitement of being with Jancey. Other than that, their partnership was working. It bothered her at first to realize Jancey was inspecting her every move, but then she decided that was a good thing because there was so much at stake. One small slip-up could cost them everything. Rather than be annoyed about it, she began doing the same to Jancey.

A quick check of her Sinn confirmed it was only a quarter after ten. She had two choices. Lie in bed for two more hours pretending to sleep, or get up and endure Jancey's ire for having so little control over her cycle. Neither would be pleasant.

Cold air hit her when she threw back the blanket, but that would feel good once she started her workout. Girding for Jancey's sharp tongue, she drew back the curtain at her feet and slid out.

"It's freezing in here."

"Because you're half naked," Jancey said flatly. "And also because it's twenty-nine degrees outside. Fahrenheit, of course. Coldest day of the summer so far."

The concepts of *below freezing* and *summer* didn't go together, at least not in this hemisphere. "How low is it supposed to get?"

"This is probably the worst of it. Rain on the way. That should warm things up...unless we get snow." Jancey stood and stretched.

So far no scolding. Perhaps she'd given up.

"I feel pretty rested. You can go on to bed early if you want."

"Early?"

"Yeah, it's..." Mila checked her watch again as she strapped it on...only this time, she turned it right side up. *Five minutes till three.* "Holy shit! Are you telling me I've been asleep for over ten hours? Why didn't you wake me?"

Jancey shrugged. "I figured you needed it. That's what happens when you go four nights in a row without a full night's sleep."

"Great. Now they're going to think I'm a lazy slacker."

"Not if you get it straightened out. Sleep is part of your job. You stay awake when you have to, you sleep when you're supposed to. It says that right here in the log." She pointed indignantly to the tablet on the table. "That needs to happen starting tonight. Take the zolpidem and go to sleep. All the astronauts do it. That's what it's for."

Mila groaned. It was one thing for Jancey to insist she eat poi but this was different. She had no use for medications, especially ones that screwed around with her brain. "Have you read those studies? That stuff stays in your system for half the next day. The warning label clearly says not to operate heavy machinery. That probably includes a spaceship, you know. You can't get much heavier than that."

"If you're going to read the label, read all of it. It says some of those side effects were observed in study trials, but it doesn't happen to everyone. This is the perfect place to try it out because there's no heavy machinery to operate."

If not for the exasperation in Jancey's voice, Mila would have dismissed it out of hand. She felt guilty for stealing two of her sleep hours. That couldn't happen again. "Fine, I'll try it tonight. Or maybe after sleeping so long, I should skip a night and start tomorrow."

"Tonight." Jancey stretched again and unzipped her flight suit. "I'm going to turn in for a few hours. Get me up by eight."

Mila hated the idea of taking a sleeping pill, but maybe Jancey was right.

Of course she was right. She'd managed on her own aboard *Guardian* for over a year.

She noticed Jancey had already completed a couple of the tasks on their morning checklist. Their daily water rations—four liters each for personal use—were already measured out in plastic jugs next to the galley area, and their planned menu for the day was already logged.

The scheduled breakfast was a strawberry protein shake. She mixed one and set it aside to thicken while she completed her workout. Jancey's earplugs would muffle the *whoosh* sound the hydraulic stair climber made with every step. Two thousand steps, to be exact, followed by two hundred sit-ups and twenty minutes of upper body exercises using stiff rubber bands.

Dripping with sweat, she relaxed in the low chair with her breakfast. The strawberry packets were her least favorite, but ever since the dressing down over the poi, she'd become rigid about eating everything she was given, no matter how disgusting. It didn't matter so much at this altitude because her sense of smell and taste were less acute. By all reports, that was even more pronounced in space.

Jancey had shared with her some of the other oddities of space. Workouts were easier in zero gravity, so it took extra effort and twice the time to engage the muscles and bones used for weight-bearing. Refrigeration used too much energy, so everything was warm. No such thing as a "bed," just a floating sleeping bag tied down on both ends like a hammock so it wouldn't bump into controls and equipment.

Eight months of that. Most people would consider that a hardship, maybe even some of their fellow candidates camped alongside them on the hillside. Mila, on the other hand, could hardly wait. Alone in a space vessel with Jancey. It was quite literally a dream come true.

After breakfast, she took a sponge bath and changed into fresh underwear before sliding back into the same flight suit she'd worn since the first day on Mauna Kea. Sturdy and durable enough to wear for three weeks before changing into the second one.

Underwear was a different matter. They'd brought along a washing machine—a five-liter plastic bag with a zipper seal. One liter of water with no-rinse soap was enough to wash six pairs of underwear and socks at a time. All she had to do was squeeze for ten minutes to swish the water around, and then wring it out and pour the wastewater through their filter, where it would then be used in the garden.

There is no waste in space.

By the time she finished, the cloudy sunrise had lightened the room through the hatch's porthole. She quietly set about the daily routine of measuring the plant growth and transcribing the data into their log. Four days and already everything had sprouted—Bibb lettuce, green onions, carrots and snow peas. That's what happened when you handed an expert in food production a tray of sprouts and a hydroponics kit. Jancey estimated they'd be eating fresh food in only three weeks as long as they were able to generate the power needed for the grow light—not a sure bet with rain on the way.

One by one, she ticked off the other items on their morning checklist. Water, food and power supplies, all of which Jancey had taken care of. She conducted a careful inspection of the interior of their habitat. All that remained was the walk-around outside, which she couldn't do until Jancey was up, since they were required to be in constant contact.

Someone on the staff had visited their habitat two nights ago to strip off a few pieces of the reflective exterior of their dome. Obviously, the objective was to keep them vigilant with regard to inspections and repairs, since maintenance of their equipment on Mars was a matter of life and death. Mila had discovered and repaired the sabotage within hours. While it may not have earned them points for being reliable, it hadn't cost them any for being negligent. Or as Jancey had put it, "You don't get points for doing it right. You lose them for doing it wrong, or for not doing it at all."

Every time they faced a challenge, she wondered how the other groups responded. Had any of them failed to notice or report the exterior "damage?" Had they shrugged off the repair as inessential? Were they managing their resources? Were they getting along?

It was hard to imagine anyone handling the analog better than they had so far. Marlon and Jean-Paul were probably on top of things, as were Jerry and Wade. Perhaps the Fagans too, since Libby had gone through NASA training and knew exactly what was expected of her. The fact remained that no matter how well they executed during the analog, none of them could get by on as little as she and Jancey when it came to water and food.

They were the only logical choice. It was no longer a question of whether or not they'd go to Mars. But would they be first?

* * *

Jancey awakened to an unpleasant sound—rain—and knew immediately Mila had let her sleep too long. Nine fifteen to be precise. Turnabout was fair play.

The other sound she heard was Mila talking in a low voice as she recorded their daily video report. If she crawled out of bed at that moment, she'd appear in the background of the transmission dressed in her thermal underwear.

"We have sixty-eight liters of water remaining. Power packs are at one hundred, ninety-two and forty-six percent. We'll be implementing strict conservation measures in anticipation of continued rain for the next two days. That is all."

Jancey slid out to find the habitat chilly and damp. They could close the air vents along the floor, but then it would be chilly, damp and stuffy.

"What happened to my eight o'clock wake-up call?"

"Seriously? You let me sleep all night and you think I'm going to wake you up after five hours? Besides, there's nothing to do. I'm caught up with everything except the walk-around."

"So I heard. I wonder if anyone else has more than half of their water supply left. We're supposed to be restocked day after tomorrow."

"I wonder if anyone else is watering their food with pee-pee."

It struck her as funny to hear a grown woman use the word "pee-pee," made even sillier by the Slavic cadence. Jancey snorted with laughter and swatted Mila's head with a rolled-up T-shirt.

"I know. Two parts hydrogen, one part oxygen. It's all the same."

They'd collected rocks, gravel and sand to construct a water filter so they could get by on less. On their journey to Mars, the ship's dehumidifiers would recycle not only their urine, but whatever floated around the compartment, including their sweat and the condensation from their breath.

"Did you get your workout done?" Jancey asked as she peeled out of her thermals and into her shorts and T-shirt.

"Workout, bath, breakfast shake."

"Better get used to cold food. Our stove's off-limits as long as it's overcast. Something tells me we'll be drinking a lot of shakes over the next couple of days."

She stepped on the stair climber and began marching.

"Do you ever take a day off?" Mila asked.

"No."

"Not ever?"

"Even if I did, I wouldn't tell you about it because then you'd want a day off too. You can't have a day off."

Not long ago she'd have said that sharply, a stern warning not to slack off. After watching Mila work, it was no longer a concern. She performed all of her duties without complaint and even looked for more to do.

"Trust me, Todorov. When we get to space, the last thing you'll want is a day off. That's the whole reason we're doing this analog—to make sure we can handle hours on end with absolutely nothing to do." She'd had very few long stretches of downtime on her solo mission, but even a few hours with nothing to do left her listless. "The real question is whether or not you can manage to stay alert when you're bored out of your mind."

Mila snorted as though jarring herself awake. "I'm sorry, what were you saying?"

"Smartass. I was going to offer to do the walk-around, but now you can forget it."

"You were not. You never do the walk-around in the morning."

"And now I never will."

It relaxed her to trade barbs with Mila. Not only did it break up the all-business dynamic of their partnership, it relieved the pressure she'd put on herself after realizing Mila viewed her as infallible. No one could live up to that sort of idealized vision. Joking around took it down a notch. There was an undercurrent of mutual respect with Mila she'd found difficult to sustain with men. Men wilted under criticism, even if it was delivered with a dose of humor. They acted wounded or henpecked, or their competitive nature kicked in and they escalated the barbs to the point of viciousness. Mila held her own and seemed to know right where it needed to stop.

"Someday you're going to beg me to let you do the walk-around, and I'm going to mock you." Mila held up a plastic bag filled with clothes and water. "I washed a few things. Except now I'm going to take yours outside and rub them in the dirt."

CHAPTER THIRTEEN

Mila couldn't deny she felt better. The zolpidem had kicked in within fifteen minutes and knocked her out cold. When she awakened at half past eleven, she was rested and alert. It was stupid to have resisted so long.

She slowed the pace of her workout to drag out an extra hour, and then caught up on all the laundry. Now she was left with nothing to do, nothing to read, nothing to see in the dark. Jancey wasn't due to get up for another three hours.

After three days of rain, they were squeezing the last of their electricity from the third power pack. Everything had been shut down except the comm, which they kept on standby only for incoming messages. No grow lights, no cell phones except when one of them went outside, no headlamps, no e-readers. They'd kept their logs by hand, scribbling in the margins of the handbook, as that was the only paper in their hut.

The good news was the rain had stopped sometime around two, and by four, she could see stars through the porthole. If the sun cooperated just for two days, they'd have their power packs back at max. Hot food. Jasmine tea. Something to read to while away eight hours alone in the dark.

She had gained a new appreciation for Jancey's thirteen-month solo mission. It was nothing like this, Jancey had explained. Not once had her power supply dwindled, and though her water was rationed, she'd never worried about running out. Her communications with Mission Control were so frequent and extended, it was a relief to be left alone.

A sound outside caught her attention. Crunching gravel. Slow, deliberate steps meant to conceal the presence of someone approaching their habitat. Another "emergency" in the offing, courtesy of the staff. Dr. V had promised to keep them on their toes with repairs, something they'd have to do regularly on Mars. That was why Mila and Jancey took turns three times a day conducting an inspection around the outside of the habitat, during which they adjusted the solar panels for maximum absorption. So far it was only "broken tiles" and a loosened wire on the south-facing communication dish that kept them in contact with Mission Control.

This time, it sounded as though someone was climbing the rungs on the side of their dome, probably to inflict damage to their solar panels. That was cruel, considering they'd just suffered through three days of rain.

Careful not to make a sound, she crawled to the porthole and looked outside. The figure stepped down from the ladder and walked quietly away in the direction of the Fagans' hut. A man, judging by his height, and dressed in dark clothing. He disappeared into the darkness thirty meters away.

Mila laughed to herself to recognize yet another advantage she and Jancey shared with the other non-married teams. The couples were likely to be sleeping at the same time. They wouldn't have heard the staff screwing around with their solar panels, and if they weren't vigilant, they could lose a whole day of recharging. If the rain returned tomorrow, such a lapse could mean the difference between success and failure.

"I think I heard Santa Claus on our roof," Jancey mumbled from inside the compartment.

"I know. I bet they screwed around with the solar panels. By the time you get up, I'll be ready to go out and see what they did. Now go back to sleep."

She complied, or so it seemed, until she started stirring again forty minutes later at first light. "I'm getting up so you can go fix the panels. We need those two extra hours to charge."

Mila began the methodical process of getting into her spacesuit. She had everything on but the helmet before Jancey tumbled past her to her lavatory. "Good morning." No response, so she continued the conversation on her own. "Good morning to you too, Mila. Don't you look dashing in your spacesuit! Why, thank you, Jancey. You look dashing when you're dashing."

A minute passed and Jancey emerged from behind the curtain, glaring at her with undisguised scorn. "This is the best I can do without coffee. If you get our power grid up and working again, I promise to say something civil."

After snapping her helmet in place, she exited the hatch to inspect the damage. It took only a glance to diagnose the problem. One of their panels was missing, though the other three appeared to be intact. With their capacity to generate power now down by a quarter, it would take longer to fully charge their power packs. They'd have to cut back on their typical usage to stay ahead. Communications and grow lights were priorities. Everything else—cooking, reading, headlamps—would have to be rationed.

Bastards. Clearly they wanted to test their ability to entertain themselves without going mad.

Before climbing up to the panels, she conducted her usual walk-around, meticulously inspecting the condition of their exterior tiles and water supply, all the while keeping an eye out for the stray panel in case it had been discarded. No such luck.

She climbed atop the dome and confirmed the remaining connections were still in working order. With a simple twist of a wing nut, she aimed the three remaining panels toward the morning sun.

From her perch atop their dome, she could see all seven of the habitats though only the closest three were clearly visible.

She did a double-take to notice none were missing panels. Not the Clarkes, the Fagans, nor Jerry and David. It didn't seem right the committee would single out only one team for a hardship.

The phone crackled through her earpiece. "Solar flare in three minutes. Get in here now. Do you copy?"

"Copy."

Bastards.

As quickly as she could, she backed down the ladder, and tumbled through the hatch as her cumbersome feet became entangled. She'd already lost almost a minute and had yet to get undressed.

Jancey was hurriedly stowing equipment and supplies inside the sleeping chamber. "I've got your clothes. Hit the head and get your ass inside."

Leaving pieces of her spacesuit strewn all over the hut, Mila rushed into the lavatory.

"Forty seconds!"

"Don't rush me!" She didn't bother to recycle, not with the clock ticking down. Out of breath and dripping with sweat, she climbed into the chamber and latched the door behind her.

Jancey fired off her message confirming they were secure inside the radiation shelter. "That might be the most realistic test we've had so far. Three minutes is probably all the warning we'll get for a solar flare. We're going to have to do better than that."

Mila stacked her clothes, toiletries and water jug against one end of the chamber and covered them with her pillow. A makeshift lounge chair. "How do we beat it? Besides the obvious, that is. I don't expect to be walking around outside on the way to Mars."

"Let's hope not."

She relayed the news about the missing solar panel, not that it mattered at the moment. A solar flare could knock out electronics, so they'd shut down everything but communications just to be on the safe side. "I think we were the only ones who lost one. Why would they single us out?"

"Hmm…could be they're hitting everyone in a vulnerable area. It wouldn't surprise me if they shorted everyone else on their water ration." Jancey was still dressed in the thermal underwear she'd slept in, and it hugged every rise and curve on her body.

"I wonder how the men will handle being cooped up for the solar flare," Mila mused as she tried not to stare. "For that matter, I wonder how many of them are actually where they're supposed to be right now. It's not as if the staff are coming by to do a bed check."

"You never know. They sneak around and do everything else." Jancey peeked out the small porthole, which looked up toward the summit. No view of the other habitats, nor of the access road. "My guess is they're all sitting in bed just like we are, backs against the wall and facing each other. But yeah, they're probably more anxious about it than we are."

"You're okay then?"

"Sure, why not?"

Mila shrugged. "I just wondered if it bothered you being stuck in here with me. I know you'd rather be by yourself like you were on *Guardian*."

"I didn't mind being by myself. In fact, at that particular time in my life, it was a pretty good idea. I was so focused on getting into space, I wasn't of much use to the people around me."

"What about now? Do you ever wish *Tenacity* was a solo mission?"

"I might have at one point," she said. The accompanying sheepish look made it sound like a confession. "I'd rather go to Mars by myself than be stuck with someone who made me uncomfortable. I don't feel that way around you. Don't let this go to your head, okay? There are a lot of things I like about you. You're smart and you work hard. You pay attention to details and study everything before you do it. That's impressive considering you haven't been through astronaut training. I also like that you don't play around when it comes to your work, but at the same time, you aren't a robot either. I feel good about you and me as a team. Grace told me I would, but she had other motives."

"Grace? Grace Faraday?" Mila could no more stop Jancey's compliment from going to her head than she could stop the sunset. "What kind of motives did she have?"

Jancey chuckled softly and shook her head.

"Don't even think about not answering. You're the one who started this."

"Let's just say she was playing matchmaker. No way was she going to let me go with Marlon, not when there was a woman available. A capable woman, I might add."

"A capable lesbian," Mila clarified, watching closely for a reaction. "Just like you."

No reaction at all, unless she counted avoidance. Jancey never even looked up as she replied, "A lesbian who is much, much younger."

"Age is irrelevant to me. No, that isn't true. It's actually quite important because I prefer older women. You're…forty-three, right?" It was a silly question to ask. She knew Jancey's birthday as well as her own. "My former girlfriend is now forty-eight. That's a twenty-one-year difference."

"Hunh. That strikes me as quite a lot."

"My mother would agree. Frederica is her colleague in the philosophy department at Humboldt."

"Awkward."

"Tell me about it. It took two years of pleading and professing my undying love before Frederica would even let me kiss her. And then another two years before she let me touch her. I nearly died of old age."

"I have to hand it to you, Mila. That's persistence. I can't believe you waited that long."

"I had no choice. She was perfect." The old perfect. The new perfect was sitting across from her.

"Where is this piece of perfection now?"

Mila shuddered. "Probably doing disgusting things with some man she met only this morning. I try not to think about it."

"One of those." Jancey made a face as if remembering her own tale of being on the losing end of someone else's gender identity search. "You have my sympathy."

"It's done. It's over." She would never again feel longing for Frederica. Her future was going to Mars with Jancey. "Besides, I have a new idea of perfection now, Major Beaumont."

* * *

Jancey could hardly pretend to be surprised with where the conversation had gone. She'd practically pushed it there. "Perfection? Please."

"I'm just telling you how I see it." Mila stared at her unabashedly, her mouth turned up in apparent appreciation. "All those things you said about me...I do those things because you are my partner, because you deserve the best. And remember, I promised never to let you down."

"In other words, all the things I just said I like about you aren't really you at all. You're pretending to be someone else just to impress me."

"I never said that. But I've become the person I am by striving toward an ideal. Like it or not, you've always represented many things about that ideal. Ever since I was thirteen years old and watched the sky through my telescope to see you go by in orbit."

Years ago, Jancey had relished her chance to be a role model who could excite girls about the STEM fields. But other than Grace and Lana, she'd never confronted its impact on such a personal level. "That's a lot of pressure, you know. I'm far from perfect. I make mistakes like everyone else. The difference is my science training has taught me to keep trying until I find the right answer. It's not good for you to be a lemming and follow me off the cliff."

"You don't have to worry about that. I have science training too. What I plan to follow is your example. Scientists don't always end up in the same place, but the good ones can always tell you exactly how they got there." Mila shivered in her shorts and T-shirt and pulled the blanket up around her shoulders. "What would you have me do differently?"

One part curiosity, the other part challenge. Many of Mila's questions were like that, yet she genuinely seemed to want an answer. "Nothing, of course."

At the same time, Jancey had the feeling they both were dancing around their true motives. The hero worship flattered her, but it felt like something more personal. That flattered her too. She couldn't let it come to anything, no matter how intriguing. Not now. Probably not until they got to Mars and found themselves together forever. By then she'd be Frederica's age.

But definitely not now.

"Keep doing what you're doing, Mila. Just don't forget you're here as a partner. You're as responsible for our success as I am. Speak up when you think you have a better idea. Keep your head. Don't lose focus on why we're here."

"Understood." Mila stretched forward and pulled the blanket over Jancey's bare feet. Then she pulled them into her lap and warmed them with a massage.

Nice. Both casual and intimate. And proof that Mila didn't understand at all.

* * *

"…and even though I worked at NASA, I was still in the air force. Those were the days when being gay resulted in a dishonorable discharge, even if you happened to hold the American record for consecutive days in space."

"But they didn't kick you out." After two hours of strategizing how they'd handle another day with a dwindling power supply, Mila had managed to steer the conversation back to their past relationships. The thrill of getting to know Jancey more intimately was irresistible. It made no sense at all that she was single, not when she could have had her pick among all the women in the world.

"Because they never initiated an investigation. They weren't going to discharge a national hero."

"World hero."

"Whatever. I wasn't outed until after the mission, and Monica was long gone by then. No one asked, and I didn't tell. It didn't matter anyway as long as I was assigned to NASA."

"I'm glad you were outed. Gay kids need to see what's possible. Even in Europe, most of the focus is on the flamboyant."

"I didn't mind it so much when it was just *The Advocate*, but then the tabloids picked it up and turned it into a *shocking scandal* in sixty-point type. One of the grocery store rags even had me in an affair with an alien."

Mila laughed and nodded along. She was too embarrassed to admit she'd saved those clippings too. "You have to admit, it made you a household name. Most people weren't ever going to read about you in a science magazine or an actual newspaper."

Jancey huffed. "I guess that's right. You can charge more in speaking fees if they think you've had sex with ET."

"Did you have a girlfriend after Monica?"

"Not for a while. I laid low for the next four years until NASA killed the long-term space program. Then I left the air force for a teaching post at Harvard. Or as they say it, *Hahvahd*. That's where I met Lindsay. She taught public policy at the JFK School of Government, and they had me in as a guest on a panel about science agencies. We tangled right off the bat when she accused NASA of wasting billions of taxpayer dollars with nothing to show for it."

"Please tell me Lindsay didn't become your girlfriend."

"Oh, but she did, and that was after I fired back that NASA wouldn't have needed a dime if it had been able to patent the things it developed. Water filters, smoke detectors, scratch-resistant lenses. Then I went on to list the medical technology, the computer science and telecommunications. You wouldn't believe how much of that stuff can be traced back to NASA engineers."

"I would actually." Mila would have given anything to see that, a fiery Jancey Beaumont taking on a roomful of bureaucrats. "You would have melted me on the spot. I'm sure you did the same to her."

"Something like that." She chuckled and took on a faraway look as she gazed out the porthole into nothingness. "We ended up spending the night together. And the next three years."

A most erotic scenario. Armed with a first name and affiliation, she would have to Google this woman to fill in the blanks of her voyeuristic fantasy. "What happened to her?"

"Stanford University happened. Sir Charles funded a program on space sustainability and brought me in. He was laying the foundation for Tenacity and Grace was already on board. It was pretty clear by that time that funds for space travel were going to have to come from the private sector."

Jancey settled against her pillow and stretched her legs alongside Mila's under the blanket. Still sitting with her back to the wall in their sleeping chamber, she was the most relaxed Mila had seen her since the analog started.

"Why didn't Lindsay go with you?"

"There are things you don't give up for someone else, and apparently one of those is tenure at Harvard. She was already living her dream when I met her."

"That's kind of sad."

"It is what it is." If she was heartbroken, it didn't show. "So where's Frederica? You gave up on her to do this, didn't you?"

"That's different. She didn't love me." Their last encounter had been so vicious, Mila wondered if she'd ever erase the memory. "That's probably not true. She loved me in her own way, but she hated that she did. Even if I'd done everything perfectly, I still would have been a woman. That wasn't how she wanted other people to see her."

"That's just screwed up. If there's one thing I've learned in my life, it's not to give a damn what anyone else wants of me. I always made selfish decisions…Monica, Lindsay, Jill. And I felt bad every time. But it would have felt a lot worse trying to be someone else."

"Who is Jill?"

"Jill. Palo Alto. Investment fund manager. Big house. Fast car. I liked her a lot."

"Yes, I've noticed your affinity for big houses and fast cars. Tell me again why you want to go to Mars."

Jancey laughed. "To break my addiction. What's your excuse?"

"I thought it would look good on my résumé." She held a straight face as long as she could as she watched Jancey's face contort with confusion.

"For whom?"

Their laughter was interrupted by a sharp beep from their tablet.

"That's the all clear," Jancey said. "Six hours and eight minutes. That gives us about five hours of sunlight to charge our power packs."

Mila slid out of the chamber and flipped the switch on the solar panels. After being cooped up in their bunk for so long, she was unexpectedly disappointed by the all clear. The personal time with Jancey had flown by too fast. "I'll go out and turn them west."

She gathered the pieces of her spacesuit that she'd strewn about the hut while hurrying to get inside the chamber. No one in their right mind would be wishing for another solar flare, but she was. Anything for another chance to sit and talk like friends.

"I was thinking, Mila…it's obvious that bunk is plenty big enough for both of us. If you think it would help you sleep better, we could try turning in at the same time. That would cut down on the noise and distractions. As long as we're up by first light, it should be okay."

Okay. It was all she could do not to shout her excitement. "It would save power too since we wouldn't need light."

Jancey nodded seriously. "Good, good. It's settled then. We'll turn in around ten and see how it goes."

Mila knew already how it would go. Perfectly. Even if she had to pretend to sleep.

CHAPTER FOURTEEN

The predawn light filtered through the porthole, barely illuminating their sleeping compartment. Jancey had slept soundly for seven hours, more than enough to feel thoroughly rested.

Near as she could tell, Mila had slept peacefully as well. All week, in fact. Her lanky frame took up slightly more than half the space, but only because of her propensity to drift diagonally in the night, away from the edges of their enclosure and toward the center of the bed. Since their pillows were at opposite ends, Jancey sometimes dealt with feet that came to rest on her stomach.

It was almost comical how quickly they both had adapted to sleeping together. Or, as she'd phrased it for the logs, syncing their sleep schedules.

She studied Mila in the gray light. A youthful face on the body of a woman, not a child. If she needed a reminder of that, she had only to dwell on the curve of her breasts beneath the thin shirt that fit her body like a layer of blue skin. Temptation.

And why shouldn't she give in? There was no reason to resist something that was inevitable. Already they were committed to living together forever. Mila wanted her. Jancey could feel it, just as she felt Mila's eyes on her every time she undressed.

She sat up and plotted her exit strategy from the chamber. With Mila sleeping so close to the doorway, the only way out was to crawl over her. Poised on all fours directly above her face, she was startled when Mila opened her eyes and blinked.

"This is certainly interesting," Mila murmured with a faint smile.

"You're dreaming. Go back to sleep."

"I'm afraid I'll miss something."

Jancey continued her maneuver, but with less care. Her knee crushed Mila's shoulder, causing her to howl in pain. "You won't miss a thing. I promise I'll put it in the log."

Since they'd begun sleeping together, she too had taken to wearing shorts and a T-shirt instead of her long thermal underwear. Even when the temperatures outside dropped overnight to freezing, their small compartment stayed warm from their breath and mutual body heat. Not so with the rest of the habitat. The low fifties, she guessed as she pulled on her flight suit and zipped it to her neck. She followed with her spacesuit, taking over Mila's usual job to conduct the morning walk-around.

It had been several days since their last disruption from the staff. The fact that they'd been sleeping soundly at the same time made them even more vigilant about checking for sabotage.

Mila had pulled the blanket over her head, signaling her refusal to get up.

Jancey passed her comm and headset through the opening. "Put this on. I'm going out to look around. Listen for anything coming in from Mission Control."

No obvious changes to the exterior of the dome. Water supply intact. She climbed the ladder to inspect the connections to the solar panels and turned them toward the rising sun. From the top, she could see a vehicle parked on the service road near the habitat two spots away from theirs—Jerry and Wade's. Two staffers emerged, each lending support to one of the astronauts as they walked them to the vehicle.

"You aren't going to believe this," Jancey said into her comm. "Jerry and Wade are being evacuated. Looks like they're very sick."

"Can you tell what's wrong?"

"No, but it's both of them. Probably something in their food supply. We should go through everything again."

In their first examination, conducted on the day they arrived, they'd found a handful of suspicious items. Sealed pouches that appeared swollen, an indication that bacteria were growing inside. Vacuum-wrapped meat that was discolored. They'd used their microscope to examine a packet of dried potatoes with suspicious black flecks. Bug droppings. Seasoned pros like Jerry and Wade should have caught those things, so it was worrisome to think something had gotten by.

"I'll be out here a while longer. I need to collect some materials for a new water filter."

"Keep me posted. I'll start the food check."

The selection committee had promised not to disqualify anyone with a genuine medical emergency. That might not be the case if their health issues sprang from carelessness. She and Mila had a lot more flexibility when it came to food because they ate less than the others. They could afford to discard anything that appeared marginal.

She removed a plastic bag and trowel from her tool pouch and stooped as low as her spacesuit would allow to scrape up a layer of rocks and gravel. As she filled a second bag with fine sand, another vehicle pulled in, this one even with the dome three sites down from theirs. David and Kamal.

"Mila, I don't think it's the food. Stay away from the water."

* * *

Mila finished the last of her oats, which she'd heated to boiling from their emergency water supply. That had been Jancey's idea. Always thinking two or three steps ahead.

The hot breakfast warmed her up, so much that she unzipped her flight suit to her waist and slipped it off her shoulders, leaving her in a tank top.

Jancey, on the other hand, still looked practically crisp in the same outfit, despite having worn it twenty-two days in a row. She was studying a sample from their water tank through her microscope. "There's the culprit right there. Fecal coliform. Want to see?"

"I'd rather not, thank you." Biology wasn't Mila's forte, but even an idiot knew what the word "fecal" meant. "Reminds me of your little energy tablet test on the first day of orientation."

"This is worse. It would be like drinking water from a cow toilet. No wonder they were sick."

That was way more descriptive than Mila would have liked. She'd grown accustomed to recycling her urine, but didn't care to think what lay in the bottom of their compost lavatory. "So how did it get there?"

"It had to be in the water supply wherever they're loading the delivery truck. That's the only way it could have infected all of us. They could have gotten a blockage in their stack vent. It causes the sewer or the septic tank to back up into your tap."

"Stop already. I'm sorry I asked."

"Basically, we need to chlorinate and boil."

"That's going to drain our power packs, especially since we're down a panel."

"I'll say this...it would have been a lot worse if it hadn't been so cold up here. That stuff thrives in warm weather."

"You don't think Mission Control would do something like this on purpose, do you?"

Jancey turned off the light on her microscope and leaned back in her chair, rubbing her eyes. "Seems a little risky. Infections like these can be deadly if they aren't treated right away. I should write up our findings and send it in."

While she did that, Mila added chlorine tablets to the water they'd drawn for the day's use. "We have to assume this is part of the trial, don't you think?"

"Unless we hear otherwise. We should collect more gravel and sand. If we filter and chlorinate, we may not have to boil."

Which meant saving their precious power packs.

Mila dressed in her spacesuit and stepped into the bright sunlight. After trudging several dozen meters up the hillside to a fresh area of scree and silt, she paused to catch her breath. From her vantage point, all eight habitats were clearly visible.

Four huts away, one of the Norwegians was climbing atop their dome. Had he been suffering ill effects from the water, he likely wouldn't be out and about.

"Hey, Jancey. If the problem was at the water source, wouldn't everyone be sick?"

"Depends on how much they drank. To tell you the truth, I'm surprised they haven't sent out a notice."

"Me too. It makes me wonder if they did this on purpose. But not to everybody." She clicked off her comm as she entered through the hatch and removed her helmet. "Like when they stole our solar panel. Maybe they're just trying to see how we respond."

Jancey dipped a medicine dropper into the bucket of water that had run through their rock and sand filter. Peering into the microscope, she said, "Good news. Between the chlorine tablets and the filter, we're under one part per million. That's well under the threshold for potable. But to be safe, we should use a new filter for every two liters."

"That's a lot of time outside scraping up rocks. I had to go about fifty meters up the hill to get enough sand for two of these." Their two-hour limit outside was barely enough to stay ahead of their needs. The whole plan would collapse if another emergency arose, or if they lost time due to another solar flare. On the other hand... "Should I feel guilty for appreciating the fact that we have something to do?"

Jancey huffed. "You should feel grateful I went outside at just the right moment to see those guys taken out. Otherwise we probably would have been puking our guts out right about now...or worse. I can't believe we still haven't heard anything from Mission Control. It's been over an hour."

Mila dressed again in her spacesuit and went back outside to collect more materials for another filter. No one else outside this time, and no vehicles in sight. After climbing the dome to adjust the solar panels to the midday sun, she reentered and stripped out of her space suit.

"I only have about fifteen minutes left outside. I can go again this afternoon but—"

The tablet beeped with a message from Mission Control.

"That better not be another solar flare," Jancey said, climbing over Mila's discarded suit to read what it said. *"Fecal coliform contamination is suspected in water supplies that were delivered to habitats yesterday. For safety reasons, you should chlorinate and boil all water before drinking it or using it in food preparation. Staff will be onsite today to chlorinate tanks and replace current supplies."*

"Looks like this wasn't part of the trial after all," Mila said.

Jancey frowned, obviously not sharing her relief. "No, but something about this feels off. We just got our water delivered yesterday. How did those guys get sick so fast? It should have taken at least three or four days for them to get bad enough to be evacuated."

"What are you thinking?"

"That they must have been contaminated earlier. Which means we dodged a bullet. That could have been us. I don't know about you, but it makes me wonder what else we've been careless about."

"We have nothing but time," Mila said. "We might as well double-check everything."

"Agreed. No excuses for missing the details. All it takes to knock us out is one small mistake."

Mila recalled her promise to Jancey when she chose her for a partner. *I will not let you down.* This was a reminder to make good on that promise.

* * *

Jancey chuckled to herself as Mila stabbed a morsel of food and twirled it around on her fork, studying it from all sides.

"I've never seen a spam in the wild. What do they look like?"

"They're small, rectangular shaped. A very hard shell on the outside."

"Sedentary, I bet. They seem to have a lot of fat."

If Jancey had to describe her mood in one word, it would be satisfied. Working together throughout the day, they'd inspected every single piece of equipment. Every morsel of food. Every item on four different checklists. She was confident they were in great shape.

Tenacity staff had delivered the new water supply and chlorinated their tank. She still felt guilty for not catching it earlier. The test strips they used weren't one hundred percent reliable. It wouldn't have been a big deal to follow it with a look under the microscope.

Mila held up another spear of meat. "When we get to Mars, will you be breeding these little spams? I envision dozens of them climbing around on the furniture, nesting in our shoes until we're ready to snatch one and cook it for dinner. Then they all scurry under the bed."

"Do I detect a tongue in that cheek of yours?"

Although Mila's question was indeed posed with humor, Jancey knew her well enough by now to recognize a genuine curiosity. She was a sponge when it came to science.

"We won't need to breed our meat. Cloning technology is further along than you think. The Japanese have been working on this for decades. By the time we launch, I'm willing to bet the pilot's seat we'll be able to replicate similar types of protein, and I have no doubt our three-D printers can be programmed to crank out tin shells for the little critters."

Mila's eyebrows arched in obvious surprise and her mouth had formed a perfect O. "The pilot's seat? What makes you think it's yours to wager?"

"You can't possibly think I'm going to let you drive. I have seniority."

"I have sharper vision and better dexterity."

"JanSolo would disagree."

Her cocky face fell flat instantly. "You said yourself my scores would be higher if those chickenshit men had stuck around to be annihilated. I'll take on JanSolo anytime, anywhere."

"You're on. And don't expect me to show mercy just because you're my partner and I'm worried about undermining your confidence."

"Oh, I get it. Just in case I win, you want me to think it's because you let me."

Jancey grinned triumphantly. Of all their accomplishments in the past three weeks, the one that pleased her most was their rapport. A welcome surprise. Mila had turned out to be the perfect partner. She had determination and curiosity. A dry wit that moderated her impatience and frustration. And all of it in a package that piqued the imagination.

Grace had been right to urge her toward Mila. Marlon would have been competent and professional, whereas Mila was all that, plus the little something extra she could never have gotten from a man.

"I like how we handled the water issue today," Mila said. She'd finished her dinner and was wiping down her utensils with an antiseptic cloth. "We think alike and that makes us very good partners."

Jancey cleaned her dishes and set them back in the bin with their galley supplies. "It's always easy when we agree. The real test is how we'll deal with it when we don't. We need to challenge each other. It makes us work harder to think things through. What will you do when we disagree?"

"I'll make my argument and try to convince you. That's what you did to me with the poi. I still gag just thinking about it, but what you said was irrefutable. Isn't that what you would do?"

"I suppose. You convinced me to choose you instead of Marlon. You made some very good points, especially about the committee not wanting to select a pair of Americans. That was persuasive."

Though it wasn't as compelling as the realization that both of them likely would have been shamefully disrespected as colleagues had they gone with one of the men. As much as she'd tried to dismiss it, there was little doubt she'd have been miserable sharing the rest of her life in a small space with a man, even one as honorable as Marlon Quinn. She had Grace to thank for sowing those doubts.

"What if we disagree and neither of us wants to give in?" she asked.

Mila shrugged. "I can't imagine that happening very often. We both look at things through a scientific lens. Besides, I made you a promise. You're the commander on this mission, and for good reason." She held up her hand to ward off the protest that was already on Jancey's lips. "I know what my job is. I'm as responsible as you are for everything we do together, and I don't plan to follow you blindly off the cliff. Ultimately though it comes down to trust. Once I've gone through training and actually experienced what it's like to live in space, I might—*might*—trust myself as much as I trust you, but we both know that won't happen for quite some time."

Jancey appreciated her honesty as well as her confidence, but was more worried about personal differences than professional. "What I want to know is do you fight fair or dirty?"

"Oh." Mila smiled slyly. "So this is about fighting. Like when you get angry and won't speak to me."

"What makes you think I'd do that?"

"Because you don't strike me as the type who goes ballistic and starts screaming and slapping. You're too cool for that. I'm the same way. I listen quietly and think about everything that's said. Even if I don't agree with it, I usually modify my behavior to avoid having to hear it again."

Jancey shook her head. "No one is that reasonable."

"I am. I've had a great deal of practice with Frederica. Mind you, my goal was to avoid her criticism, and I discovered many ways to do that, including ways that didn't involve changing the offending behavior at all. Like coming home when she was already in bed, or putting on my headphones and pretending I was listening to a lecture. Or agreeing to meet her only when there were other people around because I knew she wouldn't criticize me in front of them."

"That's passive aggressive. Very uncivilized."

She shrugged. "It worked. But you won't have to worry about it."

"How's that?"

"I won't give you anything to criticize, at least not more than once. If there's something about me that upsets you, tell me what it is and I'll change it on the spot. We don't have a lot of room for disagreements, Jancey. Literally. We won't have enough space to pull away, nor the luxury of me doing it my way and you doing it yours." By her businesslike expression and methodical tone, she could have been talking about propulsion systems. "The moment we selected each other as partners, we began a relationship where the only way to break up is to die. The way I feel about you, I'm certain I'll make the changes you need me to make."

"The way you feel? You've only known me for a month."

"Not true. I've known you since I was thirteen years old. Dreamed of you, adored you, loved you. If it weren't for you, I wouldn't even be here."

"That isn't love. It's hero worship. All thirteen-year-olds do it, but they usually outgrow it when they step into the real world."

"Not if the real world they step into is the same as their fantasy world."

Jancey shook her head vehemently. "No, you can't put that on me. The Jancey Beaumont you knew when you were growing up is a media creation, not a real person. All those hero stories were meant to sell newspapers and magazines, and to get more funding for NASA. The real me was just someone doing her job, someone who was pretty pissed off about having her mission interrupted by a couple of bumbling Cossacks."

"You were someone who actually accomplished something I only dreamed of. And all because you set your sights on it and followed through. I read your personal story. Princeton, air force, NASA. You showed determination. Tenacity. What part of that wasn't real?"

"I'm saying it's not realistic for you to call it love."

Mila's fingers rapped the table and her knee began to bounce. Unmistakable agitation. "There's no other word for it. To me, it's the most powerful, all-consuming feeling I could possibly have. When being with someone makes me deliriously happy,

I call that love. When that happiness is so great I'm willing to shape my life around having it and keeping it, that's love. When I care about someone else more than I care about myself, that's love."

The last one landed like a slap across the face. There hadn't been a single time in Jancey's life when she cared about anyone more than her own ambitions. She always chose the same thing—whatever got her closer to going into space.

What made being with Mila different was not having to choose between one or the other.

"All I'm saying, Mila, is the hero you know…the one who inspired you, the one you think you love…that isn't all there is to me. It's only the good parts, and you'll be disappointed if you expect to find that person all the time. You have to let me be myself."

Mila folded her arms and tipped back on two legs of her chair, her face just short of a scowl. "Whatever gave you the idea I expected you to be perfect? This conversation started with you asking how we'd handle something when we disagreed. I would have thought we'd handle it with honesty but now I'm not so sure. Should I have kept my feelings to myself?"

An excellent question, Jancey had to admit. As she knew from Don't Ask, Don't Tell, there was nothing honorable about hiding the truth. "No, the truth is always better. If I have a problem with it, that's on me."

Ironically, their entire discussion had been a disagreement of sorts, which they'd managed by putting everything on the table and working through it on the way to a conclusion they both could live with. Except Jancey hadn't confessed her own feelings. She hadn't told Mila how she looked forward to growing closer. How she wanted to let go of her reservations. How she was waiting for her emotions to catch up with her libido because she wanted Mila to mean more than anyone in her life.

"Mila…I appreciate everything you said. Really, I do. And believe me, you have my attention now. I'm flattered you feel that way about me, but it's also unnerving to know I'm under your microscope."

"I don't want you to be flattered. That's condescending."

"I don't mean it to be. I enjoy the feeling, and I'd be very disappointed to lose it." That was the closest she could come for now to admitting how she felt. "Just keep in mind that you've had many years to develop your feelings. I haven't. But I know this much—I don't want to be on a pedestal. I can't respect someone I look down on, and I can't love someone I don't respect."

With her chair back down on four legs, Mila rested her elbows on her knees and stared blankly at the floor. Chastened. "That will be very hard for me to do."

"You can start by taking stock of your own accomplishments. I don't deserve credit for those. You're the one who followed through. You put in the hours and the brain power. The propulsion system—that was brilliant. And you're the one who shot up to the top of the candidate list without any prior training whatsoever. If one of us should be in awe…" She tapped her chest.

A scarlet blush crept from Mila's cheeks to her neck as she struggled in vain to suppress a smile.

"I'd say that's how we're going to handle differences," Jancey said. "We'll work them out. But let's not forget why we're here. Our priority for the next three weeks is to finish on top. If we don't do that, nothing else matters."

CHAPTER FIFTEEN

Eight lettuce leaves, four pea pods, a chopped green onion and one tiny carrot created the most mouth-watering salad Mila had ever seen. The fresh, crisp display had been plucked directly from their hydroponics garden. Jancey also had boiled pasta and covered it with meat sauce from a vacuum-packed pouch. It was by far their most elaborate meal of the analog.

"It's too beautiful to eat," Mila said, salivating with anticipation.

Jancey took a photo with her tablet. "I'm sending this to Mission Control so they can see how well we've done. It'll take at least another week to grow enough for another one like this."

"Too bad we don't have a nice merlot to enjoy with it."

"I don't see us producing a lot of wine on Mars. Grapes aren't a very efficient use of garden space…though I suppose we could make it from something else."

Mila shook her head. "No, I'll eat poi if it happens to be on my plate, but I draw the line at drinking wine made of watermelon or sweet potatoes."

Since their revealing talk the week before, there had been a marked change in Jancey's demeanor. Softer, more personable. She'd talked of her upbringing in Charlottesville, where she'd been the only child of a bitter divorce. Her father remarried a fundamentalist Christian, and together they maligned her career and faith in science over God until she no longer wanted them in her life. Her mother's new husband was a businessman. Once Jancey became famous, they'd pressed her relentlessly to endorse his company's arthritis cure. Snake oil, she called it.

It was little wonder she held the world at arm's length. The women who were smart enough to be interesting to her weren't willing to take a back seat to her ambitions, and if they did, they were no longer appealing. Her closest friend—her only true friend, she said—was Grace Faraday. Grace supported her unconditionally, understood her dreams and wanted for her what she wanted for herself.

With their futures now inextricably bound together, Mila knew the day would come when she'd be all things to Jancey, perhaps sooner rather than later. Friend, family, lover. A partner in every way. Every day, she moved further past the thrill of realizing her fantasy to embracing it as a responsibility. Jancey deserved the best.

"Give me six months in the garden on Mars, we'll eat like this every night," Jancey said. "With fresh fruit for dessert."

"Remind me to pack some of those fake candles that flicker. A meal like this should always be a sensual experience. Don't you agree?"

She studied Jancey's face for the answer, hoping to add another expression to her list. A narrowing of her eyes was skepticism. A tilt of her head was curiosity. When her mouth curved upward at one corner, she was trying hard not to smile.

This time, her eyebrows arched and she lowered her chin to glare at her sternly. Mila had no clue what that meant.

By now, Jancey had to know her intentions. While she hadn't explicitly commented on any of Mila's flirtations, she hadn't pushed back either. Just this look that probably said now was not the appropriate time. So the only real question was when.

As Mila cleaned up their dishes, Jancey took out her clarinet and began to play the scales, something she did two or three times a week. A warm, mellow timbre. Rounded notes, each giving way to the next.

"That's a lovely sound. Were you serious about teaching me to play? I don't know the first thing about music."

"Nonsense. Complex diaphony? Dissonant harmony? You know plenty."

Mila studied Jancey's fingers and tried to copy their movements as if playing an imaginary instrument of her own. "Or maybe I should learn something else—like a saxophone or French horn—so we can play duets."

"Oh, no. Brass is deadly in small spaces. Besides, there are plenty of duets for clarinet. Mozart loved them. Telemann, Rossini. Here, give it a try."

Mila looked at her warily. "It looks hard."

"It is. Are you afraid you won't be able to do it?"

"No, I'm afraid wild animals will begin throwing themselves off the mountain in a mass suicide ritual."

"It's all about the lips, Mila. You're good with those, aren't you?" She punctuated her question with an overt batting of the eyelashes.

"My lips are superb, but this isn't the demonstration I had in mind."

"Always an innuendo, Todorov. Have you forgotten we have more important priorities?"

"I'm pretty sure that was your innuendo, not mine. And I know for a fact my lips won't interfere with our priorities. If you and I had met six weeks ago under other circumstances and spent this much time together, you would know very well by now how truly superb my lips are. I seriously doubt any of the married couples have hit the pause button during the analog, and they have the same priorities as we do."

Jancey shuddered and shook her head. "I make it a point not to think about what other people do in their bedrooms...or in their solar flare chambers, as the case may be."

Taking the plunge, Mila spoke the unspoken: "You know as well as I do we'll become lovers eventually. We're just postponing the inevitable. Suppose we win first place and we're set to launch for Mars in four years. How will that affect our priorities? Do you really expect to hold off until then? Or what if we come in fourth and our launch is seven years from now?"

"Oh, please. I couldn't stand to wait that long."

"To go to Mars? Or to sample my superb—"

A sharp blast from the clarinet cut off her final word. "You've convinced me of one thing for sure. You have what it takes for this mission. Tenacity."

"Thank you. I think so too."

"And so humble."

At no time had Jancey's face or tone suggested she was genuinely uncomfortable with anything she'd said. Yet Mila's goal wasn't to win her over by wearing her down. As much as she wanted a hug, a kiss—any physical sign of affection would do—she didn't want her giving in because she was tired of the pressure. What she wanted was for Jancey to realize her feelings and act on them instead of shooing them away.

"I'll try not to do it anymore…the innuendo. I'll say this though. The more time we spend together, the more I get to know you…the more I want to show you how I feel. And not just with my lips. I want to hold you while you sleep…feel your skin next to mine. I'm not able to stop those feelings, but I'll try not to talk about it if you find it annoying. Just know if you ever get to the same point, I'm already there."

"So they're feelings, not just urges."

"They're both, but I can control the urges."

"Interesting. I find it much easier to control the feelings than the urges." Jancey stood and raised the table into its notch against the wall.

Mila had only a split second to ready for Jancey's next move—a full-on kiss. The suddenness of her actions, the force of her lips, the tug of her hand on the back of Mila's neck. It left her disoriented. Not once had she thought Jancey would make the first move.

Which was utterly ridiculous, of course. Women like Jancey were used to being in charge. That was fine as long as it happened again. And again. And again.

"Not bad, Todorov. A little practice and you could be pretty good at that."

Seriously? Mila didn't know whether to be flattered or insulted. "I'm willing to put in lots of practice."

With her arms around Jancey's waist, she held her in place and initiated another kiss. Slow and easy this time, gently teasing with her tongue until Jancey's lips parted and took her in. Exquisite.

Then sharp teeth tugged at her lip and she remembered who was boss.

* * *

Not bad. The words had tumbled out instantaneously, a defense mechanism against admitting her true feelings. Jancey had been overwhelmed to feel another woman's power.

Then again, Mila wasn't just another woman. More than anyone she'd been with, she was very nearly her equal in all the ways that mattered.

It was unsettling.

The air inside their dome was suddenly steamy despite the falling temperature outside. Under any other circumstances, she might have unzipped her flight suit to cool off. Then Mila would unzip hers. Then chaos.

Self-control. Concentration. Priorities.

"We need to focus," she said, though her tepid tone left even her unconvinced.

"I am focusing," Mila murmured as her warm lips nuzzled Jancey's neck.

"On our analog." It took every ounce of willpower she could muster to extricate herself from the embrace. "We can't let ourselves get distracted."

It had nothing to do with distraction and everything to do with feeling out of control. Her urges, and yes, her feelings—

they were nothing compared to Mila's obvious hunger to have her inside and out. She wasn't ready to lay herself bare like that. She had to be the one in command, the one doling out pleasure, the one setting limits.

She'd start by dictating the terms. No fooling around until they'd taken care of business. No matter how much her body disagreed.

With both hands on Mila's shoulders, she held her at arm's length. "Rest assured, you have my attention now. When we finish this—"

"We're never going to finish this, Jancey. There will always be a mission, a reason we have to focus on our work. We can do both." Mila leaned back against the wall of the dome and dropped her hands to her hips, no longer posturing for an intimate advantage. "I already told you. I won't keep pushing you if it's something you don't want. But after the way you just kissed me, I think it is what you want. In fact, I think you want it even more now."

"Is that so?" It was so, and it was frightening how well Mila read her. "That was only a test drive. I had to know if you were worth it."

Mila's face brightened. "Was I?"

"You have serious potential." And just like that, she felt back in control. She'd handle Mila with both humor and an inflated sense of superiority. "Think you could use that potential to file the activity logs while I test tomorrow's water supply?"

"Should I log that kiss?"

"Do I seriously have to answer that?"

Just when she thought she'd regained the upper hand, she readied for bed with a sponge bath and her body betrayed her once again. Though her back was turned, she could feel Mila's eyes on her. It aroused her. Even before a much younger woman, she was confident of her sensuality. All the women she'd known had loved her firm thighs and butt, and especially her breasts. Just the thought of Mila watching her made her nipples stand on end, and she flaunted them by stretching her arms high above her head to allow her shirt to fall slowly into place. Taunting, teasing, titillating. *Look all you want.*

She crawled into the sleeping chamber with her reading tablet, knowing sleep would elude her until her body cooled off and her mind emptied of its lustful thoughts. It was cruel to put on such a show. As though her mouth were saying one thing and her actions another.

Mila joined her without a word, taking up her usual position at the other end of the mattress so they faced one another. She too had washed and put on a freshly laundered T-shirt and shorts.

"You're all spruced up. What's the occasion?"

"It's Saturday…I think. Or maybe it's only Friday."

"It's Tuesday."

Mila huffed. "Who can tell? I don't even know if I'm early or late, but I feel better."

"I suppose that counts for something." Jancey forced her attention back to her tablet, having read the same page several times already.

Again, she could feel Mila watching her, though it appeared for the moment she'd tabled her desires. She looked relaxed, languid. Sexy. Beneath that thin shirt was taut skin unmarred by age. A flat belly and small breasts that sat high upon her chest.

Jancey couldn't seem to focus. More than a year had passed since she last made love. Too long. No matter what she told herself about concentrating on their work, her body didn't want to wait.

"What are you reading?"

The question caught her off guard. "I'm, uh…it's an old classic, *Daughters of a Coral Dawn*. I've read it half a dozen times. I always find something new."

"Sounds interesting." Mila abruptly switched her pillow to Jancey's end to lie alongside. "What's it about?"

She was surprised by the move but not bothered. They had kissed, after all. Surely they could sleep side by side instead of head to foot. "A lesbian utopia on another planet."

"If a certain pair of lesbians I know ends up on another planet, that will be utopia."

"Hmmm…and if it follows the book, the trouble will start when the men show up."

"That's why we need to go first, to establish superiority." Mila lay on her side, her face only inches away. "Does it bother you for me to be this close?"

"No, you're fine." Her words came out with an irritating squeak, not at all the voice of control. "As long as you don't mind that I keep reading."

Mila scooted closer, brazenly resting her head on Jancey's shoulder.

The audacity was astonishing, and yet she had no urge to pull away.

Focus. Book. Utopia.

The words on the page ran together like so much nonsense no matter how many times she read them or how hard she tried to concentrate. Mila's hand had come to rest on her stomach, and her fingertips danced the way they had when she pretended to play the clarinet.

"A Payrungasmad curse on the neighbors. Can you do that again, dear?"

She'd read that sentence six times and was no closer to understanding who said it or why. The hand was underneath her shirt now, tickling her skin. Why wasn't she stopping this?

"Is this all right?" Mila asked.

Afraid her voice would squeak again, Jancey managed only something between a grunt and a moan. That's how she'd handle it. Pretend it didn't matter, that Mila's actions were having no effect. The ultimate in self-discipline.

That worked until Mila's hand worked its way upward, where her knuckles brushed the underside of her breasts.

Still pretending to read, Jancey swung her tablet to the opposite hand, allowing Mila unfettered access to her torso. With her near hand, she began stroking Mila's hair. It was getting harder by the second to feign disinterest, especially with her nipples now standing erect as though ready to burst through her shirt.

"How's your book?" Mila murmured, tugging Jancey's shirt upward.

"I have no idea."

The chamber had grown so warm over the last few minutes that she actually welcomed the exposure, and abruptly sat up to pull her shirt over her head and toss it aside, along with her tablet. Her pretense was over.

Her torture, however, had just begun. She'd fully expected Mila to devour her begging breasts immediately, but the woman clearly had her own deliberate schedule, one designed to drive her insane.

After several minutes of lightly stroking the outside of her breasts, Mila finally made it to her areolas. They pebbled, drawing so tight that her nipples stood like soldiers.

Then Mila abruptly broke away. Without a word she pulled off both her shirt and shorts, and burrowed again along Jancey's side.

Her cool skin was like a mountain stream against Jancey's rising heat, and she too tugged off her shorts to feel it more completely. With a deep gasp, she inhaled a trace of soap and mint, and a growing essence of Mila's arousal. Or maybe it was her own arousal. Her legs were open. When had she done that?

Mila was above her now, suspended somehow so that her weight rested elsewhere. Like zero gravity. That enabled her to slide her warm mouth all around…across Jancey's ribs, up her sternum and all around the curve of her breasts.

Everywhere except where Jancey wanted it most.

When she could stand it no longer, she clutched Mila's head and guided her to a nipple. Even then, the expected onslaught didn't come. Mila's lips grew hard and closed her nipple in a firm vise. Tugging, squeezing, warming with her hot breath. The only moisture came from her tongue lightly flicking the tip. It cooled instantly when she left it to move to the other side.

The torture went on interminably as though Mila were waiting for a signal to proceed. But it likely wasn't permission she sought. It was surrender, an admission from Jancey that she needed this.

As if her whole body weren't screaming loud enough.

Then suddenly Mila sucked her nipple deep into her mouth, raking it with her teeth.

A rapturous explosion of pleasure and pain filled her entire body, and she arched upward to ride the wave. Squeezing her eyes tightly, she shut out everything but the sensation of a warm, wet mouth.

Mila chose that moment—the perfect moment—to enter her.

"God, you're so wet."

How could she not be after such an unhurried assault? She wanted to feel everything all at once, so badly that it was all she could do not to stroke herself.

For once, Mila seemed to sense her desperation—maybe it was the fingernails digging into her back—and rolled her thumb across the taut bundle of nerves.

Jancey could hear herself making noises—moans, hisses, half-words—but she had no control over their utterance. It didn't matter. Mila needed no coaching. With every thrust, she ground her thumb, increasing the speed and pressure until Jancey thought she might explode.

Then she did. Bursting pulsing pounding. Her hips high off the bed, with one leg wrapped tightly around Mila's thigh and her face buried into her neck. Sweating throbbing.

Spent.

Mila eased her back to her pillow and finished with a deep kiss.

Still gasping for breath, she tucked Mila's hair behind her ear and cupped her cheek. "You can't be trusted, Todorov."

"Not true, Major Beaumont. My priority is you. Your goals are my goals. Your wants are my wants. And you can always trust me to put you first."

Jancey pushed her onto her back and straddled her leg. "I've decided I want to be your commander after all."

CHAPTER SIXTEEN

From atop the dome, Mila could see a smattering of snow on the peak above. Unusual for September, but not unheard of at nearly fourteen thousand feet. Some people had been known to ski down the slope, if only to brag they'd skied in the morning and sunned on the beach in the afternoon. Neither appealed to her. All the adventure she could ever want was inside the habitat.

Though Jancey had insisted she wouldn't become the commander, she'd had no problem pulling rank at sunrise.

"Time to turn the solar panels."

"I did it yesterday," Mila answered sleepily.

"My wants are your wants. That's what you said. I want you to go out and turn the solar panels."

Cheeky. The next forty years would probably be filled with conversations like that, a realization that made her smile.

Another hour or three of sleep would have been nice, but she wouldn't have traded a minute of their night for it. From the moment they'd become lovers two weeks ago, Jancey left all her reservations behind, and they'd made love every night.

Sleep should have come easier for Mila. Even with Jancey beside her, she still struggled to fall asleep. At Jancey's insistence, she'd taken a sleeping pill the night before after lying awake for over an hour. A practice she'd have to accept. At least they didn't leave a morning fog.

As she inspected the habitat, she noticed one of the Fagans walking around their dome. Brandon, she guessed, since he was considerably taller than his wife. He appeared to be looking directly at her but she had no compulsion to wave. The guy was an asshole.

She finished her walk-around and noted that Mission Control hadn't terrorized them in over a week. No broken tiles on their dome, no stripped wires on their panels, no more trouble with their water supply. Only three solar flares in five weeks. With only four days to go, the committee apparently was content to let them limp toward the finish line.

On her second pass around the dome, she called in to Jancey. "I'm happy to report we're in good shape."

"Maybe they've forgotten we're here," she replied sleepily.

"I'm giving it one more look."

There was danger in becoming complacent, especially now that their relationship was soaking up so much of their attention. She'd promised Jancey becoming lovers wouldn't affect their work.

Returning to find Jancey still inside the sleeping chamber, she stripped off her spacesuit and stowed it. "I saw Brandon Fagan out there. If they get picked for Mars, would it be socially awkward to have a dinner party and not invite them?"

Jancey emerged already dressed in her flight suit. "Not for me. I never understood what Libby saw in him. He always rubbed me the wrong way. All the women at NASA had a special connection. We weren't part of the old boys' club, but that was cool. We had our own club. I remember one night in Houston…a bunch of us went out for a beer. Brandon Fagan showed up at the door and made a big deal about looking at his watch, like he was pissed off at her being late. Couldn't even be bothered to come over to our table and act like a human being.

Libby just got up and followed him out. Left her dinner, stuck us with the bill. It was like she didn't have his permission to be there. Weird."

"Creepy is more like it. If she were my friend, I'd have to kick his ass."

"Same here. We weren't great friends in those days, but there was a connection. Like a sisterhood."

Mila liked the idea of NASA's female astronauts hanging out together at a bar. It was that special brand of camaraderie she'd longed for all her life—brilliant, accomplished women who loved adventure the way she did. "It's amazing to me to think of so many women together at NASA. I would have given anything to be part of that."

"It took a long time for us to get there. We didn't have *the right stuff*, if you know what I mean."

Mila cupped her crotch. "This kind of stuff."

"Exactly. The Russians saw fit to put Valentina Tereshkova in space twenty years before Sally Ride. Seven Mercury astronauts, sixteen Gemini and twenty-four Apollo. All men. But once the shuttle missions opened the ranks to women, our odds were actually better than the men's because there weren't as many women competing for the slots."

Jancey mixed a vanilla protein shake and poured it into Mila's cup. Then she repeated the process for herself.

"I thought my chances would be better with the ESA," Mila said. "Except they don't choose that many women. Thousands of applications and they pick maybe one. Claudie Haigneré is the only European woman who's ever flown."

"All the more reason Tenacity should choose us." Jancey tapped her cup to Mila's in a toast and downed her drink in several gulps. "Four more days, Todorov."

"Forty more years, Major Beaumont."

"I'll be a very old woman by then."

Since they'd become lovers, Jancey was quick to smile, easy with the flirtations. Deeply confident.

"I promise I'll still find you fascinating."

Their suggestive gaze was broken by a high-pitched signal from their comm.

"I was just thinking not ten minutes ago that it's been a long time since Mission Control messed with us. What do they want?"

Jancey spun around to study their tablet. "They aren't kidding around this time. It's a big one. Super X-class."

The largest class of solar flare ever recorded. A coronal mass ejection directed toward Earth could potentially—

"CME coming our way. Blackout in three minutes."

They went into motion instantly packing as many supplies as they could fit into their chamber. Food, water, clean clothing. The dreaded diapers, which they'd managed to avoid so far. An X-class solar flare could last a couple of days—or longer— and wipe out electrical grids on Earth, causing weeks or even months of chaos.

Mila took one last look around the habitat as the seconds ticked off, and then crawled into the chamber opposite Jancey, who had taken up her usual position, back against the wall with her legs stretched out in front. "How long do you think they'll hold us here?"

Jancey shrugged. "My guess is four days, all the way to the end of the analog. Maybe even longer if they want to twist the knife. We can't go anywhere without the all clear, so if they play this like the CME knocked out their grid, we're down for who knows how long."

Their abundant food supply was encouraging. Plenty of precooked, vacuum-packed casseroles, vegetables and desserts, all of which they'd have to eat at room temperature because they couldn't use their power packs to warm them. The biggest challenge would be stretching their water supply—ten liters apiece—should they be confined longer to their chamber.

"This is the real test," Jancey said. "It's not about survival or self-sufficiency. It's about how we get along with each other when there's literally nothing to do for days on end. They've got us totally isolated from social stimuli. No books, no challenges, no work to keep us busy. This is how they think we'll crack."

Mila chuckled as she tapped her foot against Jancey's. "Little do they know that alone with you is exactly where I want to be."

Jancey shook her head. "Don't give me that look. Despite anything I might have uttered recently in a moment of delirium, I can't possibly do that for four straight days. Besides, this is supposed to simulate being aboard *Tenacity* in the radiation chamber. Weightless sex can be awfully frustrating, to say the least."

"Is that a confession I hear?"

"I'm not admitting anything, but it's a fact that blood behaves differently in zero gravity. Plus there's lots of sweat and not much friction."

"It doesn't matter. There's a lot more to making love than orgasms."

Jancey tipped her head to one side. Skepticism. "Convince me."

"Okay." Mila leaned forward with her elbows on her knees, leering as she took in every inch of Jancey. "I'm making love to you right now."

"Sorry. Not feeling it."

"But you will once you realize you love me. Just being together will be enough. You'll look at me and feel everything there is between us. All the emotions, all the physical memories. You'll think of our future together. Things you want from me, ways you can bring me pleasure."

"I will, huh?" Amused. "What makes you so sure I'm going to love you? I do lust very well. Love…not so much."

"I don't believe you." It was Mila's turn to laugh as Jancey gave her an incredulous look. "When I fell asleep last night, you were holding me…brushing my hair with your fingers, kissing my ear. That's not lust. You've already begun to love me."

"I was trying to help you fall asleep. You were keeping me awake."

"I think you like touching me that way, and it has nothing to do with sex. It makes you feel good. It's what we do when we love someone. Am I right?"

Jancey glared at her through narrowed eyes, an obviously exaggerated scowl. She wasn't the sort to let anyone call her a softie.

"You can deny it all you want, Jancey, but I won't believe you. You think you have control over your feelings. I've got news for you. You don't. Not when it comes to me."

"You're awfully sure of yourself, Todorov. In fact, I'd say you were cocky."

The use of her surname was a defense mechanism. Jancey did that when she needed to assert herself, to regain a sense of authority and self-control. It was almost an endearment.

"I'm not cocky. But I know you're starting to fall in love with me. I should think that's a good thing. We're bound together for life, you and me. Day in and day out forever, hundreds of millions of miles from everyone else."

She scooted across the chamber and took Jancey's hand. As usual, it was warm, even a bit damp from perspiration. She raised it to her lips and gently kissed the knuckles before bringing the palm to her cheek.

"No use fighting it."

"For your information, I'm not fighting it," Jancey said, this time seriously. "What I'm fighting is you telling me how I feel. If and when the day comes when my feelings are so strong I can't keep them to myself anymore, I want to be the one to say so. In fact, I think I'd enjoy that. But not if your reaction is to say you already knew."

This time, there was no teasing in her voice, and Mila regretted pushing too far. "You're right...everything you just said. I'm sorry." She unleashed a new flurry of kisses on Jancey's hand. "Forgive me."

Jancey didn't answer at all, instead freeing her hand and scooting sideways until she was out of reach.

* * *

There was something far more irritating than a cocky Mila—a brooding Mila. For the last fifteen hours, she'd kept mostly to herself, dozing or staring out the small window. Either she was feeling chastised and afraid to rock the boat, or she was sulking.

By Jancey's watch—which provided the only light in their chamber, but only when she pressed the button—it was nearly midnight. Normally they'd be asleep by now, but napping off and on throughout the day had screwed up their sleep schedule.

Whatever was going on with Mila, it had dragged on long enough. The inflated sense of confidence she'd displayed earlier had been off-putting, but it didn't deserve the doghouse. Besides, she'd already apologized.

"Talk to me, Mila. What's the first thing you'll do when this analog is over?"

"Take a very hot shower, wash my hair, shave my legs. What about you? No, let me guess…you'll go somewhere to get as far away from me as you can."

Jancey bit her tongue to keep from pointing out that Mila was doing it again, scripting her every thought. "Funny you'd say that…I'd swear it wasn't all that long ago you were pretty sure I was secretly in love with you."

Mila huffed. "Obviously I was wrong. I think too much of myself sometimes."

"And now you're pouting."

"I'm not pouting. I'm trying not to be annoying. When I don't know what to say, it's usually best not to say anything."

"Also known as walking on eggshells," Jancey said. "You don't have to do that around me. We talked about this weeks ago, remember? We're going to have disagreements every now and then. It's perfectly normal. What matters is how we respond to them, how we treat each other. I don't want you shrinking into a cocoon because you're afraid to talk."

After a long moment of silence, Mila said, "You can't see me nodding in the dark. I get what you're saying. But I still feel bad about today, like I disrespected you. I can't help it."

"Forget about it. I already did." Not actually true. It had stayed with her because of a surprising realization. "Did you ever hear that saying about the definition of insanity?"

"You mean doing the same thing over and over and expecting different results?"

"Exactly. All my relationships were like that. I'd meet someone and put myself out there a little at a time. I took, I gave, I took some more. All the while knowing the whole thing would come crashing down when it was time for me to chase that one thing I really want." Those were Monica's words. Lindsay's words. Jill's words. "It's different this time."

"Because I'm chasing the same thing as you?"

"Yes, and because everything we do is an investment. We have to work through all of it together when we're playing for keeps."

"I agree." Her face was a silhouette as she peered out into the night. "What is it you want me to do?"

"I want you to relax," Jancey said. "I'm not Frederica. I'm not holding back to be cruel to you. You can trust me."

Mila sighed and scooted close enough to draw her into an embrace. "I do...and I needed to hear that. Thank you."

"You're welcome." She planted a kiss on her nose. "Do you want to join me at Grace Faraday's house when we get done? Now that the students are back, there won't be any rooms at the university. And I have no intention of moving into a hotel, not when I have the world's greatest guest house and a Jaguar convertible at my disposal. Besides, it might be good to show everyone we aren't in any hurry to get away from each other."

Another extended silence.

"Mila?"

"Sorry...I'd love to. As long as it's okay with Grace." There was a welcome excitement in her voice.

"It will be. She also has a guest room in the main house if you want your own space for a while."

"I don't need space from you, Jancey."

"We all need space sometimes. It's not a reflection on you, but I'll tell you something that is." She spun around and lay her head in Mila's lap. "I don't feel the urge to keep parts of my life separate from yours. That's a brand-new feeling for me."

Mila stroked her shoulders with cool hands that penetrated her thin T-shirt. Calming.

"When I say I need space," Jancey went on, "it's to spend some time in my head, not to get away from you. I can do that when you're with me as long as I have quiet."

"I understand."

"But what's really amazing to me—and this has never happened before—is that I don't want you to go very far." She covered one of Mila's hands with hers. "I want you close enough that I can pull you back when I need you…or close enough that I can get to you when you need me. You have no idea what a big deal that is for me."

Mila inhaled sharply and leaned forward so her hands slid across Jancey's stomach. "It gives me chill bumps to hear you say that. It's what I've always wanted."

Jancey guided the cool hands under her elastic waistband. Perhaps Mila had just learned the value of waiting for her to put her feelings into words.

CHAPTER SEVENTEEN

"Thirty-nine."

"Forty," Mila grunted as she lunged to her left to bat the makeshift ball back to Jancey. Four socks rolled up in duct tape, their improvised volleyball.

"Forty-one."

It sailed out of reach before she could right herself. "Crap. We'll never make it to fifty."

"Depends on how much longer they leave us stranded here," Jancey said, her voice flat from boredom. "I can't believe we're still here."

"Maybe it's not a drill. Earth actually got hit with a real Super X and half the planet's power grid is down."

Six days had passed since the onset of the "solar storm." Two days beyond what should have been the end of their analog. With the help of their precooked dinners, they'd been able to stretch their water supply. It would shrink faster now since all they had left were dry protein bars and powders. And less than two liters of water between them. They'd be lucky to last two more days before having to drink their filtered urine. *Only if I'm about to die*, she'd said, opening herself to Jancey's mocking and scorn.

There were worse things than being confined in a space of less than four cubic meters with the woman she loved. Still… their chamber became unpleasant after two days, disgusting after four, and bordered now on hazardous. A lightning strike might launch a new life form.

"I'm not sure which is harder," Mila said. "The tedium of being stuck here another day or the agony of having to wait even longer to find out who's first to go on *Tenacity*. We should have known that by now."

"I don't think they'll know right away. Mark my word, the first person we'll see when we step off the bus is Danielle Zion. She's going to put us through the whole battery of tests to see how we held up."

The mere mention of Zion sent both of them into exercise routines that included sit-ups, push-ups, planks and bicycle kicks.

Mila's voice cracked as she held her plank with one bent arm. "I bet they've already picked the first team. Probably the second too, because they didn't all agree on the first one and second was the consolation prize. The real contest now is for third and fourth."

"Maybe…but we'll still have more hoops to jump through. Calloway's probably going to drill down into our darkest places to find out how we got along."

"What are you going to tell them?"

Jancey stopped her sit-ups and touched Mila's hip with just enough force to tip her over. "That I think you're the perfect partner. That my impressions of you during this trial make me feel even more committed to work together."

"Your impressions of me? You make me sound like your student." She wanted Jancey to publicly acknowledge her—something Frederica had never done. "Are you worried somebody on the committee will freak out about sending two lesbians into space?"

"The thought had crossed my mind," she said, her tone heavy with sarcasm. "When we walk out of here, anyone with half a brain will figure it out, but that doesn't mean we should acknowledge anything. I don't see an upside to sharing our feelings publicly. How will the Russians feel when we go there to train? Or the Chinese? What if they pull their support?"

A real possibility, Mila conceded.

"Look, Mila…I don't want to hide it—I got my fill of that in the air force—but I don't want us to throw our chances away."

"So we do what? Pretend we're friends?"

"We don't have to pretend that. We are friends." Jancey straddled her and leaned down for a kiss. "Trust me, the people who matter will know. I won't be able to hide that I'm proud of you."

Jancey was right about one thing—words like those were far sweeter when they came without prodding.

She stared up into green eyes that glinted from the light coming through their porthole. So beautiful…her emotions overflowed. "I love you, Jancey."

"I know you do." Her half-smile was confident, lively. "I feel it from you, and if I'm honest with myself—"

The comm suddenly beeped, its first sound in six days. Both of them scrambled across the chamber to read the message.

"Simulation concluded. Prepare for evacuation."

* * *

Carrying a backpack that held her clarinet case and tablet computer, Jancey strode alongside Mila to the edge of the dirt road, where the bus was making periodic stops to pick up the teams. She held a hand to shield her eyes from the sun. It was the first time she'd been outside in weeks without her helmet, which had tinted glass.

The bus bypassed the hut on the other side of the Fagans.

"Whoa! Did you see that?" Mila exclaimed.

"Jerry and Wade. Looks like they never made it back after the water episode." Unlike Kamal and David. It was shocking that a pair of NASA astronauts would fail to complete a six-week analog that required so little.

"They looked pretty sick when they left. Must have hit them hard."

"That's very bad news," Jancey said. Water contaminated with *E. coli* was known to cause irreversible kidney damage. She wouldn't wish that on anyone, even if it meant one less competitor.

The Fagans were next to board. Brandon's beard was bushy and dark, clearly visible from a hundred yards away. Even more noticeable was his arm around Libby's shoulder. They were exactly the sort of team Sir Charles envisioned for the Tenacity Project—a competent pair who supported one another.

She'd expected the Fagans to earn a slot on the launch schedule. If they'd performed well on the analog, they were sure to get serious consideration for the top prize.

As they took a step toward the bus, she caught Mila's arm. "Sit beside me on the bus."

"It never occurred to me not to."

When they stepped aboard, her suspicions were confirmed. Only the Fagans and the Hatsus were sitting together. The others had spread out as if relieved at the chance to get space from their partner, including the Norwegian couple.

Marlon also sported a beard, but his looked as though it had been scissored without benefit of a mirror. His jaw set firmly, he stood and stretched out a hand as she walked by. "Good to see you, Major."

"You too."

As she took his hand, he tugged her closer and whispered, "I thought about you every day."

She chuckled to herself as she continued toward the rear of the bus, casting a glance at Jean-Paul, who had slumped in his seat and pulled a cap over his eyes. The last six days in their sleeping chamber must have been pure hell.

As she took a window seat, Mila relieved her of the bags and stowed them in the shallow bin above them along with her own. In a low voice, she said, "I see what you mean about sitting together. These people don't seem to like each other."

The Clarkes were the last to board and there was no mistaking the acrimony between them. Courtney Clarke tossed her armload into the window seat and sat on the aisle as her husband Phillip pushed past her to sit four rows behind.

Jancey suppressed a smile. If anyone on the committee was here and taking notes, the Clarkes were history. Another competitor gone.

The bus rode past the residence buildings near the visitor center and continued down the slope to University Research Park in Hilo. The Tenacity Project had built its sprawling two-story headquarters among the academic facilities for the twelve telescopes atop Mauna Kea. Tenacity Centre, Grace had called it. It was constructed in the traditional Hawaiian style, and painted the color of rust. Like the Red Planet, she said. Horizontal planks with shuttered windows that jutted out from the bottom. A gently sloping roof that extended out to cool the air close to the building.

"Definitely looks like we're done with the university," Mila said.

"I guess we don't need so much space now that there aren't many of us left."

The driver parked and stood to face them. "Leave your personal belongings on the bus. They'll be inventoried and returned to you inside."

Inventoried. They probably were checking for contraband, something prohibited, like a personal cell phone or food wrappers. Staff assistants were still on the mountain making a list of leftover supplies and waste in each habitat.

The building had a "new" smell. Fresh paint, carpet, varnish. They filed in and were led to the fitness center in the basement where none other than Danielle Zion was waiting.

"Told you so," Jancey whispered.

"Drop your gear. Shoes off. Let's see how many of you got fat and lazy."

Fat and lazy wasn't the problem in space. Given the monotony of the rations and the loss of appetite that came from being weightless, most astronauts lost weight and muscle mass regardless of how much they ate or worked out. High altitude would likely have the same effect, especially given the repetitive food choices.

Mila was first to step on the scale. One-thirty. Not much for someone five-seven, but only a pound lighter than before the analog. She flashed Jancey a thumbs-up.

Jancey dreaded her weigh-in. She could tell from the way her flight suit hung from her shoulders that she'd lost a few pounds, despite her conscious efforts to eat more than she wanted, especially over the last few days when they'd been confined.

"Pockets empty, Beaumont?"

"Now *that* would have been a great idea." She slapped her thighs and stepped up.

"One-twenty-five, down three."

Not as bad as she'd expected, and not nearly as bad as Courtney Clarke. She'd dropped nine pounds, and Libby Fagan had lost four. Suki Hatsu, like Mila, was down only one.

The men fared far worse, most of them losing more than ten pounds. Brandon Fagan, however, surprised everyone with a two-pound gain. Impressive.

As a team, she and Mila were second only to the Fagans in maintaining their weight. Their advantage, however, was being able to do so on less food and water, and with very little waste. Even a small amount of savings over six weeks would substantially impact the size of their three-year supply, which was the minimum they had to carry on their vessel.

"That's it," Zion said. "We'll run through the fitness test tomorrow morning. Right now, there's a brown bag lunch waiting for you on the lower level in the conference room. If anyone's interested in grabbing a shower first, you'll find fresh clothing in the locker rooms, which are located through that…"

Jancey didn't stick around for the rest of her instructions. She could practically smell the soap and water.

* * *

Mila didn't dare tell anyone how much she appreciated the lush foliage in the courtyard behind Tenacity Centre. Though she'd lived most of her life amidst urban concrete, she enjoyed parks and gardens more than she'd realized. The bleak landscape of Mauna Kea had left her sensory deprived, something she'd have to reconcile in preparation for Mars. Nothing but rust-colored rocky terrain, all of it framed from inside the tinted glass of her helmet. In fact, once they launched, the only green she'd see for the rest of her life would be in the hydroponics garden.

And in Jancey's eyes.

The conference room looked out on the courtyard, so she could enjoy the greenery while they debriefed. Several tables had been arranged in a large rectangle, and she sat beside Jancey directly opposite the podium.

Dr. Calloway, who reminded everyone to call him Cal, passed around several documents until everyone had a neat stack. He held up one for display. "The first form you're asked to sign is the Compliance Agreement. Read and initial each line, then sign your name at the bottom and pass them back to me."

One by one, Mila checked off the items on the list. No, she hadn't taken any prohibited materials to the habitat. No, she hadn't communicated with anyone other than Mission Control. Yes, her reported logs were accurate. Yes, she'd worn her spacesuit each time she left the habitat. Yes, she'd remained inside the sleeping chamber during the entirety of each solar storm.

A formality for everyone, apparently. Even if someone had cheated, it made little sense to expect them to confess. A cheater would also lie.

The next form was a self-assessment of her mental health. No feelings of depression. No anxiety. Calm and peaceful, plenty of energy.

Another formality. Even if anyone had awakened this morning depressed, a hot shower and warm, humid air had surely cured it. If the committee hoped to tease out psychological problems, they'd have to find another way.

The third form was a short-answer questionnaire that promised more nuance. What creature comfort had she missed most? *Very hot black tea.* To whom would she make the first call now that the analog was over? *Her grandmother in Bulgaria.* What was the best thing about working with your partner?

Mila glanced over at Jancey to find her puzzling over the same question. How to show the committee they were well-matched without saying why?

The best thing about working with my partner was that it gave me the chance to become her friend—a friend for life, no matter what happens to us.

With that out of the way, the rest of the questions were relatively straightforward. Her least favorite meal was the strawberry protein shake. The most difficult aspect of the analog was learning to sleep on a rigid schedule, but she emphasized that she'd managed to do it with the help of a sleep aid.

Jancey was first to finish and stepped away from the table to visit the courtyard.

Mila turned in her paper and followed her into a corner where they were hidden from view by a thick bird of paradise. Expecting a smile, she was surprised by Jancey's look of concern. "Everything all right?"

"I'm worried about Marlon. I've never seen him so agitated."

"You think he had problems with Jean-Paul?"

"I think if they launched for Mars together tomorrow, they'd kill each other."

Mila felt a pang of guilt for not sharing Jancey's concern. Marlon was one of her oldest friends, someone she liked and respected. But the way Mila saw it, their disarray meant one less rival. "Is there any way we can help him?"

Jancey shook her head. "No, he knows what he needs to do. If they want Mars badly enough, they'll make peace with each other. And if they don't...they might as well bow out and let someone else go. I'm only worried because I know what kind of sacrifice that would be for a guy like him."

"Would you have done that? I mean...what if I'd driven you so crazy you'd wanted to kill me?"

"I'd have killed you," she deadpanned before smiling. "Relax. There was never a chance we were going to have trouble. Once I chose to go with you, I was prepared to do whatever it took to make it work. I would have done the same thing with Marlon. The difference for those guys is they both chose someone else first and they never mentally committed to work together."

"You would have killed me?" Mila placed her hands over her chest, feigning shock and heartbreak.

"Probably not." Jancey grabbed the collar of Mila's T-shirt and yanked her close enough to kiss.

Before that could happen, the sound of a throat clearing broke them apart, and Jean-Paul stepped from behind the palms, leering in a way that made Mila want to smash his face in. "Cal has another exercise for us."

She started to follow him and found Jancey gripping her shirttail.

"Hold on a second," she said. "I'm not walking out of here looking like I've been caught doing something wrong. Just give it a minute." Her defiance notwithstanding, there was no doubt she was annoyed.

"Forget it, Jancey. If you're right about him and Marlon, it won't matter anyway. They'll be gone in a couple of days."

They returned to their seats to find Cal sitting on the edge of the table with his legs swinging underneath. His relaxed posture suggested the formal part of their evaluation was over. That was certain when the department heads began to file in, taking seats along the perimeter so they could listen in during the debriefing.

There was no mistaking at this point why they all needed to be there—they were the selection committee. Sir Charles, Dr. V, Svein Helland, Moriya Ito, Danielle Zion. All the department heads who'd had a hand in their testing. Today they held legal pads for taking notes, not on their test scores, but on their subjective observations.

The last person to enter the room was Grace Faraday. She also had a notebook, which could mean only one thing—she was on the selection committee as well, and would help decide their fate.

And it didn't hurt that she was Jancey's oldest, dearest friend.

CHAPTER EIGHTEEN

Jancey stared at her reflection in the bathroom mirror, relishing her brief moment of pseudo-solitude. Pseudo, because there were nearly three dozen people on the other side of the door, but solitude nonetheless. By her recollection, she hadn't been completely alone in seven weeks.

Outside on Grace's lawn, the committee mingled with the other fourteen final candidates ahead of the formal announcement of who would launch first. Wade Hackett was still being held in Hilo Medical Center after suffering complications from the water contamination. Apparently they'd discovered an undiagnosed kidney condition, one that undoubtedly would have proved fatal had he encountered a toxic bacteria after launch.

The catered dinner party Grace had arranged—another extravagant luau that should have been a delightful improvement over powdered shakes and precooked casseroles—would have been more enjoyable had it not been for the butterflies everyone suffered as they awaited the news.

They'd spent two days debriefing at Tenacity Centre, discussing as a group their successes and failures. All had suggestions for how to make the eight-month flight to Mars more stimulating, and their gradual colonization a social success. Intranet video games. Instructor guides for books so they could talk about what they read. Musical instruments. Art programs on their tablets. Digital puzzles they could work together.

After the group sessions, they'd been hauled in for team and individual interviews that seemed designed to uncover negative feelings related to the project or their partner.

Jancey knew enough to approach the entire exercise with professionalism, treating every question as though her selection depended on her response. She framed their success as "just doing our job," and challenges as "interesting opportunities."

She exited the bathroom to find Grace in the hallway, Duke and Sasha by her side.

"Do I get to say I told you so?" Grace asked.

"This is more of your torture, isn't it?" She was already annoyed that Grace was holding out on her as to what the committee had decided during the day's deliberations behind closed doors. Now she was gloating about Mila too.

She'd had no chance to talk with Grace about Mila, other than to acknowledge they were sleeping together now. Hard to sneak that by when she brought Mila to stay with her in the guest house.

"I think she's adorable, and you're adorable with her."

"Let's hope you still think so tomorrow. If we aren't ecstatically happy, neither of us will be adorable." She said it pointedly and stepped nose to nose with Grace.

"Give it up, Major Beaumont. I'm not allowed to tell you anything or Charles will have my hide. Wait for me." She disappeared inside the bathroom with the dogs.

Jancey cooled her heels as much as she could, pacing the hallway anxiously. By now, the music of the luau had stopped, which meant the announcement was imminent. "Quit stalling."

Grace and her canine entourage emerged and she looped her arm through the crook of Jancey's elbow. "Very well, let's go find out who's going and when. But first, I have a question for you."

More beating around the bush.

"I want to know what happens to you and Mila if you aren't chosen."

Her heart began to pound. "Are you serious, Grace?"

"Don't read anything into that. I just want to know if it's the real thing or just a marriage of convenience."

As far as Jancey was concerned, it was a moot point, one she'd never even entertained. There was no way she and Mila would be completely shut out of the launch schedule. Even if they weren't first, it was unfathomable they'd finish in the lower four. Or lower three, since Jerry and Wade were out.

"If by some outrageous act of idiocy we get axed from the program, I'm off to Sedona. I'd like it just fine if she came too, but I'd never ask her. She needs to stay on with the project and get herself in position to try again in a few years. If anyone understands that, it's yours truly. Space isn't something you give up on, not when you're only twenty-seven."

They reached the patio, where all eyes turned in their direction. Sir Charles was at the podium ready to make the announcement.

"Does that mean you love her? Or does it mean you don't?"

"They're waiting for us, Grace."

Grace stopped cold. It was clear she wouldn't take another step until she got a reply.

Jancey turned her back to the group and lowered her voice. "If the time comes when I want to say how I feel, she should hear it first. Now can we please go sit down?"

Her dodge worked, and they finally made it to their seats.

Sir Charles, wearing an aquamarine Hawaiian shirt and white pants that matched his goatee, gripped the sides of the podium and cleared his throat. "I know everyone is presently at the end of their tether, and there is probably nothing you want to hear from me other than the results of our deliberations. However, I want to take this opportunity to thank each of you for your dedication, your enthusiasm and your contributions to the Tenacity Project. We hope to be standing here again four years from now to announce the next class of colonists. Those of you who are not selected for the first wave are strongly encouraged to reapply."

Four years. Jancey would be forty-seven. Still inside the window but would she have the heart to go through this again? She'd given it her best. Her partnership with Mila should have put them over the top.

Would they choose two women? As members of the selection committee, Grace and Danielle would champion that. But two lesbians? Yes, but maybe not first.

Jancey wanted to be first. That's where the adventure was, the danger.

"Let me ask that you refrain from public announcements until after our press conference, which is scheduled for..." He checked with his assistant on the front row. "Tomorrow afternoon. I'm so very fortunate to be surrounded by well-organized, competent staff. I remember one day last spring when Melissa came into my office. I'd left my..."

An excruciating side story no one wanted to hear. Groans all around.

"Very well. Our fourth place team will launch in approximately seven years. That team is Kamal Sidhu and David Pillay."

Kamal let out a whoop as both men jumped from their seats and shared a bear hug, slapping each other on the back.

That was a huge surprise, considering their early scores on concentration and fitness had landed them in the third group. On the other hand, Kamal was a trained astronaut from the Indian Space Agency, and they'd performed well enough on the challenges to vault several teams from the top two groups. These guys had their act together.

"The previous year, we'll be gathering in Kamal's home country of India to wish Godspeed to...Fujio and Suki Hatsu."

Applause erupted for the couple, who stood together, all smiles, and bowed to the group.

A Japanese team. How many married couples would they choose? All of a sudden she was second-guessing her decision to fly under the radar. What if sharing her feelings for Mila had been the one piece of assurance the committee needed to know they'd work well together?

"Now it's time for my beauty pageant speech, the one where I say if for any reason our winners cannot fulfill their duties, the runners-up will take their place. That is precisely our plan, ladies and gentlemen."

Jancey listened for her name. Second place. It would be all right.

"Brandon and Libby Fagan."

Her stomach dropped as she turned toward Grace, who refused to look her way. *What will you do if you aren't chosen?* It was clear now why she'd asked. The board would never pass over a man like Marlon Quinn, nor shut out the European Space Agency.

She was barely aware of Mila's cool hand clutching hers beneath the tablecloth as Sir Charles prepared his final announcement.

"And four years from now, we'll be sending the first two humans to Mars. A team of very...very competent women. Jancey Beaumont and Mila Todorov."

A tidal wave of relief washed over her as all the tension drained from her body. She couldn't have stood if her chair had been on fire, but it didn't matter. Everyone else was on their feet applauding. Even Marlon.

"We're going to Mars," Mila said, resting her forehead on Jancey's shoulder. "I might cry. Tell them it's an allergy."

* * *

Mila twisted from side to side, luxuriating in the leather executive chair in Grace's study. It was perhaps the finest chair her butt had ever known, so fine the designers of *Tenacity* needed to come right away and take down all the specs so they could replicate it for the ship.

Sir Charles had asked them not to make public announcements, but Grace assured her it was fine to tell her family.

True to her word, she'd Skyped first with her grandmother, whose reaction was equal parts pride, alarm and despondency. Pride would win out over alarm eventually, but she would never be okay with Mila leaving the planet forever.

The next call went to her mother, who failed to answer. Ten a.m. in Berlin. She probably was giving a lecture. Mila had sat in on a few of those and found them far more interesting than the lectures she got at home. Her mother would be annoyed she'd chosen Mars over Humboldt, but relieved she'd be a hundred-million miles from Frederica.

She couldn't wait to introduce her mother to Jancey, a woman nearly as old as Frederica. A woman whose accomplishments put her in a class by herself. A woman who wouldn't be intimidated by disapproval.

Her third call went to Vio, who refused to believe her news.

"Seriously, dude. I'm going to Mars with Jancey Beaumont. You get to say you knew me when."

Vio stared back from her kitchen. "When what?"

"Never mind." It was hard to tell sometimes whether Vio was trolling her or legitimately having trouble with English idioms. Mila had always insisted they speak to each other in English, since her comfort level with Dutch left something to be desired. "We're going on a press tour starting next week. They expect me to wear a dress on TV in front of the entire world. Yet another reason to leave this planet."

"You'll rock it."

"Rocket?"

"Yes, that's what I said."

"You were making a pun."

"I wasn't," Vio insisted flatly. "When are you coming back to Europe?"

"We don't have the training schedule yet. They've built most of the robotics in Cologne, so we'll have to go there for training eventually."

"Rotterdam's only three hours by train," Vio said. "I'll come visit. It would be fun to see the robotics engineers' faces when The General and JanSolo start taking down everything in sight."

"You're weird sometimes."

"It makes me interesting."

Mila couldn't deny that, as their shared interest in unusual things—video games, fantasy worlds—was the foundation of their friendship. "Don't ever change, Vio. I need to go. I'm still trying to reach my mother before she hears about me from one of her colleagues at Humboldt. She'll pin the poor fool down for hours to tell him how ridiculous it is to go to Mars."

"I have to go too. I need to study for my astronaut test so I can be the first person on Jupiter."

Mila opened her mouth to spew forth the litany of reasons that would never happen but decided instead to leave Vio's fantasy intact.

* * *

Jancey sat on a wicker love seat by the pool, mesmerized by the sight of the Red Planet rising in the eastern sky. Home.

When the last guest had gone, Grace turned out the lights on the patio so they'd have a better look at the night sky. Now she was walking out with a tray holding three snifters and a decanter. "I've already poured you a Hennessy so don't even try to say no."

"I wouldn't dream of it." A rare indulgence, one she'd enjoy without guilt now that the trials were finished. "Mars is up."

"To Mars then," Grace replied, raising her glass. She had changed from her floral dress to pink silk pajamas and a light robe. Her gray hair was down from its twist, hanging softly around her shoulders. "I know you're going to ask, so I'll save you the trouble. It wasn't even close. You and Mila were nearly perfect."

Though Jancey had known that in her gut, having it confirmed swelled her with pride. "Nearly?"

"Well...there was the matter of not securing your solar panel."

"You mean so your little troublemakers couldn't steal it? We couldn't very well sit on the roof all night and guard it. Even if we had, I'm sure you'd have found another way."

"We didn't steal it. We were very careful to treat everyone equally. You all got the same equipment, the same supplies. All the same drills and conditions. If we tampered with your habitat, we tampered with everyone's."

"Are you serious?" She distinctly remembered Mila saying she'd seen someone climb onto their dome just before dawn. If that wasn't the staff…then who was it?

"The important thing was you managed without it," Grace said. She looked past Jancey as the dogs ran to greet Mila. "Here comes your new roommate."

Jancey chuckled at her choice of words, and slid over to make a space on the love seat. "Did you finish your calls?"

"Never got my mother, but I wrote her an email. I apologize in advance if my phone rings in the middle of the night."

"It's okay." She lifted Mila's arm and scooted under it. A wave of nostalgia enveloped her as she recalled sitting in this very spot with Jill only two years ago. It wasn't Jill she'd missed. It was the warmth and comfort of resting in another woman's arms. "Grace was just saying we ran away with the vote."

"That's good, because I don't think there's anything we could have done better."

"I felt that way about all the NASA people going in. Too bad about Jerry and Wade though." And Marlon, though she didn't want to put Grace on the spot by asking where he and Jean-Paul had fallen short. It was hard not to notice their discord.

"I'm just glad they're all right now. Jerry will get another chance in four years when we draw the next crew." Grace shook her head and sighed. "But Wade…I suppose he's lucky he found out about his kidney condition now instead of later. That was very frightening for all of us."

"Did you ever find out where the contamination came from?"

"No, the water truck was clean and so was the source."

"It couldn't have come from anything Jerry and Wade did because all of us had it."

"Not all of you. Just the last four teams." That was Jerry and Wade, the Fagans, Jancey and Mila, and the Clarkes.

"That's bizarre." And it went against everything she knew about the concentration of microbes in a closed water source. The only rational explanation was contamination by the worker who'd delivered it. A moot point now.

Grace tossed back her drink and set the glass on the tray. "As much as I'd like to stay and help you plan where to put the furniture in your new home, I need to get horizontal and let my Hennessy do its job."

* * *

The warm breeze fluttered in off the ocean, a welcome change from the frigid nights on Mauna Kea. Mila lounged lengthwise on the love seat with Jancey leaning against her chest.

"I'll never be able to look at the night sky the same way again," she said, relishing the soft tickle of Jancey's fingertips along her forearms. "Especially Mars."

"Space draws me every day. It's like being homesick...except I've never been homesick for any place here on Earth. I always had an insatiable longing to go out there, and once I did, all I could think about was going again."

"And all I've ever dreamed about was going with you."

"Thank you for keeping your promise."

Mila chuckled and nuzzled the smooth skin behind Jancey's ear. "Which promise was that? I made so many."

"All of them. But mostly the one about winning. You promised me we'd win if I picked you."

That seemed like a century ago. "We both know I rode your coattails. I'd never be sitting here if I'd teamed with anyone else."

Jancey wasn't so sure of that. Mila with someone else would have been stiff competition, a real challenge for her and Marlon. Even if they'd finished first, she wouldn't have this feeling of exhilaration, this sense that everything in her life was now perfect. Not only was she returning to space, she was going with someone who could turn out to be the best thing ever to happen to her. That's what Grace had tried to tell her—Mila was her chance to have it all.

* * *

Mila had nearly dozed off when Jancey left her arms, allowing the breeze to cool her chest. She would have been content to sleep under the stars, but it soon became apparent Jancey had something else in mind.

With an almost robotic gait, she followed Jancey to the poolside cabana, where a platform bed with half a dozen overstuffed pillows was positioned so it faced the ocean. The canvas curtains that covered three sides of the structure shielded them from view of the house.

Jancey eased her onto the bed before stepping away to light several candles. When she returned, she crawled slowly until she straddled Mila's waist. "It's time we had a talk."

Talking was the last thing on her mind when Jancey sat back on her heels and removed her shirt and bra. Then she hovered above, allowing her breasts to brush her face.

She reached up to cup them but Jancey abruptly pulled away. "No hands," she whispered.

Again Jancey draped her breasts across her face, leaving one in place above her lips long enough for her to pull a rigid nipple into her mouth.

And then she took it away.

"I love you, Mila."

Though spoken as softly as the breeze, the words thundered through her. Words she feared she might never hear, now spoken like a solemn vow.

"I'm sorry I didn't tell you sooner. My heart felt it, but I wanted to be sure it was about feelings, not urges."

"You were right to wait." She ignored Jancey's earlier admonition, clutching her hands to hold them over her heart. "And you were right about how it would feel to hear it."

"I'm going to make sure you know it."

Mila had never been one to submit in bed, and it was all she could do to keep still while her body was covered with kisses. Each effort to assert herself was met with a firm hand, a hardened thigh…whatever it took to hold her in place. It was only a matter of time before she lost the battle for control, and Jancey dictated the terms of her surrender.

Jancey's lips tightened to tug on her nipple as her hand slid into the moisture between her legs. She used the essence on her fingers to paint a trail from her breast to the inside of her thigh, leaving no doubt what she intended to do next.

With her eyes tightly closed, she envisioned the path of Jancey's mouth. From her breast to her ribs. To the concave hollow just above her hip bone. Along the smooth crease at the edge of her pubic curls that led to the source of her wetness. Lips smacked softly, halting and deliberate, but ending in a flurry as Jancey reached her ultimate target.

Mila opened her legs and dug her heels into the foam mattress to thrust herself upward.

Ever in control, Jancey was there to hold her down, wrapping both arms around her thighs and spreading her outer lips with her fingertips. Mila could do nothing but wait for the mercy that would come only when Jancey felt she had teased her enough.

She pictured Jancey's tongue as it changed shape and texture. One moment it was soft and flat, lapping her as if to drink every drop. Then it went rapier-thin, stroking her inside and out. Plenty of pressure to stir a climax if only it would linger long enough over her swollen core.

Mila was bursting with want. When Jancey's lips finally touched her where she needed it most, she broke the "no hands" rule again by gripping her head and holding it in place. "Give me this before I stop breathing."

Jancey looked up, smiling with her eyes, and answered her plea. Voracious. Unrelenting. Emphatic.

They both lay still long after the tremors ceased, with Jancey resting her cheek on Mila's thigh. The balmy air cooled her damp skin but it wasn't unpleasant. Nothing could lessen her comfort, nor her happiness at being the one Jancey loved.

CHAPTER NINETEEN

Jancey awoke to the sound of voices on the veranda, a wide porch that overlooked the pool. She slid out of bed without waking Mila and peered through the slats of the shutters to see Sir Charles leaning against the rail as he spoke with Grace.

Seven thirty a.m. Pretty early for a social call. The press conference wasn't until two in the afternoon.

As quietly as she could, she laid out her clothes for what would be a media day, a freshly pressed flight suit.

By the time she stepped out of the shower, Mila had joined her in the bathroom. From her half-closed eyes, she wasn't yet fully awake. "Any idea what all that yelling is about?"

"Who's yelling?" Jancey asked.

"Sounds like Grace, but I can't make out what she's saying." She rubbed her eyes and looked at Jancey. "How come you're dressed in that?"

"We have a press conference this afternoon. Did you forget?"

"Evidently. You killed all my brain cells when you took my head off last night."

Jancey stretched up on her tiptoes and kissed Mila on the nose. "You are such an amateur. I'll go up and see what's going on while you revive your poor little brain."

She found them sitting in overstuffed bamboo chairs around a low table, each nursing a cup of coffee. Sir Charles and Grace. Though Duke and Sasha met her with wagging tails, the others were clearly upset.

It was too early in the morning for them to be having a bad day already. Whatever their problem, it appeared to be a private matter. After a cordial greeting, she poured herself a cup of coffee and turned to leave.

"Something's come up, Jancey," Grace said. She held out a glossy photo.

Jancey hesitantly approached, noting their grim faces. It was an eight by ten color shot of their analog habitat. A sunny day. Morning, given the shadows tilted toward the west. Mila was outside in her spacesuit, apparently conducting her walk-around. Then she noticed what made it remarkable—she wasn't wearing her helmet.

That was a cardinal sin, enough to disqualify them from the competition.

Obviously it was taken with a telephoto lens from the east. Not a perfect photo but clear enough. With everyone positioned along the same altitude, it could have come from the Fagans, from Jerry, or even someone farther away. "Where did you get this?"

"I received it via email last evening when I got back to my room," Sir Charles said.

The Fagans had left immediately after dinner. "Do you even know if it's real?"

"It's been authenticated," Grace replied softly. "No evidence of Photoshop."

Authenticated. At least they hadn't simply accepted it outright.

This didn't make sense at all. Why wasn't Mila wearing her communications cap? They'd been in constant contact every time one of them went out. Every single time. "This must have been taken before the analog ever started. I remember we tried

our spacesuits on when we were up there setting up the dome…
we walked around a little to get used to them. Maybe Mila
walked outside, but it shouldn't have counted against us then."

Sir Charles shook his head. "My staff tells me it's geocoded
and time-stamped for last Thursday, just before we announced
the Super X solar storm."

Jancey recalled the morning clearly. She'd stayed in bed
while Mila had done the walk-around. In fact, she was still
inside the sleeping chamber when Mila returned, so she hadn't
actually seen her in her spacesuit.

She picked up the photo to study the details. No sign of
Mila's phone. No earbuds. No wireless device affixed to her ear.
Her hands were encased in thick gloves, so it wasn't feasible that
she'd been using the tiny keypad on her cell phone. How was
she communicating?

"There's something wrong here."

"I couldn't agree more," Sir Charles said. "A simple mistake
might have been forgiven had Ms. Todorov admitted to doing
this accidentally. Instead, she signed a form indicating she had
obeyed all the rules and restrictions, and that clearly is false. I'm
afraid there is no alternative but to disqualify your team."

His words hit her like a physical punch to the gut.

Grace sat forward and shook her finger. "You're being
hasty, Charles. This is a decision for the committee. The entire
committee. Regardless of this single incident—which could
never actually happen in space—I would still argue that Mila
and Jancey represent the project's very best chance for success.
At the very least, we should hear from Mila."

"Hear from me about what?" Mila walked casually onto
the veranda and poured hot water over a teabag. She too was
dressed in her flight suit, its sleeves rolled to her elbows. Her
hair, still wet from the shower, was pulled back in a tie.

Jancey could barely contain her pique at her casual demeanor.
"You need to get over here and explain yourself before we get
disqualified."

"What?"

Grace took the photo from her hands and handed it to Mila. "This was sent to Sir Charles last night. Jancey was just telling us there must be a valid explanation for this."

Mila studied the photo in silence, her face growing redder by the second. "When was this taken?"

"Last week…right before they called up to announce the Super X. You went outside that morning to do the walk-around."

She needed to hear Mila offer an explanation, however feeble it might be. Her helmet was broken. A bee had flown inside and she'd been forced to rip it off.

"I have no memory of this. As far as I know, I always put on my helmet to go outside. It was automatic."

Under the circumstances, that was as good a response as any. An oversight was better than a deliberate flouting of the rules.

Grace turned to Sir Charles. "Which means she was being honest when she signed her form saying she'd adhered to the rules. That's something the committee should consider."

Jancey's question was more pointed. "But do you distinctly remember wearing it? You talked to me while you were outside. Did you have it on?"

"I…" She hesitated too long to be convincing. "I thought so."

"Your uncertainty is problematic," Sir Charles said, and then turned to Grace. "The issue was raised by one of the competing teams, along with charges of favoritism. Everyone knows about your friendship with the major. That was something we all were willing to overlook when it became obvious they were the better team. This clouds that. I worry the press will focus on infighting among our astronauts instead of the mission. Or worse, they'll criticize the whole project based on the selection process. We can't allow something like this to undermine our integrity."

Jancey felt her panic rise as she whipped her head from Grace to Sir Charles and back.

Grace shot her a worried look before pressing her case. "With all due respect, Charles, we owe it to all the members of the committee to allow them to make the decision together. Perhaps there is something short of disqualification…Jancey and Mila could forfeit their position and fly later in the rotation."

He lumbered to his feet, leaning heavily on his cane. "There's very little time to act. We have reporters flying in this afternoon from all over the world. Call the other members of the committee. Tell them to come to Tenacity Centre right away."

If his dour tone was any indication, the meeting would be a waste of time.

* * *

Mila drew in a deep breath and grasped the door handle of their bedroom, relieved to find that Jancey hadn't locked her out. She was shocked to see her stuffing her belongings into a suitcase.

"What are you doing? Nothing's been decided. They're taking it to the whole committee. We might get bumped down but Grace won't let them disqualify us."

"Don't kid yourself," Jancey spat, not even looking up from her task. "You heard what Sir Charles said. We went in with a strike against us because Grace was my friend and they didn't want anyone to think they were playing favorites. And don't think for a minute they wanted the first two people on Mars to be a pair of lesbians. We *made* them choose us. Our scores were so high, they had no other credible alternative. And now we've lost that advantage."

"I don't know how this happened. I have no recollection of going out without my helmet but…"

"But what?" The brusque tone wasn't frustration or disappointment. It was anger.

"It's just that I'd taken that zolpidem a few hours earlier because I couldn't get to sleep. It's possible I did something without being aware."

"Great, so it's my fault for making you take a sleeping pill. That's rich."

"I didn't say that. I'm just trying to figure out how it happened. I remember when I came back in telling you about Brandon Fagan staring at me. We joked about how creepy he was, how we wouldn't ask him to dinner if we all ended up on Mars. I think he's the one who took the photo. Maybe he was looking at me like that because I didn't have my helmet on."

"It doesn't matter who took the photo." Jancey dumped the contents of the nightstand's drawer into a small bag, zipped it closed and tossed it into her suitcase. "What I find so maddening, so…excruciating, is that I watched you go in and out two or three times a day for six weeks, and the *one time* I didn't see you, you went out without your helmet."

It hurt to see her so quick to believe the worst, though it was hard to argue with the evidence. Brandon Fagan obviously had caught her outside bare-headed. And being the jerk he was, he took a photo in order to bring her down.

She shuddered to recall the night she'd exited the library and he'd all but accused her of cheating during the underwater exercise. The confrontation had unnerved her and caused her to doubt herself. It was Jancey who'd assured her then she'd done nothing wrong, but for all Mila knew, Brandon had taken his concerns to Zion, since she'd supervised the test. Now he was taking them to Sir Charles.

One thing she remembered with crystal clarity was seeing him outside his habitat when she first stepped out. It pissed her off to think he just happened to have a camera and telephoto lens at the very moment she appeared without her helmet. He probably carried it with him all the time just waiting to catch her.

Or what if all of it was a setup?

It was perfectly rational to believe he had it in for her. Even though it supposedly had been authenticated, Brandon was too smart to get caught Photoshopping. He could have tweaked the time stamp on a photo that was taken before the analog ever started.

"I need to figure this out," she said.

Jancey rolled her eyes dramatically and continued to pack.

Mila grabbed her shoulders and forced her to pay attention. "Seriously. If I did this, I'll take full responsibility. But I need to be sure."

"You can't take full responsibility, Mila. You can only take half, and I have to take the other half. And you know what? I'm not even angry at you. I'm angry at myself. Protocols matter in space. Even the smallest mistake can kill you, and it was my job to check you. I let sex get in the way of that. I knew all along we needed to focus, and I didn't. I let down my guard to satisfy my stupid libido. Whatever happens to us, I deserve it. *We* deserve it." She jerked her shoulders free and stomped into the bathroom to collect her toiletries.

"Where do you think you're going?"

"I don't know and I don't care. But I'm not going to sit on a stage smiling and clapping for somebody else when it should have been me."

"Yes, you will, Jancey. You can't throw a tantrum for the whole world to see and then expect people to respect you. The Tenacity Project is bigger than us. It's Mars! Besides, you don't know yet what the board will decide. They might only bump us down, but we'll still get to go. Fourth is better than not going at all. If you don't believe me, ask Marlon." A risky thing to say, since right now Jancey probably was wishing she'd chosen him instead.

Jancey stopped abruptly and sat in a heap on the bed, looking as though she might cry. "I've never wanted anything so much in my life. I'm not going to apologize for that."

"You don't have to. I've never wanted anything more than to go into space with you, and I'm not going to give that up. No matter how long that takes, we'll make it happen." She summoned every ounce of courage to join her on the bed, ever so slowly drawing her into a hug.

Jancey resisted at first, stiffening at her touch. Then gradually she relaxed, laying her head on Mila's shoulder. She allowed herself one sob before straightening and pulling away.

CHAPTER TWENTY

Jancey had taken a long run along the coastal highway to burn the adrenaline her body had produced to fight or flee. Now freshly showered for the second time today, she felt the energy building inside again as they prepared for the announcement.

For all her bluster about remaining loyal to the program, Mila's face was a mask of gloom as they walked together into the lobby of Tenacity Centre, which had been set up with a podium and several rows of chairs.

Mila had spent the entire morning hovering over her computer after receiving a digital copy of the photo from Grace. She had to see it for herself. If her incoherent grumbling was any indication, she'd grudgingly come to terms with its genuineness.

"You were right. It's not over yet," Jancey said as they took their seats on the second row. "If it were an open-and-shut case, we'd have gotten our answer by now."

Grace had promised to text her about the committee's vote. They'd been meeting in the conference room for over four hours, something Jancey took as a hopeful sign. Any discussion lasting this long meant others besides Grace were fighting for her. They needed only two or three members to force a compromise—perhaps launching in third or fourth place instead of first. She could live with that.

Marlon slid into a seat beside her and looked around at all the reporters and cameras. "Pretty exciting, isn't it? I bet you didn't sleep at all. I, on the other hand, got my first good night's sleep in six weeks."

She couldn't bring herself to tell him about the controversy, not when the jury was still out. Once the rumors began to spread, she'd share with him the truth, no matter what the committee decided.

"I'm so sorry about you and Jean-Paul. I know how much this mission meant to you. I hope you won't give up."

After peering over his shoulder to see his partner conversing with Jerry, he lowered his voice. "It's just as well. I'm not sure I could have endured a life in such a small space with someone so moody. I'll try again in the next round. Maybe I'll draw a better match."

"I hear you. I lucked out with Mila." Notwithstanding the fact that they were on the brink of disqualification thanks to her carelessness.

Their carelessness. It would haunt her forever that she'd been too lazy to get out of bed that morning, that she'd lolled around in a sensual haze while Mila went outside on her own.

Cameras began flashing as the committee entered en masse with Sir Charles in front.

Jancey's heart sank to see Grace slip out the front door. Only one thing would have caused her to skip the press conference.

"Ladies and gentlemen, I'm sorry to keep you waiting." Wearing the faintest of smiles on what should have been the project's most triumphant day to date, Sir Charles walked the press and visitors through the basics of the selection process, details they probably knew from the briefing materials. Next was the launch schedule. "Without further ado, I'd like to announce our four teams. The first two people to colonize Mars...Americans Brandon and Libby Fagan."

"What the hell?" Marlon bolted upright in his chair and swiveled toward her.

Jancey couldn't bear to look at him. Nor could she take Mila's hand, which tapped against her thigh.

"They'll be joined twelve months later by another couple, this one from Japan. Fujio and Suki Hatsu."

It wasn't even close. You and Mila were nearly perfect.

So how far would they fall?

"...Kamal Sidhu from India and South Africa's David Pillay."

She was shaking so hard, she gripped the table for support.

"And our final team, representing America and France, Marlon Quinn and Jean-Paul Robillard."

It was all Jancey could do to breathe. Marlon was up and back-slapping Jean-Paul as if they were long lost brothers.

At least her humiliation was confined to their colleagues, since the earlier results were never publicly announced. That said, it was only a matter of time before it was leaked why she and Mila had been disqualified.

Already, Shel Montgomery had spotted her and was inching closer with her notepad.

Jancey had no intention of sticking around for an interview. When Sir Charles opened the floor to questions, she took advantage of the reporters' forward surge to slip out the side door.

Grace was sitting on a teak bench beneath the portico, primly dressed for the press event in a pale yellow pantsuit and floral scarf. Judging from her red-rimmed eyes, she was as devastated as Jancey.

"I'm so sorry. I did everything I could."

"I know you did. As bad as I feel right now, you have no idea how much it means to me to know I have a friend like you who would fight for me like that." She tugged her from the bench. "Now let's get out of here before the press finds out what happened. I left the keys to the Jag with Mila."

"For what it's worth, Danielle Zion was in your corner too."

"Good to know." Though it meant they were outvoted by the men. As much as that stung, at least this time there had been women in the room with a vote. "I had a feeling from the very beginning Sir Charles would want to send a couple…a straight couple. Looks like he got his wish."

A steady rain was falling, but Grace was prepared with a large umbrella, which she opened as they exited the portico toward the parking lot. "There's still a chance, Jancey. I don't think anyone on the board believes Marlon and Jean-Paul will survive the training together. It's clear to everyone they rub each other the wrong way. If you and Mila stay close to the project, you might—"

"Oh, no. I'm not going to hang out playing fifth fiddle. This was it. My last hurrah."

"Now you're just being stubborn. Isn't it better to launch seven years from now than not at all?"

Jancey mulled over that question as they drove the seaside highway back to the house. "I could wait that long if I knew for sure if it would happen. But not with the uncertainty. I don't think I could stand watching another open seat given to somebody else. Especially after we did everything we could to earn it."

"You did earn it. If not for that one mistake…you must be furious with Mila."

"Actually, I'm not." Holding her emotions in check, she explained how she blamed herself for not performing a proper check. "If I'd done my job, we'd be getting ready for Mars."

"How is she taking it?"

"We haven't talked much. She spent most of the morning commiserating online with her friend in the Netherlands. If I had to guess, I'd say she's in total denial."

"She'll come around in a couple of days," Grace said. "Sir Charles is very interested in having her stay on as part of the engineering team. And he wants you to join the training staff. That would put you both in perfect position to step in if there's an opening."

"The answer's still no."

"If you won't consider staying in the program for yourself, at least consider Mila. You two made the perfect team. She deserves another chance."

"I couldn't agree more, but not another chance with me. If there's one thing that's abundantly clear, it's that Mila and I do not make the perfect team. We make a terrible team. She's a distraction for me. I'm a distraction for her. And astronauts can't have distractions." She huffed sarcastically at the thought of Brandon Fagan tapping his watch in the bar to hurry Libby along. "I think the only reason the Fagans made it so far is because they don't like each other enough to be distracted."

Grace whipped the car into the driveway with such force that Jancey's seat belt locked and dug into her shoulder.

"Whoa! When did you turn into Danica Patrick?"

"I hate it when you pretend you don't have any feelings," Grace fumed. "We both know it's an act, so just stop it."

"Who cares if it's an act? Feelings don't matter in this business. All any of us really care about is getting to space."

Grace parked under the portico and got out and slammed the door.

"Come on, Grace. Do you honestly think Mila cares more about me than going to Mars? If she does, then she doesn't deserve to go."

"At least she cares about something."

After nearly twelve years of friendship, she could tell when Grace was deliberately pushing her buttons.

"I know what you're doing, Grace. What do you want from me?"

"I want you to be true to yourself. The Jancey Beaumont I know doesn't quit."

"Until now. Look at who they picked. Jean-Paul's the oldest, and he's forty-six. That's only three years older than me. Do you seriously think they're going to send me to Mars when I'm fifty?"

She also feared the collapse of the Tenacity Project. If the first colonists failed to thrive—a reasonable concern since they weren't sending their best team—the funders would pull the plug.

Konani appeared in the kitchen and offered to fix chi-chis, but Grace waved her off, storming into the lanai where she poured a pair of Bushmills over ice. Jancey declined and watched her pound the first one back and carry the second to an overstuffed teak chair.

It was tempting not to follow her but she knew it was expected. "I don't get why you're so angry at me. I'm the one who ought to be throwing things."

"So why aren't you? You've just totally disengaged. You're walking away from the chance to go to Mars. You're walking away from Mila. I suppose you'll walk away from me next."

"Why would I do that? You're practically the only friend I've got."

"You have Mila. She loves you. That's obvious to anyone with eyes." She threw off her jacket and loosened her scarf before slumping deep into the plush cushions. "The first time someone comes along and gives you everything you claim to want, what do you do? You move the goalpost. What is it you want now?"

"Right now I just want to screw it all. No more space program, no more university politics. And no more dead-end relationships." She cringed at the self-pitying dejection in her voice. "I've got my property in Sedona. Maybe it's time I put a house on it."

"So now Mila's just a dead-end relationship. Do you really expect me to believe you aren't blaming her for this? You're throwing your whole future away so you can punish her. But on the outside, you're putting on a face. You want everyone to think you're noble...that you're the one taking responsibility."

The accusation stung, especially coming from Grace, who had always been on her side, even when she was being borderline unreasonable. Was there truth to what she said about Mila? Undoubtedly yes. It was Mila's fault, even though Jancey could have prevented it. Mila should have been responsible for herself, and she should have taken double care because she also had an obligation to her partner.

Finally she'd met someone who could give her everything. Instead, that woman had taken it all away.

"I need you to do something for me, Grace. You don't have to like it."

* * *

Mila found herself terrified behind the wheel of the expensive sports car. Four vehicles were lined up behind her, itching to pass at the first opportunity. When she reached a long stretch with a dotted yellow line, she slowed and let them around.

She'd have been completely at ease piloting someone's billion-dollar spaceship, but not Grace's Jaguar. If something happened to it, she'd have to look her in the eye and take the blame.

It annoyed her that Jancey had bailed on her with Grace, leaving her to talk to reporters on her own. She'd answered Shel's questions by dancing around the truth, chalking up the results to the excellent performances of the four teams that were chosen. Not that her deflection would matter—word would get out eventually. Maybe Jancey had the right idea after all. She should have bailed too.

She carefully squeezed into the garage, getting out twice to check the proximity of her rear bumper so it wouldn't be crushed when the door came down. If she'd exercised this much care on Mauna Kea, they'd be readying for their trip to Mars. She'd never forgive herself for blowing the chance to be first, but was more determined than ever to ace the next trial.

Grace and the dogs met her in the foyer. "Come into the lanai. Would you like a drink?"

Until that moment, she'd never really understood the appeal of getting drunk. "No, thank you."

She expected to find Jancey in the lanai but she was nowhere to be seen. "Where's Jancey? I should go talk to her."

"That probably ishn't a good idea. Sh-she's in a very bad mood." A noticeable slur.

"That makes two of us. I really thought they'd let us fly, even if it was third or fourth. Jancey always said we had to make them choose us because they wouldn't want to."

"Probably some truth to that. Men!" Grace poured an amber drink from a decanter. "What really happened?"

Mila wanted the answer to that as much as anyone. "I don't know. It's not like I did it on purpose. I can't even remember it. Putting on the suit was automatic. Same order every time—from the bottom up. I just can't believe I would have walked out before I put my helmet on."

There were other things that stood out as strange. The collar on the spacesuit was stiff. Without the helmet weighing it down, it would have stood up awkwardly. Surely she would have noticed that—just like she would have noticed the sun in her eyes as soon as she stepped outside. Her instinct would have been to retrieve her sunglasses. And Jancey was right about her cell phone. How could she have used it without her comm cap?

And yet she had. A picture was worth a thousand excuses.

"I should go talk to Jancey," Mila said.

"Let's jush give her a while. She's upset."

"Who could blame her?"

Jancey had hardly spoken three words to her at Tenacity Centre, dismissing her apology by taking the blame herself. Then she'd put on a brave face right up until the moment Marlon and Jean-Paul got the nod.

A single lapse so small she couldn't even remember it. Their only chance was to try again in four years.

"You know the committee, Grace. Is it worth coming back to try again?"

"Absolutely! They didn't want this to happen. It wasn't the *photo* that upset everyone. It was the *note*...the note that came with it. It accused us of *favoritism*. *Me* in particular because Jancey was shtaying here." The effects of whatever was in the decanter were becoming more and more apparent with her emphasis on certain words and dramatic hand waving. "They shaid it was *obvious* we picked Jancey before the competition ever *shtarted*."

That was bullshit, the kind of trash talk that spewed from sore losers. Even if it were true, why should the committee have to defend their choice? It was their money. They could send whomever they wanted.

"Charles has the skin of a boiled onion," Grace spat. "Completely withers at the least bit of criticism. He couldn't bear to have people say mean things about his *beloved* Tenacity Project. The child he never had. And everyone kishes his *butt* because they want to keep their jobs. All but Danielle…she's got guts, that girl. I like her. I like her quite a lot," she added, her lascivious look making her meaning clear.

"Did you ever find out for sure who sent it, Grace? Was it Brandon Fagan?"

"Who   else?   Sniveling…self-righteous…brown-nosing *ashwipe*. You should have heard him this morning when they called him in." She slugged the rest of her drink and stumbled to the wet bar to pour another. In a whiny voice meant to mock him, she added, "This is so difficult for me, Sir Charles. I was worried if it got out later, people would question the overshight of the project."

"That almost sounds like a threat."

"I thought so too but Charles bought his pearl-clutching. Told us all it might jeopardize our support with funders. That's what really shcared him…having his competence questioned. He had to look tough."

The whole episode sickened Mila, but she couldn't push back at all. Faced with graphic evidence of someone skirting the rules, she might have voted the same way. She rose with dread and said, "I better go out there and talk to Jancey."

"No, no! Shtay here and talk to me. I want to know what you're going to do next."

Her plea was so emphatic, Mila hurriedly sat back down. "To tell you the truth, I'm not sure. Svein Helland wants me to stay with the program, but now I'm not so sure Sir Charles really wants that."

"He will if he wants my support."

"Let's hope it doesn't come to that." Her greater concern was Jancey. From the very beginning, she'd vowed to call it quits if she failed to make the launch team. "I really need to see what Jancey's going to do."

Grace let her leave this time, and she realized why as soon as she entered the guesthouse. Jancey's blue flight suit, T-shirts and khakis—everything issued by the Tenacity Project—were folded neatly on the bed. But her suitcase was gone.

CHAPTER TWENTY-ONE

The United Airlines ticket agent was postcard beautiful. Silky dark hair, bright teeth and creamy Polynesian skin. "I'm so sorry, Ms. Beaumont. We aren't allowed to accept your baggage until four hours before your flight. You'll have to return at six thirty."

Jancey tried to smile through her disappointment. It made sense the airline didn't want her suitcase cluttering their baggage room all day. The problem was it left her nowhere to go for the next two hours. Her overnight flight to Los Angeles didn't board until ten, and she'd mistakenly assumed she could hide out in the departure lounge all afternoon and evening.

The exterior of the Hilo airport was one long portico with the occasional concrete bench, but no shops or vending machines where she could get even a bottle of water.

At least she was out of the rain.

And out of the house. It was a cowardly escape but still preferable to a confrontation with Mila. The way she was feeling right now, she probably would have hurled foul-mouthed abuse and blame, no matter that she knew their disqualification was as much her fault as Mila's. She was spoiling for a fight and in no condition to fight fair.

Hurting Mila wasn't something she wanted to do. Both of them were devastated, and Mila already had the burden of feeling responsible.

She shook her head sardonically when a taxi door opened to deposit the Clarkes at the curb, their dream shattered too. They walked past on their way to the Hawaiian Airlines counter, staring at the ground as though lost in thought.

Jancey made no move to engage them, turning slightly on her bench so they wouldn't see her. Genuine misery didn't love company at all.

By the dour look on their faces, they'd reached the same decision as she to bail on the Tenacity Project. The still-hopeful candidates—Mila and some of the younger ones from the earlier rounds—would hang around on the periphery to try again in four years, while the NASA and ESA alums would likely move on. This was their closing act, one last gasp at hanging onto their fading space careers. The Clarkes were probably heading to high-paying executive jobs in the aerospace industry. Jerry too, and the Norwegian couple as well.

A chair like that was waiting for her if she were willing to kiss political butts. She'd had enough politics at the university. Besides, she couldn't work in the industry if it meant preparing others for space while knowing she'd never launch again.

No, the time was right to make the move to Sedona. Experiments to run, books to write. She'd be the foremost authority on self-sufficiency, the go-to expert on food production in hostile environments. No more tedious meetings. No public relations. No dress shoes.

And no one to share her bed, to appreciate her music. No partner in her work, in her life.

For a very short time, Mila had made her believe she could have it all. And overnight she'd lost it.

"You weren't even going to say goodbye?"

Jancey closed her eyes and pinched the bridge of her nose at the familiar voice behind her. So much for her escape. "I was going to call you."

"And now you don't have to." Mila sat next to her on the bench, looking around casually as though taking in the scenery. "So what would you have said?"

Her challenging tone was irksome but the question was fair. "I would have encouraged you to stick with the Tenacity Project and try again. I'd have wished you luck…and probably told you to call me if you ever needed anything."

Mila bobbed her head in agreement, still not looking at her. "But nothing about us. Nothing about you and me making love. Or me promising to love you forever no matter what. Surely you understood 'no matter what' meant even if we failed to make the cut this time."

This time. The frustrating truth was Mila believed they still had a chance. She was unshaken by their disqualification. Still devoted to their shared dream, unable to grasp that eight years—the time before the second round of teams began to launch—was an eternity for someone already forty-three.

"The future isn't about our feelings for each other, Mila. I'll be forty-seven years old the next time trials roll around. They aren't going to choose someone that old."

"They will if we make them. If we do everything just like we did this time—but with no mistakes."

"I can't spend the next four years of my life sucking up to a selection committee that's willing to throw reason under the bus for the sake of public relations. Tenacity isn't a scientific mission—it's a circus and Sir Charles is the ringmaster. You and I both know there wasn't anyone better qualified for a lifetime space mission than us. I can't function in a system that would ignore such a basic fact as that."

The same way she couldn't function in a university setting where faculty meetings, exam schedules and office hours were more important than research and sharing what she knew with her students.

Mila finally turned to face her. "It was my fault this time and I learned from it. I promise you it won't happen again. Every minute, every second…I'll focus on the mission."

Jancey shook her head vehemently. "You're missing the point. You don't just decide not to make mistakes. They happen, and they can happen again no matter how careful you are. Grace said it wasn't even close—we did better than all the other teams in practically everything. If one inconsequential mistake outweighs six weeks of that, then you can be sure they'll pull it out and use it against us next time if there's somebody else who serves their PR purposes better. It's their chess game and we're just the goddamn pawns."

A young couple walked by, the mother herding two preschoolers while the father pushed an infant in a stroller. He gave her a scolding look.

Realizing she'd practically shouted a curse word, Jancey mouthed an apology.

"So as far as you're concerned, we don't stand a chance no matter what we do." Mila began pacing the small courtyard in front of the bench. "Fine, then I might as well come with you. Where are we going?"

Now Mila was being obstinate, obviously thinking she could make her change her mind by pretending to sacrifice herself. It wasn't going to work.

"I'm going to Sedona. You're going to stay and ingratiate yourself to Sir Charles and the rest of the committee until it's time for the next trial. Your chances will be better without me."

Mila looked skyward and blew out an exasperated breath. "Now who's missing the point? I don't want to go if I can't go with you."

"That's insane. This is Mars we're talking about. Opportunities for something that big only come along once every hundred years. You'd be crazy to pass that up." As soon as she said it, she braced for Mila to throw those very words back in her face.

"I'd be even crazier to pass up the chance to live out my life with the one person who means more to me than anything I could ever dream for myself." She squatted in front, pinning her in place with eyes darker than night. "If I have to choose between you and Mars, I'll choose you. Every time."

The heartfelt declaration warmed her only for an instant. Then it became an accusation—not from Mila, but from Monica, Lindsay and Jill. She'd never chosen one of them first.

"I've never done that for anyone, Mila, and I'm not going to let you do it for me."

"You don't get to make my decisions. The only way you could possibly make me stay with Tenacity is convince me you don't love me. Good luck with that. You took a long time to say it, but I knew you meant it. And I know you didn't suddenly stop loving me over something you call an inconsequential mistake. You can't control your feelings about me, no matter how much you wish you could."

"That's pretty arrogant"—she briefly considered biting her tongue—"even for you."

"So tell me I'm wrong."

Simple enough. All she had to do was say it. With conviction. "What difference does it make what I tell you if you've already decided I'm lying?" Feeling suddenly claustrophobic, Jancey pushed past her to stand.

"I asked you to convince me. Can you do that or not?"

Jancey knew she couldn't pull that off for one simple reason—it wasn't true.

"If you're trying to make me say it again, fine. I *do* love you. But that isn't some magic word that solves everything. We want different things."

"I want you. That's all that matters." Mila took her seat on the bench, clearly energized after forcing the admission.

"But it solves nothing. It's because I love you that I can't let you give up on Mars. I know what it's like to have that kind of dream burning inside you for as long as you can remember. You're only twenty-seven years old. If you stick with Tenacity, you'll have at least three more chances to make the cut, and I can't be the one to take that away from you."

Mila bolted to her feet and grabbed Jancey's shoulders. "Did you not hear what I just said? I don't want to go without you. If you plan on spending the rest of your life out in the middle of nowhere, I want to be there too."

"You can't possibly mean that." How could anyone with Mila's expertise in astronautical engineering give up the chance for a future in space?

"I love you, Jancey. And it's not because you're that daring astronaut that gave a little girl something to dream about. It's because of who you are underneath. You're intense…passionate. Righteous about everything you do. Do you have any idea how weak that makes me? I'm your prisoner. I'd follow you into the freaking Kool-Aid volcano."

"Kilauea," she said absently. There was no point in pushing back. What could she possibly say to someone so devoted? It was what she'd wanted all her life.

Mila snatched the handle of her suitcase and took a step toward the parking lot. "I don't care what you do from this minute forward. I plan to do it with you. So you can't leave yet. You have to wait for me."

Jancey gripped her wrist, freezing them in place. "You win, Todorov. If you aren't going to take no for an answer, I might as well let you come with me."

Her feet suddenly left the ground as Mila swept her into a bear hug. "You won't ever be sorry, Jancey."

She was sure of that. For the first time in her life, nothing mattered more than proving herself worthy of a love so deep.

* * *

Mila stowed the suitcase in the closet of their bedroom at the guesthouse and returned to the kitchenette. For all her effort to appear cool and confident, she still quaked inside over almost being left behind. The disappointment of being cut from Tenacity was trivial next to the heartbreak she'd have suffered from losing Jancey.

Even though Jancey had capitulated on her decision to leave without her, their agreement to settle together in Sedona still felt tenuous. Jancey had warned her not to trust declarations or promises that were coerced. Nothing said arm-twisting like storming off with her suitcase.

"Did you see Grace when we came in?" Jancey asked, handing her a glass of lemonade.

"She's probably resting." *Probably passed out* was more like it. She'd been knocking back at least her third drink when Mila left for the airport.

"She'll be surprised to find me back here."

"Don't bet on it. I told her I wasn't coming back without you." She followed Jancey outside to a shaded area of the patio, and was pleased when she chose an oversized chaise lounge that would accommodate both of them. The rain had stopped, and the setting sun was painting the clouds in colorful pastels.

Her cell phone chirped, a text from Vio. The third one today asking her to Skype.

"Do you need to get that?"

"Later. Right now I want to hear about how we're going to live off the grid in Sedona."

"It's not about living off the grid. It's about putting all the theories of sustainability into practice and proving they can work in any environment. We do that and we're one step closer to perpetuating a colony. That's my whole life's work."

"A real-life Rubik's Cube," Mila said. She wrapped her arm around Jancey's shoulder.

"Exactly. There are many ways to solve it, but one's more efficient than the others. I was on my way to answering that question on *Guardian*, but I had to jettison everything I'd built to make room for the cosmonauts. What's waiting for me in Sedona is my chance to finish what I started."

Mila didn't doubt for a moment Jancey could do everything she said. It was ridiculous that she wasn't leading the first team to Mars. "Sir Charles is an idiot. The Fagans are going to starve to death before the next ship arrives with supplies."

"Don't get me started," Jancey muttered testily.

"Sorry. So what's my job going to be? It doesn't sound like you'll have much use for an astronautical engineer in the Red Rock Country." She'd Googled it the first time she'd heard Jancey talk about it.

"What would you like to do?"

"I think my first job should be to supervise building our house. I want to make absolutely certain it has a flush toilet and a hot shower."

"Pfft. Only five days back and you've gone soft already."

"I'd give it up for Mars, but Sedona? I don't think so." Joking about toilets and showers was easier than contemplating how she'd fit into Jancey's plans. "Where's the nearest university? Maybe I should take some chemistry and biology courses so I can help you with your research."

"That sounds like a..." Jancey squirmed free and swung her legs over the side of the chaise, running both her hands through her hair. "That's a terrible idea, Mila. I'm not going to turn you into a lab assistant. You could be one of the top engineers in the space industry."

"Not in Sedona."

"It isn't right. I can't let you waste that, no matter how much I want you with me." She pushed herself up and began to pace.

"We already had this conversation. It's decided."

"No."

Mila's gut tightened again, the same as when she'd entered the bedroom and found Jancey gone. "What do you mean no? I told you I don't care what else happens. All that matters to me is being with you."

"That isn't all that matters. Tenacity needs you...and as much as I hate to say it, it needs me too. We certainly earned our chance to be a part of this." She hung her head and muttered, "God, I can't believe I'm going to say this. Fine. We stay. But only if they let us work in the same place. I'm not going to Japan while you go to Germany."

"Yes!" Mila pumped her fist triumphantly. "And we try again in the next round?"

"If that's what you want."

"You've just made me the happiest person in the world. No, the universe."

CHAPTER TWENTY-TWO

Jancey zipped her khakis and took a moment to study her reflection in the full-length mirror. Not twenty-four hours ago she'd left her Tenacity Project clothing folded neatly on the bed, retired forever. Now she was relishing the uniform again, feeling good about belonging to a team, about having a mission.

Amazing how Mila Todorov had changed everything.

She leaned into the bathroom where Mila was taking a shower behind a frosted glass door that showed her outline but no details. "I heard Grace talking to the dogs up on the veranda. Think I'll go bang some pots and pans and see if her head hurts."

"Don't give her too much grief. She was right about us, you know. We need each other."

"The woman knows me better than I know myself. You have no idea how annoying that is." And reassuring, especially when she needed a push in the right direction. "Oh, and you told me to remind you to call Vio."

"I will."

Jancey found Grace at an umbrella table by the pool and bowed deeply to her applause. Obviously, she'd expected Mila to bring her back.

Outwardly, she'd recovered from her bout of the "Irish Flu." She was dressed elegantly in a white turban and pale blue pantsuit, with a linen napkin tucked around the collar to protect her from breakfast spills.

The table was set for three.

"Konani made breakfast," Grace said, gesturing toward a side table. A fruit tray, a bread basket, egg cups and a large carafe of coffee.

Jancey noticed a leather folio on one of the chairs. "Heading out?"

"Dog and pony show with some of the astronomers at ten o'clock." Grace eyed her outfit. "I take it from your choice of T-shirts you've decided to join our team again. That'll make everyone happy. Especially yours truly."

"I've decided to do what's best for Mila, and that's to give her another chance to fly. She's too young to give up on her dreams."

"And so are you. I promise you I'm going to stay after Charles until he fixes this. Both of you need to stay ready."

As much as Jancey wanted that to happen, she couldn't hold Grace to such a promise. Too many egos, too many variables. All she could do was give Mila her best effort.

"What I care about most right now is being with Mila. If you have any strings to pull, see if you can get us assigned together somewhere. I don't care if it's Germany, Japan or Houston, as long as both of us are there."

"How about Hawaii?"

An island paradise to share not only with the woman she loved, but also with her best friend. "That wouldn't suck at all."

As she leaned over to toast her orange juice glass to Grace's, a shriek came from inside the guesthouse.

"What the hell?"

They didn't have to wait long for an answer. Mila burst through the palms. "Get in here! You have to see this."

* * *

Mila was shaking with excitement when Jancey and Grace reached her room. "You aren't going to believe what Vio found. We were set up. The photo is fake."

"I knew it!" Jancey said.

Grace shook her head. "That can't be. Charles said his people authenticated it."

"They were probably looking for Photoshop," Mila explained. "That's what most people use. This one was done with something called Bulwark. It's architecture software. They use it to add details to their computer renderings, like furniture and landscaping. It automatically sizes everything…makes it look seamless. My friend Vio—she's an architect—I sent her the picture and she opened it in Bulwark. Look what happens."

She played a video clip from their Skype chat with Vio describing the process as she demonstrated on a second laptop. *"Notice how I move my cursor all over the photo and it's an arrow. But when I get to your head, it turns into a hand. That tells me I can grab it."* A halo of red dirt that blended into the background encircled her head as she dragged it to the side, revealing a helmet underneath.

"I'll be damned," Grace mumbled. "You had your helmet on the whole time."

Jancey pounded the desk with anger. "It has to be Jean-Paul. He's the architect."

"That's what I thought too until I saw this."

Vio continued with her demonstration. *"Then I noticed I got another hand when I passed over the name tag. I was able to blow up what was underneath. I'm sending you a screen grab."*

Mila stopped the video and clicked on an icon on her desktop. The close-up photo of the tape was clear—*L FAGAN.* "It wasn't even me. You remember when they gave me her flight suit by mistake? That's because we're exactly the same size."

Grace started for the door. "I'll get my car keys. We need to show this to Charles right away."

Jancey's hand on Mila's shoulder kept her from rising. "My god, Mila. Do you know what this means?"

She wanted to scream with joy but didn't dare. "I'm trying not to get my hopes up. There aren't any guarantees Sir Charles will make this right."

"Don't be so sure. Something tells me Grace won't take no for an answer this time." Jancey planted a kiss atop her head. "I'm so sorry. I should have believed in you."

"You don't have to be sorry. I didn't believe in myself either. I should have been able to say for sure it wasn't real, and I couldn't do that. I got caught not paying attention to details."

"So did I. But we learned a lesson about looking out for each other. That's something I won't ever forget. And I won't let you forget it either."

* * *

"I'm telling you, something weird's going on," Jerry said. "Are y'all sure we haven't landed on Mars already?"

Jancey had a gut feeling about why Jerry and Wade were included in the group of finalists who'd been invited to the private meeting at Grace's house. Also present were Marlon, the Hatsus, David and Kamal. Changes were in the offing for the Tenacity Project, changes in the launch schedule and expedition teams. At least that's what she hoped. Her fear was they would scrap the results altogether and restart the selection process from the beginning.

The whole project had come to a grinding halt for the last three days while the selection committee huddled with lawyers and public relations consultants to discuss the fallout from their investigation. Grace had been feeding them tidbits. No details yet, but she confirmed they were in serious damage-control mode, and Sir Charles wanted everything fixed before reporting anything to the board of directors.

Konani had set out a tray on the veranda with drinks and snacks, but Jancey was too anxious to eat. Wade, on the other hand, was ravenous. His bout with *E. coli* had left him down more than twenty pounds. Though his infection had been physically devastating, he was relieved to have his dormant renal condition now under medical control. A blessing in disguise, the doctors called it.

Duke and Sasha suddenly ran to the front door barking.

"They're here," Mila announced as she peered through the shutters at the driveway. "Grace and Sir Charles."

Jancey and the others scurried to seats on the veranda, all trying to appear calmer than they were.

Grace and Sir Charles joined them, the latter leaning on his cane and looking a decade older than his seventy-five years. He removed a silk handkerchief from his breast pocket and mopped his brow. An uncharacteristic sweat for a man who usually was composed.

"Thank you all for meeting here," he began. "And thank you, Grace, for the offer of your home. We find ourselves in need of privacy. Utmost privacy."

Under the circumstances, Jancey couldn't blame them for wanting to keep the scandal confidential. The Tenacity Project didn't need controversy, certainly not the sort that would cause potential investors to question the board's oversight.

Marlon spoke up. "I believe I speak for everyone when I say you can count on our cooperation."

Heads nodded all around.

Sir Charles visibly relaxed and seated himself in the chair Fujio Hatsu had offered. "I can't tell you how refreshing it is to sit down at a meeting that isn't hostile. The events of the last several days have shaken my faith somewhat in human nature, but I am confident we have at last assembled a crew of which we can be proud. You are that crew."

Just as Jancey had suspected.

"I'm going to let Ms. Faraday walk you through what we discovered in our recent investigation."

Jancey was still in shock over what had transpired, unable to reconcile how a NASA colleague—a woman who'd worked inside an honorable culture where they always supported one another in pursuit of the mission—could stoop so low as to cheat another astronaut out of the opportunity to fly. It just wasn't done. Clearly, she'd put too much stock into Libby's supposed professionalism and too little into her resentment about being passed over for *Guardian*. That jealousy had festered for a very long time.

Grace accepted the offer of Marlon's chair while he stood off to the side. "As you all know, Jancey and Mila finished first in the competition and were awarded the distinction of the first launch. The next morning, however, the committee received a photo from Brandon Fagan showing Mila outside the habitat on Mauna Kea without her helmet, a clear violation of the rules. He indicated to us when he submitted the photo that he had concerns—concerns he maintains were shared by others—that Jancey and Mila were always favored to win because of Jancey's friendship with me. Within his message was the implication he and others would go public with charges of favoritism if Jancey and Mila were not completely disqualified from the program for breaking the rules."

"Son of a bitch," Mila said under her breath.

"We were not aware of any such grievances among other candidates, and in fact are not convinced they exist outside of the persons involved in this incident."

The revelation made Jancey sick to her stomach. Professionals didn't grumble about petty gripes, real or perceived. They focused on the mission and waited for their call. How many of the people sitting around her right now had groused privately about her having the inside track? How many had assumed their win was unearned, that she and Mila couldn't possibly have performed better than the others? She wanted to know…no, she didn't. Screw them. She had one job—getting ready for Mars.

Sir Charles was speaking again. "I want to make perfectly clear the allegation of favoritism is baseless. In fact, it's fair to say the committee subjected Major Beaumont and Ms. Todorov to even more scrutiny in order to overcome that perceived bias. Anyone who doubts that is invited to examine our selection data. I assure you, you'll come to the same conclusions as we did. They exceeded all of our performance expectations, and used far fewer resources than any other team."

"That is irrefutable," Grace added. "The Fagans' accusations began to unravel when it was discovered the photo in question was manipulated using a software commonly used by architects. That led us to question Jean-Paul Robillard. When confronted with the evidence, the Fagans and Jean-Paul implicated one another in what was a conspiracy to have not only Jancey and Mila but several other colleagues disqualified."

"In other words, they cheated," Jerry snarled, giving voice to what all of them were thinking.

"We have secured their resignations," Grace said as a chorus of angry voices rose in protest. "And we're confident there are no other conspirators involved. However, several questions remain…questions only you can answer. That's why we wanted to meet with you privately. I'll let Sir Charles explain."

"First, let me say there is no evidence whatsoever that Ms. Todorov broke the rules going outside without her equipment, so she and Major Beaumont will be reinserted into the launch schedule."

Jancey cast a quick glance at Mila, who gave her a thumbs-up, but Sir Charles's choice of words made her uneasy. *Reinserted into the schedule?* Why hadn't he mentioned their place in the order?

"With Mr. Robillard leaving the program, the board made the decision to team Colonel Quinn with Major Huffstetler."

"Outstanding!" Jerry said, stretching to shake Marlon's hand.

"I was trying to figure out why you were here, bro."

"Now you know. They're sending me to Mars with you to make sure you don't get lost."

"One thing I forgot to mention," Grace interjected, "Jean-Paul also admitted to stealing solar panels from the Hatsus and from Jancey and Mila. They were discovered yesterday afternoon buried near his habitat."

Another mystery explained.

"And in the course of our interviews," Sir Charles said, "Mrs. Fagan became exasperated with her husband. She expressed strong regrets about her role, and also a willingness to provide more information...including some that involved potentially criminal behavior involving the electrical box in the submersible that mysteriously caught fire. The attorneys who were present advised her at that point not to elaborate."

Mila abruptly sat up straight, her jaw dropping. "They could have killed us!"

Jancey vividly recalled her feelings that day. Concern for Mila and Andi's safety, and pride in the way they handled themselves under pressure. The idea that the Fagans had caused a near-fatal catastrophe by tampering with the box filled her with rage.

Sir Charles thumped his cane loudly on the tile floor to quiet the outcry. "That's precisely why we're having this meeting—to discuss how to proceed. The police department's investigation of the fire was inconclusive. Our attorneys have advised it will be very difficult to prove culpability without a confession, which we did not receive. Similarly, we have reason to believe the Fagans grew *E. coli* bacteria in their habitat and used it to contaminate four water tanks, including their own so as not to raise suspicions."

"Whoa!" It was Wade who was riled this time. "Are you saying someone deliberately poisoned our water? You can kill somebody like that."

Kamal and David reacted angrily as well, though they'd been able to return to Mauna Kea shortly after receiving treatment.

"Brass necks, the lot of them," Sir Charles said. "If any of you wish to pursue criminal or civil charges, the Tenacity Project will support that decision and assist in your investigation. There is, however, an alternative the committee would ask you to consider."

"As long as there's accountability," Jancey said. "They don't get to walk away and point fingers back at us."

"Yes, the committee found that possibility quite troubling as well. We proposed an accord that requires them to withdraw from Tenacity, stating personal reasons, and to refrain from pursuing future employment in the aerospace industry. It isn't Jersey justice, but it guarantees our paths shall not cross again.

All three of them accepted those terms in order to avoid public humiliation and criminal charges."

They were smart to accept it, Jancey thought, considering the difficulty they'd have had getting jobs in the first place if their employers found out they were scumbags.

Sir Charles continued, "Furthermore, the confidentiality clause of our agreement prohibits them from discussing the Tenacity Project with anyone. That helps us avoid negative publicity that might inhibit our ability to develop further support. Negotiations for additional funds are at a critical point, and it wouldn't do to raise questions." He peered over his glasses to emphasize his point. "These funders could well mean the difference between success and failure of the entire project."

Jancey grasped what was at stake. The last thing they needed now that the world's media were paying attention was a managerial disaster that would cause potential investors to question their overall competency.

"What it requires from you is waiving your right to hold them publicly accountable, and criminally liable." He made eye contact with all, lingering especially on those who had reason to want them prosecuted. "The decision is yours, but I hope you'll consider this entire incident water under the bridge."

"I wasn't impacted the way you guys were," Marlon said. "I'll back you a hundred percent if you want to see them in jail. But we all know what it's like to dream about space every minute of every day. Cutting me off from that would be the worst thing you could do to me, so think about what their lives will be like now."

Mila set her jaw and nodded. "Agreed. There's justice in a deal that totally shuts them out of aerospace."

As the others signed off, Jancey entertained a couple of niggling thoughts. "What does Wade get out of this? He spent two weeks in the hospital and lost his chance to fly forever."

"A seat on our board of directors," Sir Charles answered, not missing a beat. "We've assembled the leaders in the space industry with not one astronaut. A serious oversight on our part, corrected with his addition. He'll guide us on behalf of all of you."

Jerry was first to offer a pat on the back. "No more of that squash soup, buddy. You hear me? That stuff is nasty."

Jancey interrupted the congratulations with one final question, the bit of information Sir Charles had skirted in his plan forward. "What's the launch order? Who goes first?"

He looked down, noticeably uncomfortable. "That is a sticky wicket, I'm afraid. We've already announced the Fagans as the first to launch. If we replace them with a team not even on the rotation, it would be difficult to explain."

In other words, the Hatsus would launch first, followed by David and Kamal.

Mila abruptly rose and stomped away from the group, clearly trying to control her rage. Falling back on old habits—say nothing to avoid losing control.

Jancey understood her anger. None of this was their fault—everyone else knew it too—and yet they were being asked to step aside so the committee could save face.

"Unacceptable," Wade said emphatically. "From the beginning, the Tenacity Project said the selection process would be based on merit. We took you at your word. You want me on the board to speak for the astronauts? That's what I'm doing now. The committee can't break its faith—nor sacrifice its integrity—for the sake of public relations."

"We feel the same," Fujio said, gesturing toward his wife, who nodded her agreement. "We did not earn the right to be the first team on Mars. It would not be proper to take that honor from Major Beaumont and Miss Todorov."

David spoke up. "Fujio and Suki are right. We went through all the trials together. They came out on top, fair and square."

It felt good to get everyone's support, especially after hearing that some of her fellow candidates had been suspicious of her friendship with Grace.

Yet even Grace appeared conflicted, a sign to Jancey that it wasn't as simple as Wade and the others made it sound. The threat of losing investor support was real. If potential funders or space contractors raised questions about the project's leadership, the entire effort could crumble.

Jancey couldn't ignore those concerns. Grace wouldn't be so worried unless she believed the risk to be great.

With a slight jerk of her head, she summoned Mila back to the group. "Trust me on this," she whispered. For the sake of the project, they had to be team players. "We'll do what's best for Tenacity. What matters most—not just to me, but to all of us here—is having the resources to get to Mars, and then to support the colony once we're there. Mila and I don't want to screw that up."

Sir Charles beamed. "Splendid! We'll issue a press release at once announcing both the withdrawals and the replacements."

Grace tugged his sleeve. "Perhaps we could add that in light of our new personnel, there may be subsequent changes in the launch schedule. It is, after all, vital that we have the best team in place when the others launch."

"Yes, perhaps," he said, noticeably dismissive.

That didn't bode well for their chances, but Jancey could make peace with it. At least she had a guaranteed seat, something that wasn't true when she'd decided to return to the project to be with Mila.

As Grace and the dogs walked the entourage to the door to see them off, Jancey and Mila huddled at the rail, looking out over the back lawn and the ocean beyond.

"Kinda sucks, doesn't it?" Mila said.

"Not as much as it sucked four days ago. Look at the bright side."

"Which is?"

"I don't know. There has to be one somewhere."

"I'll tell you the bright side," Grace said, squeezing in between them. "There's no way I'm letting Charles fly anyone else first."

* * *

"Do you think Grace has any idea what goes on in her cabana after dark?" Mila asked, spreading a spa towel over their bodies to ward off the chill as their perspiration dried. Jancey's head lay on her chest, and a bare leg was wedged between hers.

"This place has been here as long as I can remember. I suspect she and Lana spent a lot of nights out here doing exactly the same thing we just did."

The second phase of training, eighteen months from now, would take them to Cologne, Germany. Until then, they'd have many more nights like this while they studied at Tenacity Centre.

"By the way," Mila said, "I feel very proud to be your partner. Watching you negotiate with Sir Charles, it just struck me what a special person you are. Everyone listens to you. You could have gone with anyone and you chose me."

"I'm proud of you too. I'm also proud of me. Here I am forty-three years old with a trophy astronaut on my arm."

"I can't even begin to know what that means."

"It means I've won a prize." Jancey burrowed deeper under the towel as a breeze rippled through the nearby palms. "You know what's interesting to me? I'm even more excited about Tenacity than I was before. All because I had it, lost it and got it back again. Isn't that weird?"

Mila chuckled. "Not really. I feel the same way about you. I'd finally gotten used to believing we were going to be together forever. Next thing I know, Grace tells me you're at the airport."

"About that…" Jancey sat up and wrapped the towel around her shoulders, leaving Mila to shiver. "It was never about leaving *you*. I was leaving Tenacity, and I didn't want to drag you with me. You deserved a shot at your dream."

"You're my dream, Jancey." She pulled her back down and held her head against her breast.

"And you're mine. I didn't know that for sure until you walked off with my suitcase. That's when I knew I needed to follow you. I've walked away from women all my life. You're the first one who didn't just let me go."

"And the last one."

"Absolutely." Jancey kissed the hollow of her breasts and stroked the tender skin below her navel. A signal she was ready to make love again. "The last one."

EPILOGUE

Four years, four months later
Satish Dhawan Space Centre, India

"Yes, I hear you just fine," Shel Montgomery said to the producer, adjusting her earpiece to make sure it stayed put. She was somewhat out of her element on TV, but *Tenacity's* official spokesperson was fielding media requests from London.

At the improvised studio desk with her was BBC's world news anchor, Rolf Kinlan, a dark-haired middle-aged English gent whose Botox injections seemed to favor one eye at the expense of the other. In front of them, off-camera, was an HD display of the scene inside *Tenacity's* launch center, which was being shown to viewers on a split screen. Family and friends of the astronauts sat alongside VIPs and press in bleachers that lined a long red carpet outside the launch center.

The network had pulled out all the stops to cover the *Tenacity* launch onsite. And why not? It was the biggest space story since Neil Armstrong walked on the moon.

"Live in three…two…one."

"In case you're just tuning in," Kinlan said smoothly, "we're coming to you live from Andhra Pradesh in southeastern India, where *Tenacity III* is set to launch three hours and four minutes from now for the first manned flight to Mars. I'm joined here by Shel Montgomery, associate director of media relations for the Tenacity Project. Shel, can you tell our viewers what we see here on the screen?"

"Sure, Rolf." Though she lacked his on-air aplomb, she made up for it with insider knowledge and the ability to communicate scientific information to a broad audience in words most could understand. "You're looking inside what we call the launch hangar. That's the forward-most structure to the launch pad. The astronauts will exit the building through that hallway. According to our schedule, they're due any minute."

"Extraordinary. The efforts of thousands over a period of ten years...all coming down to these next few hours."

"More like the efforts of millions over centuries, going all the way back to the ancient poets who wrote of visiting the heavens. Everything starts with an idea."

She was there not only to provide inside commentary and technical information, but to help fill air time as they waited for action. As she spoke of Jules Verne's 1865 story of space travel, the camera focused on famous faces as they took seats in the bleachers.

"The rover that was sent to Mars four years ago on *Tenacity I*, and the second one that followed two years later, have completed their work with the habitat preparation. We've gotten confirmation back from the planet that life support is functional...heating, cooling, water...it's all sitting there like an empty house awaiting the colonists' arrival. Maybe we can show viewers that slide again—"

Kinlan interrupted her to describe the scene. "Among the honored guests and dignitaries on hand, that's US President Warren and her husband greeting Bulgaria's prime minister."

Shel chuckled to herself at his reluctance to stumble over the five-syllable Bulgarian surname.

He turned back to her. "So tell us, Shel, what sort of morning have the astronauts had so far?"

"They've been up for about four hours." She walked him through the morning protocol. Breakfast, shower, getting outfitted by the suit techs and going through all the pressure checks.

"And what about the families? This isn't an ordinary space launch, at least not the sort to which we've become accustomed. These astronauts are leaving Earth today, and if their mission is successful, they're never coming back. I should think it's quite poignant."

"It is. Their families were on hand last night at our farewell banquet, along with a few of their close friends and a lot of the Tenacity staff, about a hundred of us in all. Not exactly an intimate dinner. Afterward, they retreated with their loved ones to say a private goodbye. Obviously, they'll have one more chance to wave as they walk out. They should be able to remain in touch through our available technology, but the signals won't allow—"

"Sorry to interrupt. I'm told they're on their way out and should be appearing…"

A security guard with a handheld radio opened a steel door and out walked Jancey Beaumont and Mila Todorov, all smiles as cameras flashed to record the historic moment. Their gait was stiff and awkward, owing to the cooling tubes and air hoses that ran beneath their royal blue flight suits.

"Absolutely remarkable," Kinlan said as the astronauts acknowledged their respective political leaders with a slight bow. "What do you suppose is going through their heads right now?"

"As you can see, it's a very emotional moment as they wave their final goodbyes." She had interviewed most of the family and close friends who had come to see the launch. "The woman in the red coat is Mila Todorov's grandmother from Bulgaria. I don't understand a word she says, but I can tell you she's quite the spitfire. It's very obvious where Mila gets her intensity."

She went on to point out Mila's mother, her college friend Vio, and her roommate from the Tenacity trials, Andi Toloti. Jancey's family was also present, though Shel was careful not to point out that her mother and stepfather were seated on one end of the bleachers, while her father and stepmother were on the other.

"I see some of the other Tenacity crew," Kinlan remarked. "Marlon Quinn...Fujio Hatsu. Here in support of their colleagues."

"Walking behind the astronauts, you also see several members of the closeout crew. Those are the people who led them through the morning checklists and got them ready to roll. And there's Sir Charles Boyd, the visionary behind the Tenacity Project. The woman pushing his wheelchair is Grace Faraday, also one of the project's key supporters, and a longtime friend of Major Beaumont."

Through their earpieces, the producer told them to cut the conversation so they could go to crowd noise. The cheers were growing louder with every step the astronauts took toward the bus that would take them to the launch pad.

Despite their smiles and friendly waves, it was clear to Shel they weren't lingering to drag out their exit. Both turned one last time to salute Grace and Sir Charles, and then strode to the bus with determination.

"Now they're riding out to the launch site, which is about six kilometers away. They'll be met there by the ingress crew to get strapped in and run through the prelaunch checklist."

"It's curious to me, Shel, and I'm sure to our viewers, that a pair of women would be selected as the first colonists on Mars. And correct me if I'm wrong," Kinlan said as he checked his notes, "that represents a change in the launch order that was announced originally. Remind us how that came about."

It was Shel's favorite question, one she'd answered in dozens of interviews. "As you can imagine, there are a number of competing positions on what comprises the ideal characteristics of a Mars colonist team. Physiologically speaking, it's a pretty even tradeoff between men and women, but the practical considerations actually favor sending two women."

She explained the benefits associated with their size and resource needs, noting how they could take nearly four years' worth of food supplies in the same space where a team of hearty men could take only two.

"Those are just the scientific reasons, Rolf. The change came about at the request of their fellow astronauts, who felt

Beaumont and Todorov were best prepared to lay the foundation for the colony. I've talked with them about this, and it means a lot to have the confidence of the teams that will follow. It's a big responsibility but they feel they're up to the challenge."

* * *

The elevator rose as high as a forty-story building and opened to three crewmen in yellow jumpsuits. The ingress team.

The crew chief was Gene Watson, a grizzled veteran of the Kennedy Space Center. "Right this way, ladies."

Mila and Jancey left their closeout crew behind and stepped onto the enclosed gangway that connected the elevator platform to the vessel.

Whether it was excitement about boarding or nervousness at being up so high on a movable bridge, Mila picked up her gait. For the past month, she'd been so consumed with safety that she could barely walk without calculating exactly where her foot would land. One small misstep…a sprained ankle, a broken toe…would have been a reason to cancel her mission. Fifteen more meters and all her doubts would be laid to rest.

"Hold up just a minute," Jancey said, grabbing her elbow from behind.

The crewmen continued to the vessel but waited by the door to allow them to enter first.

"We aren't going to have another chance to talk, at least not without the whole world listening in on the comm."

Mila nodded toward Gene to let him know they'd be there in a moment. When she turned back to Jancey, she was startled to see her green eyes reflecting the vibrant blue of her flight suit. "Wow, you look amazing."

"Me? You were born to wear that suit, Mila. Thanks for getting us here."

"I should be the one saying that."

Jancey held up a finger toward Gene, stepping closer as she lowered her voice. "Before we step aboard, I want to remind you one last time that I love you. It's okay to be scared. I'm right here with you."

"I'm not scared, Jancey. I've been waiting for this day as long as I can remember. And no matter what happens when that rocket lifts off, it's all perfect for me because it happens with you."

* * *

The HD screen before them showed the rocket on its pad against a bright blue sky. A digital clock counted down the time to launch. T-minus two minutes.

"We should be getting a signal soon from the launch director," Shel said. The stream of communications between launch control and the cockpit came in live over their television feed, most of it crackling technical jargon she interpreted for the viewers at home.

"*Tenacity, you're Go for launch. Lower and lock your visors... initiate O2. Safe journey.*"

Shel referenced her notes as she watched the clock. "Right about now, they're switching over to internal power...starting the auto-sequencing program. Everything's mechanized to the millisecond."

T-minus nine...eight...seven.

With her finger pressed to her earpiece, she repeated the words from the launch center. "Confirming a main engine start."

Three...two...one.

A billow of white smoke exploded on both sides of the rocket as it lifted from its track.

"We have ignition and liftoff."

A flawless launch leaving a mountain of orange gases in its wake.

"Once it leaves the tower, the launch center hands it over to Mission Control."

Shel went quiet for a full minute to allow the image to speak for itself. Like everyone else on the inside of the Tenacity Project, she was holding her breath for two more critical stages—the separation of the rocket booster and then the powering down of the vessel's thrusters.

"What are the astronauts doing right now?" Kinlan asked, breaking the tension.

Probably genuflecting, was the first thought to enter her head. Though in truth, it wouldn't be possible. The pressure from accelerating to nearly 18,000 miles per hour would have them pinned to their seats, unable to lift even their arms.

"Mission Control is driving this bus, Rolf. They're just enjoying the ride."

The ship was barely visible on their screen, its position noted by a vast vapor trail.

"We have Stage One separation."

She breathed a quiet sigh of relief. Inside the vessel, the violent shaking would have stopped, though they still were accelerating to reach their initial orbit. For the astronauts, that meant six more minutes of feeling as though elephants were sitting on their chests. And for Shel, six long minutes of waiting for word they'd broken through.

Tenacity was no longer in viewing range of their cameras, and their only information was the audio feed from Mission Control. Sporadic reports of altitude and airspeed. Ongoing systems monitoring. All followed by the expected one-word response from Jancey—*Roger*.

After a cue from their producer, Kinlan resumed their commentary. "While we're waiting for confirmation of orbit, perhaps you can walk us through what happens next. As travelers, we've grown dependent on navigation systems to get from one place to the other. Is it that simple for the *Tenacity* crew?"

His question would make the anxious minutes pass more quickly, and she'd brought along a diagram, which was now displayed on the screen.

"Pretty much, Rolf, but *Tenacity* can't travel to Mars in a straight line, because Mars is moving too. Eight months from now, it'll be in a different place." With a series of color-coded circles, she explained the Hohmann Transfer Orbit, which allowed them to jump from Earth's orbit to that of Mars. "It's like taking three buses to get across town."

Despite her jovial remarks, the pit of her stomach was knotted with growing worry as the seconds ticked off to T-plus eight-thirty. They should be in orbit by now…engaging the on-board life support…taking off their helmets.

Breathless seconds.

"*Woo!*"

Finally a sign, and it sounded like Mila, though it wasn't exactly an official communiqué. More like an exclamation of surprise at the sudden weightlessness.

Jancey followed, and Shel could actually hear a smile in her voice. "*Mission Control, this is Tenacity, on course for Mars. We're heading home.*"

Bella Books, Inc.

Women. Books. Even Better Together.

P.O. Box 10543
Tallahassee, FL 32302

Phone: 800-729-4992
www.bellabooks.com